The First Wave

Book One of The Secrets of Achaea

By T.J. Vincent

Kindle Direct Publishing

Edited by: Francie Futterman

Cover design and maps by: Aven Jones

Printed in the United States of America

to Elise

for introducing me to imagination

"There are no 'good' or 'bad' people. Some are a little better or a little worse, but all are activated more by misunderstanding than malice."

Tennessee Williams

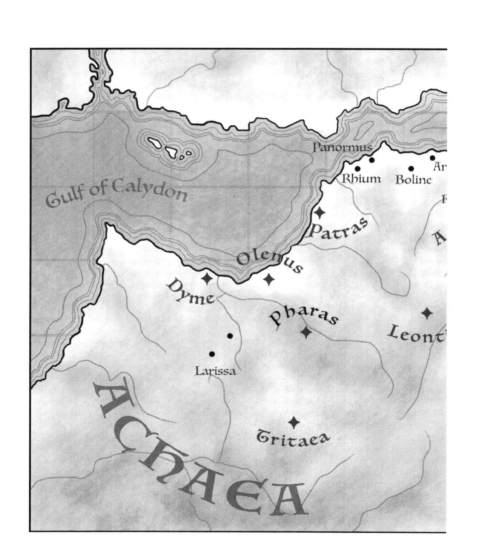

Gulf of Calydon

Panormus

Rhium Boline Ar

Patras

Olenus

Dyme

Pharas

Leont

Larissa

Tritaea

ACHAEA

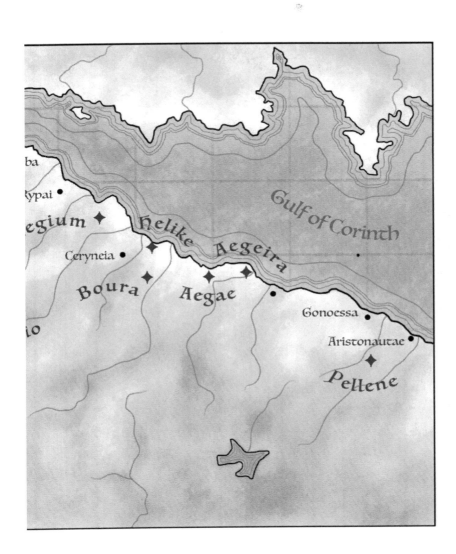

Prologue

The boy was tall for his age. His father was tall, too, so it was no surprise to anyone. In fact, he didn't even need to stand on his toes like so many other children in the square. It seemed to the boy that everyone in the city had gathered here today. Sleek leather shoes and little sandals alike stood on the cobblestones, all pointing to the man on the platform. The boy's heart skipped excitedly in his chest. He didn't usually spend time here; it was always packed with adults going about their business, and there was no space to play. His mother and father came here often though, and today they had brought him along. Father was speaking to the city for the first time in a while, so Mother said it was a good idea to come and watch. As the boy surveyed the massive crowd gazing with anticipation at his father, he felt pride and love surge through him.

"Citizens of Helike!"

He was starting! The crowd fluttered and straightened. The boy could burst – the whole city was listening to *his* dad! He had bragged to Cerwin and Elin and his other friends all week.

GHE FIRSG WAVE

"I know many have called for the Children of the Sea to be eradicated from this city, and I know many have been disappointed in the delay. As we have assured you in months past, the Children of the Sea are not our brothers. They are not the brothers of Sons who would serve our Lord of the Sea with dignity and peace..."

His father was generally a quiet man, but today his voice was booming and powerful. The boy loved the shyness and calm he always showed around him and Mother. He was the best man in the world, and he could do anything! He loved everyone, and they loved him back. They all liked how his dark hair fell curly down his back, and how impressive he looked for a priest. All the other priests were fat or old, but his father was strong like a warrior. He stood a head taller than his brothers in the temple where they lived, and had big, tan arms, just like the boy wanted.

His mother always said he was the handsomest man in the city, and that always made the boy blush. He hated when his parents kissed and hugged; it was gross. His father may have been the handsomest to his mother, but he said she was the prettiest. She was also tall, with hair the same shade of black as the boy's. She had a sharp jawline and thin face, and her brown eyes always looked at the boy with such love.

When he was around his parents, the boy was always happy. Mother made him laugh, and Father told him stories. Sometimes, Mother would tickle his back before bed, and it made him laugh so hard, he cried salty tears out of only his left eye. He never told

Cerwin or Elin any of that. They would call him a baby.

"...But they are men and women who would disrespect our order, and the Sea King who grants us such fortune as an Achaean city. Citizens, I apologize for the time it took for me to deliver this message. We, the Sons of Poseidon and our families, faithful servants of the Order, have called to the Council to rid ourselves of these vile people. The Children of the Sea, for their crimes, and their impiety have hereby been sentenced to exile from Helike. The Council has decreed that any who resist, shall be accordingly punished.... But this is not the task of a priest. I merely wish to inform you good people that your fears of –"

Suddenly, a violent crash echoed around the square. The boy's breath caught in his throat. People's heads turned wildly in panic and confusion.

One second passed. Two.

The boy could have blinked, and he would have missed everything.

Two figures exploded through the walls of a nearby shop, causing a second crash, louder and closer than before. Shattered marble and glass flew in all directions, inciting yelps of agony throughout the crowd as the shrapnel pierced skin. The boy felt a stab of pain shoot through his foot, as two young girls collided with him, and it was trapped underneath the stomp of a metal boot.

He heard bones crunch and knew that for the first time in his life, something was broken. Screams reverberated around him, and the boy felt dazed from the pain, unable to think.

ᚦᚺᛖ ᚠᛁᚱᛋᚦ ᚹᚨᚡᛖ

"Father! Mother!" he cried in anguish, hoping for an answer.

But it was fruitless. He could neither hear, nor see individual people throughout the melee, only bodies obstructing the light of his surroundings.

I have to find them! Have to see them!

With a huge effort, the boy pulled himself up. His foot was on fire, but he had to find Mother and Father, had to make sure they were okay. He shoved a rotund boy aside and threw himself up towards the steps from which Father had spoken.

There!

"Father!" he yelled again, this time with a better result.

Under piles of robes and other Sons, a hand shot out, and a strong man emerged from the chaos, back onto the steps.

It's Father! And next to him, Mother!

The boy stumbled towards them with all the energy left in his body. They were calling his name, but he could barely make it out.

"Mother! I'm coming!"

They stretched their arms to him, as the chaos continued to spread from the square to the surrounding streets in the city. The boy could feel their warmth, he could feel the danger washing away as they ran towards him.

Then the pain reached its climax. His foot must have fallen off, it burned so badly. He collapsed to the ground just as he felt the touch of his mother, and the large, calloused hand of his father began to lift him off the ground.

No sooner did he emerge from the dust than he fell gruffly

4

back onto it. He heard his mother's voice, but it was a shriek he barely recognized.

And Father dropped me? He never drops me. Never.

Two people landed on the stones beside him. Two tall, dark-haired people. He felt familiar hands grasp his, as he gazed into the face of his father, expecting to feel the comfort he always did with him. Blood trickled from the side of his father's mouth. He looked desperately at his mother, willing her eyes to meet his with the brimming love they always did; but they were empty. Lightless.

"C-c-close them," whispered the voice of his father, quieter than usual, and so strained that it almost did not sound like his.

He reached towards his son's eyes, and the boy caught one last glimpse of his serene smile before his fingertips brushed the boy's eyelids shut.

The boy kept his eyes determinedly closed, feeling tears push out of both the right and left, as his father's hand fell limply next to his face.

Chapter 1

Sapphir

She hated that scar above her upper lip. The white, jagged mark was a bold imperfection on her otherwise immaculate face. But that wasn't what bothered her. It was the memories that came with it. Sapphir studied it in her bronze mirror, moving the surface of her left cheek and lips with her tongue in revulsion. It was a stubborn thing, to be so white, yet somehow stand out from pale skin. She vividly remembered the day she had received the gift – from her father of course. How her mother had screamed...

"Mother!" A shrill voice called frantically from the yard.

Sapphir snapped back to the present, and began to move quickly to the sound, "Ivy! Is that you?"

"He's not letting go!" Ivy responded.

A wave of relief passed over Sapphir, and she slowed her pace. It was just a childish squabble.

"Cy! What did you take?"

"I never took it! Ivy gave it to me!"

The boy was dancing out of reach of his older sister, parading a small piece of wood around her.

"I made it for *us* to play with and hunt rabbits!" Ivy said, anguished as she made another wild grab for Cy.

"I'm better at hunting anyway!" Cy declared, "If you actually wanna catch any you should –"

"Cy!" Sapphir interrupted.

The boy scrunched his face. With resignation, he dropped the object and let Ivy approach. She snatched it up and began cleaning it with the hem of her smock. Sapphir realized that Ivy had made herself a stone knife, with an olive tree handle and shale from the cliff-side.

"Ivy, knives aren't toys!"

"We weren't gonna play with it! We were gonna hunt with it and catch dinner!" Ivy insisted.

Sapphir kept her amusement contained, knowing she couldn't let Cy and Ivy see how the dangerous games they played entertained her.

"Just clean it up. Dinner is all ready, we don't need to go about hunting rabbits," she said, putting on a stern tone.

Ivy saw right through it.

"Fine, Mother!"

The girl and her brother raced towards the house, neck and neck, kicking up dust as they went.

Of Sapphir's five children, Cy and Ivy were the most energetic.

ᏀᏂᎬ FIRSᏂ WAVᎬ

The two were ten and eleven. Ivy had olive skin and short black hair, while Cy was paler and blonde. Cy's eyes shone blue, contrasting from Ivy's green. Both were wiry from activity, but Cy was a head taller, and lorded the extra height over his sister with pleasure.

Sapphir's dwelling was nothing exceptional. She had lost most of the splendor of her old life after leaving the city. However, the cozy comfort of her simple abode was much preferable to the cold temple she had once inhabited.

It was not always cold.

Her new home consisted of three small caverns, each nestled into a cliff that led to the summit of the island on which they resided. The interior of each had been smoothed out and separated into a few rooms. Her kids all slept in one cave, she slept in another, and the biggest was reserved for a common space. They dined there every night.

Above all the rooms, the kitchen was perhaps Sapphir's favorite. She loved nothing more than a full table, especially when that table was full of delicious food. Tonight, Sapphir had been roasting a lamb's leg, and she could smell the perfectly seared flesh from far away. Diced onions, garlic, and cabbage surrounded the meat, soaking up the succulent juices wonderfully.

Egan was already at the table. He was not often far from the kitchen, preferring to read in the comfort of the cave; sunlight poured in through a hole in the ceiling. Egan was her oldest child, a boy of thirteen whose size defied his idle nature. He ate sparingly, rarely active like Cy and Ivy. Yet he grew like a weed nonetheless and was broader than most boys his age.

"Hello, Mother," he said when Sapphir entered, keeping his eyes fixed on the book in front of him.

"You sound tired, Egan."

"I'm not."

That about summed up most of the interactions between Sapphir and her eldest. He seemed to grow more petulant with each day.

A sudden clamor broke the quiet of the kitchen, as Cy and Ivy poured in, dragging Celia behind them, who was putting up a monstrous fight.

"No, no, no!" Celia exclaimed, "I'm not hungry! And Blackwing was just learning to say hello!'"

Blackwing was Celia's pet osprey. She had found it one day by the oceanside, dragging its wing across the rocky beach as it struggled to take flight. Sapphir remembered how excited Celia had been, hiking carefully back up the mountain with the animal in tow, its left wing streaked with black and bent at a horrific angle. Sapphir had been reluctant to let Celia keep it, but her daughter had been so happy. She couldn't bring herself to say no. The bird couldn't fly and, like most ospreys, had no speech capability other than high-pitched screeches. However, Celia insisted that she would make him do both before the year was finished. To her credit, Blackwing did seem to be quite fond of her, constantly nibbling at her curly, hazel hair and leaving tiny scratches on her delicate arms. Celia had a habit of feeding him as many treats as he wanted.

"Ma said it's dinner time though," Ivy insisted, pulling Celia to her feet in front of Sapphir.

"Celia doesn't want to eat today, Ma," Cy explained.

"Yes, I've put that much together, Cy."

Celia looked slightly embarrassed, "It's not that I don't want to eat, it's just that I don't want dinner."

"How do you plan to eat without dinner?"

"Well, I could take my food and eat with Blackwing! He doesn't like to be left alone."

Celia was only seven and had not yet overcome the construct that dinner didn't have to be eaten at a table.

"Celia, honey, why don't you just eat dinner here with us, and then you can go back to Blackwing as soon as you're done! You can even bring him a little meat."

Celia considered for a moment.

"Come on, C!" Ivy encouraged, "Just eat with us."

"Okay, but I'll eat really, really fast so I can take Blackwing his food."

"Sounds great, Celia. Where's Maya?"

Her fifth child. Maya was a younger copy of Ivy in every way, at least on the exterior. She was much quieter, almost mute, and two years Celia's junior. She, like Egan, preferred solitude. However, Maya was somewhat of a wanderer, exploring the cliffs and hillsides around the remote island. Perhaps Sapphir should not have let her venture out so far so often, but Maya was a careful child and much more responsible than the sister she resembled so strongly.

"I saw her down by the sea earlier!" Celia offered, although this didn't narrow it down much.

Sapphir was just about to begin searching for the girl, when she strolled in peacefully, a wildflower perched in her dark hair. She didn't speak, beaming at her siblings as a greeting.

"Where did you go today, Maya?" Sapphir asked.

"Water," Maya responded, presenting Sapphir with a flower like her own.

Sapphir accepted the gift and slipped it between her ear and ginger hair. This made Maya smile even wider.

My sweetest child...

"I want to sit by Mother!" Celia's declaration was followed with a scramble for the chair next to Sapphir.

Cy and Ivy sat next to each other as always, and Maya hugged Egan before joining the round table at his side. Even Egan couldn't suppress a look of warmth. The six admired Sapphir's creation hungrily, mouths watering for a hearty dinner.

"Shall we pray?"

The children nodded, each slicing off a small portion of the lamb and placing it on a plate in the center. Many traditional folks from the mainland slaughtered their farm animals for the pure sake of pleasing the gods. Sapphir had found that rather traumatizing as a young girl and was reluctant to expose her children to the same fate. Besides, the gods would probably prefer their meat cooked.

"To the Sky Father Zeus, and his divine children, we give thanks. His sisters and brothers, and the beauty Aphrodite, please guide us this day and tomorrow. May this lamb serve as an offering of our faith."

The family knew the words by heart, and Sapphir was glad to see the ease with which her children delivered them.

"And to our Lord Poseidon, protect us!"

The last part was uncommon across most of the known world, but Sapphir had been raised with the Children of the Sea, and they honored Poseidon above all others. Helike was a city by the vast ocean after all; it only made sense. Even though the city was leagues away, and the Children of the Sea were naught but a smudge Helike had attempted to scrub out, Sapphir did not forget her faith.

"Can we eat now?" Ivy asked.

"Of course, children! Enjoy!"

They dug in. Conversation did not continue for a while, as the family attacked their meals ravenously. Sapphir had spiced the lamb perfectly. She was pleased.

After enjoying her supper, Sapphir excused herself to the kitchen. She set down her own plate in the basin next to the others, as the children had finished long before and dashed off to play. Sapphir had always found the water basin humorous. A sculpture of Poseidon's upper body connected to a bowl into which the god himself spouted water. It looked to Sapphir as if the sea god was spitting into the bowl.

My dishes, every night, cleansed by a god's saliva.

A scrub brush hung from Poseidon's extended arm in an offering gesture, meaning even the gods expected Sapphir to do the house cleaning.

"You're a pain, you know that, right?" Sapphir asked the god, instantly turning upwards to the heavens, "Not you, Lord Poseidon, just the statue."

Poseidon didn't respond, not that Sapphir had expected anything. She didn't know what the gods thought or did in the average day but figured none were listening as she prepared to clean the dishes.

With a sigh, Sapphir accepted Poseidon's scrub brush, and placed it into the cool water that had collected around the dirty dishes.

She waved her hand over the basin and closed her eyes in concentration.

After a moment, Sapphir retreated to a comfortable cushion that sat in the adjacent room. She closed her eyes once more, this time for rest, and let the gentle *tsch, tsch tsch,* of the self-cleaning dishes lull her into meditation.

Chapter 2

Nicolaus

"If you will, son, fetch me some more water," Orrin requested.

"Of course, sir," Nic replied, accepting the cup from the massive hand that was attached to a proportionally large mountain of robes.

Nic was small and skinny next to most people, but the man he served was not most people. Orrin positively dwarfed the boy. Although one could only see his thick neck beneath the robes he wore for comfort, it was taut with muscle – a preview to the rest of his body.

Nic retrieved the pitcher that was filled to the brim with cool, fresh, stream water, and topped off the clay cup. He traversed the less-than-cramped living quarters and placed it on the intricate mahogany desk, laced with gold designs.

"Thank you, Nic."

Nic nodded. "Will you be needing anything else this

morning?"

"Not now, son. I meet with the Council today, yes?"

"Yes. At an hour past midday, sir."

"Agh, then leave me to my letters. I fear I am behind in my duties."

"You wouldn't want me to read any, would you, sir?"

Nic hoped Orrin would say yes. He had trained as a scribe years ago and enjoyed sifting through the chatter of the town, no matter how mundane.

"Not today. We have, well, intelligence for the eyes of the Council only."

"Of course, sir. I'll knock when it's time to convene."

"Many thanks," Orrin responded, not glancing up from the stack of papers he had already begun to unfold and unroll.

Nic walked briskly from the room, running a dark-skinned hand over wavy black hair, and shut the door behind him carefully. This task itself was one of the more difficult things for Nic to accomplish, as the door was heavier than any door should be. It was made of thick ebony wood that Nic had never seen outside the palace walls. Rough-hewn iron leaves stuck firmly to its surface, adding an unnecessary amount of weight. Without Nic's coaxing, the door would surely slam shut and place undue stress on the frame.

Nic supposed that the room needed the extra protection of a solid door, though. Orrin was one of five councilors in the city-state of Helike. Well, four now.

THE FIRST WAVE

How long has it been since the number dropped? One month? Two?

Time passed quickly and insignificantly for a man of his rank. Orrin's room was nothing impressive on the inside. The desk was the most expensive thing. The bed was a simple oak frame, with a goose-feather mattress. The frame was enormous, as it needed to fit Orrin and occasionally his wife. But other than a large bed and desk, there was only a wardrobe with two sea-green himations, formal cloaks for important men, and two flowing red robes.

Orrin rarely wore the himation unless the Council convened.

Nic descended the marble staircase that led from Orrin's wing to the main floor. Everything else in the palace was extravagant. Even alongside the staircase, pictures in swirling silver or gold frames depicted the rise of Helike and the portraits of councilors long dead. The staircase ended in the entryway to the great hall, an enormous dining atrium with a sprawling gold-tipped table, made of the same ebony as Orrin's door.

Nic hated this room. He was never actually allowed to eat here. He was only allowed to serve here.

All twelve of the Olympians had a statue somewhere in the room. They stared down at the table fiercely, daring anyone who ate there to ignore the proper table mannerisms that accompanied a royal court.

Nic particularly despised the statue of Poseidon. It was the largest, as he was patron god of the city, and it was the most obnoxiously lavish. Some famous sculptor had spent extra time on the sea god's face. It glared with an uncomfortably menacing look.

Gabrielle and Ibbie would like all these statues, even if I do not.

Nic was impious. Why should he have been otherwise? The gods had never treated him fairly, assuming they existed. He would not tell anyone this; doing so would be heresy in Helike. But when he had prayed, it had always been for his family. And where had that led him? He was still a servant, still a *slave* – an ocean away from the sisters, brothers, and parents who had raised him.

Nic missed Memphis. The memories of his Egyptian village faded with each passing day. He could recall the muddy papyrus lining the river and the way the sand felt between his toes, but he found it harder to picture the shops and stands he used to frequent. However, he remembered his family just fine. And as thankful as he was for Orrin to have chosen him as his personal attendant – at least he wasn't serving Gaios or Kyros anymore – Nic wanted to be home.

With a shudder, he continued out of the wretched hall and into the main entryway. Similar to everything else in the Palace of Helike, the room was ornately decorated. Stairwells sprung up from all sides of the room, leading to the living chambers of servants, attendants, and family of the Council. A mosaic curved across a domed ceiling high above the polished marble floors.

Nic's room, like those of the other attendants, was tucked away on the third floor. It was situated eye-level with the top of the doorframe to the castle. He was acquainted with the others on staff to the Council but was often scorned for his darker skin and therefore had no close relationships.

Well, Opi is always nice to me. But we're not friends.

His only true friend tended the tavern that lay at the bottom of the palace valley – an easy walk down, but brutal journey back. How he wished he could steal away for a midday refreshment. But alas, Nic rarely ventured past the castle gates during daylight.

Orrin's bedroom may have been plain, but it was far superior to the tight quarters given to non-Council members. There was hardly room to move between the walls, as the bed took up the majority of the room. Of course, that made the bed sound much bigger than it was.

Nic's feet hung off the end when he lay to sleep and correcting this always resulted in a painful bump on his head. A single window brought natural light into the room, probably to allow the blinding sun rays to wake Nic well before Orrin. This way, he could literally tend to Orrin's every need from the moment he awoke.

Nic figured he had an hour or so to rest before he needed to retrieve his master. *Associate* rather, as Nic was so often reminded by Gaios — he was no slave and therefore had no master. Orrin regarded Gaios as "dishonorable" and shared this opinion often in his rants after particularly aggravating Council meetings. He was careful that his true feelings about the other councilors were only voiced in private. Nic empathized strongly with Orrin's dislike of the man, but he personally felt that "pathetic" was a more appropriate term.

Nic absentmindedly prodded the firm mattress. It wasn't the most inviting thing, but rest would do nicely. He lay down wearily and let himself retreat into his thoughts.

****

"Sir!" Nic called, knocking politely on the hefty door to Orrin's room.

"It's time?" Orrin responded.

Nic heard the rustling of papers from inside the room.

"Yes sir, the Council gathers in the court."

The door opened, and Orrin, now wearing the formal himation of a true leader of the city, emerged. The himation was sea-green, the color of the ocean, with Helike's trident crest neatly oriented on the back. The garment exposed Orrin's right pectoral, and Nic couldn't help but feel slightly jealous at its size. Orrin was, indeed, a strong individual.

One day, I might not be so damn skinny.

"Well let's get on with it," Orrin sighed, taking the lead.

The two descended to the great hall, continuing past the entrance until they reached an archway that led directly to the palace's most cherished spectacle.

The Court of Helike.

The first time Nic had been allowed inside, it was to serve Kyros after a night of heavy drinking. Even compared to Nic, who fancied himself a professional drinker, Kyros was in a league of his own. The councilor had once been a great war hero of Helike, squashing an Achaean rebellion that had arisen years ago around Thebes. Nicolaus had heard wondrous stories of the fearsome General Kyros, upending the rebellion by taking the lead on the field of battle, and personally beheading the leader, Deukalius.

But now, the only battle Kyros fought was with his own love of wine and ale, or with his wife, who seemed to catch him with mistresses every day.

Yes, the first time in the Court had definitely been with Kyros. The slob had complained about his aching head the entire time, before finally unleashing his sick right in front of Nic.

What a revolting man.

Despite this unpleasantness, it had not stopped Nic from taking in the grandeur of Helike's most important room. Once again, the Olympian gods presided, standing tall above the raised platform. The councilors sat here when the room filled with Heliken citizens.

Beneath the gods were five identical thrones, each covered in sea-blue velvet and bejeweled with rubies and aquamarine. The chairs themselves were structured of gold, or some alloy that mimicked it perfectly.

However, on days like today, where the meeting was meant only for the councilors' ears, the four sat at a round table by the foot of the thrones. Nic and the other servants carried the table in and out before each meeting, a difficult task considering it was studded with iron, and weighed about as much as the men seated around it.

Orrin bowed formally to his peers, ever-courteous, as was customary for such a noble setting. Nicolaus followed suit, taking his place next to the other attendants as Orrin seated himself.

Simon's attendant, a young girl named Opi, smiled brightly, tilting her head to acknowledge Nic's arrival. She had short, black hair like Nic's, with caramel skin lighter than his. If Nic remembered correctly, Opi was from the deserts west of Egypt, close to where he had grown up. She was kind, but seemed simple to Nic. He nodded politely.

Am I supposed to smile back?

"Fellow councilors," Orrin began, "I hope you all have had a fine morning."

"Be a lot finer if I didn't have this shit to do," Kyros responded without hesitation, rubbing two fat fingers across his temples.

"Wonderful that we have you to represent the town, Kyros," Simon said, staring without amusement at him.

"Save your snide remarks, Flat-Nose," Kyros grunted, "I've got enough of that waiting for me in my chambers."

"Perhaps if you kept yourself confined to those who live in your chamber," Simon offered calmly.

"My endeavors are–"

"Silence, the both of you!" Gaios snapped, "We have real matters for the city to discuss today, as I'm sure you are all aware."

Gaios gave the Flat-Nose a strange look that Nic couldn't discern.

ᏩᏂ FIRST WAVE

"Indeed, thank you, Gaios," Orrin said, although Nic could tell it pained him to agree with Gaios about anything.

This querulous exchange was the perfect example of what Nic hated in politics. These four men were the wisest leaders Helike had to offer?

Please. Orrin deserves his position, but the others…

Kyros was a formerly impressive warrior, whose ego had blown up almost as much as his body over the years. His blond tuft of hair matched his skin tone, but his face had somewhat of a blotchy effect that came with his enormous weight. He was shorter than Orrin but heavier nonetheless – a huge disappointment after years as a dashing hero.

Simon the Flat-Nose had just that – a flat nose. His skin stretched tight over his bones, giving his face angular features that seemed gaunt, and his voice a curious nasal tone. In truth, Nic didn't know where Simon's rise to councilor began, but he had foreign features – light brown skin and thinner eyes. His wit always seemed well beyond that of his counterparts. For someone like Nicolaus, however, the Flat-Nose seemed like nothing special.

Last was Gaios. Orrin didn't like him. He claimed the man always had motives for his motives and lies within his lies. His position came from a long family line of nobility in Helike; he was a descendant of one of the founders of the great city. If Orrin represented honor and integrity, Gaios was the opposite — slimy and ruthless. People got in his way, and those people were mysteriously removed from his way, or became his greatest supporters. He had long fingers that always moved, seemingly as though they were unraveling the plots he had woven. Despite his reputation, Gaios remained; and he still received the love of the people of Helike. Perhaps it was due to his undeniable attractiveness; he possessed perfect brown hair and tan skin with brown eyes.

"Yes, the matters of our people," Gaios continued, "The farmers gripe of disease befalling their cattle and maggots ravaging their crops."

"And we should have the answer to their ineptitudes? Every day trade pours in from Patras and Olenus. We have food aplenty," Kyros offered.

It was clear Kyros had access to plenty of food.

"An interesting point to be sure," Gaios answered, "Dear sir Orrin, you seemed to have strong feelings when we last brought this issue to light."

"And why shouldn't I? The people of our city should not have to live dependent on other cities. If their crops lay in ruin, we may soon—"

"Must I explain to you how trade works?" Kyros interrupted.

"You miss my point, Kyros," Orrin responded, "These may not be natural occurrences – not the will of the gods carrying out misfortune. We should act before the situation gets out of hand. Consider the man snatching children! We have yet to respond, and it means many families living in fear for their safety!"

"And you miss his point, my friend," Gaios said, his voice

dripping with false friendliness, "Those attacks have occurred too sparingly for us to draw resources to intervene. And what are we to do if a few farmers are left struggling? Shall we come to their rescue and leave newer farms without the opportunity to grow? Shall we jeopardize healthy trade with Patras and Olenus?"

Nic watched the argument go back and forth, absorbing very little of it as his mind wandered to tonight's dinner. He was well aware of the incidents with the lost children. They were among the few events that garnered extra concern from Orrin, enough to stick out in Nic's mind. In the years since Nic arrived in Helike, young boys and girls were taken from their homes from time to time. The attacks seemed to have no particular order, but nobody had any idea how or why they were happening.

I know what it's like – getting taken from home.

"This is hardly our main concern, as I am sure you're aware. Our wise fellow, Councilor Euripides, fell victim to the blade recently... have we no idea as to who committed the deed?" Gaios asked.

Simon nodded solemnly to Orrin, "You have been tasked with this particular concern, what answer have you to offer?"

"Euripides' murder was, indeed, a tragedy. As for my pursuit of the assassin, I fear I have no idea. The knife found on the scene was nothing of consequence – not a recognizable weapon. We have reason to believe that a mage may have done it. It was Euripides, after all, who was the loudest voice against magic in the city. Although the Sons of Poseidon claim to have cleansed their sanctum of those wretches."

"And have you exercised the notion that it could have been a Bouran? Or a mage sent by the Bourans? We know many fled there following the exile," Gaios offered.

"Kyros dealt most recently with Ucalegon. What was his reaction to the murder?"

Kyros had nodded off, allowing his chin to recede into the folds of his obese neck.

"Kyros!" Orrin exclaimed.

"Huh-wha-oh. Sorry gentlemen, must have been up tending to the troubles of the city too late."

"Troubles of the city? That's no way to speak of the women you hire," Simon responded evenly.

Kyros sneered, then shrugged as if this was a fair quip. "What was the question, dear Orrin?"

"In your most recent meeting with Ucalegon, did he speak of Euripides?"

"If I recall properly, he gave quite the sweet apology. Some nonsense about how his heart went out to our city, and how he couldn't bear to see another Achaean state brought to its knees... the craven."

Nicolaus always found it funny how the councilors spoke of the Bouran king. Distaste was putting it lightly. The men hated him. Nic had seen Ucalegon twice before in person, and both times it had been when peace was being negotiated after the Bourans had been threatened by some other member of the League.

ᏝᏂᎬ ᖴᏆᏒᏚᏖ ᎳᎯᏉᎬ

It's only a matter of time...

The Achaean League was parceled into twelve different city-states, and twelve foolish rulers had decided an alliance between the strongholds would resolve conflict across the region.

If those idiots could see it now.

The way Nic understood it, twelve divisions meant more greedy men wanting more power than they had; it meant twelve different geographically adjacent governmental systems – all forced within striking distance of one another.

Nicolaus would be surprised if the League didn't implode within the next five years. However, the quibbles of Achaea meant very little to Nic. He was unsure what would even happen should war burst out between the cities. What did that have to do with being a servant? He would be a servant for Orrin or a servant for some other nobleman or woman.

Nic supposed he liked Orrin better than most.

The Golden Spear.

That's what some people called him. Nic had never seen this side of his better, only the side that was trapped in the shackles of diplomacy and politics – a place he seemed uncomfortable. On the battlefield, however, Orrin famously wielded a golden spear... and he used it masterfully.

The Achaean League had a reputation for staying out of conflicts, often to the chagrin of their more powerful neighboring regions. When Athens and Sparta had warred, Athens had taken advantage of the League's inactivity, laying siege to the cities of

26

Boura and Helike. They hoped to gain the extra strength and territory, in an attempt to increase their chances against the vicious Spartan army. The Golden Spear got his name during that time. With all the glory of heroes from the old stories, he led a fierce attack against the might of Athenian foot soldiers as they scaled the Heliken walls.

Krassen, Nic's friend who tended the bar down the hill, even said Orrin had shoved that Golden Spear right through the heart of General Piraeus of Athens, although many claimed he'd thrown the man off the wall with his bare hands. Who could say? All Nic knew was that he was a servant to a war hero.

And it would probably be just the same if I were servant to dead General Piraeus of Athens.

"Anyway," Kyros continued, "For all we care he can stick that apology up his royal ass. The man may very well have ordered the assassination. I say we assume he did and stick our swords where his words should go."

"A lovely notion Kyros," Gaios said, "I concur in a way. Boura has too long been disrespectful to our power, unappreciative of our protection, and tight with their purses in trade."

"Ucalegon is a man of independence," Simon agreed, "Although many would say his push for isolation from the League has only benefited his territory."

"Some may say his territory would benefit if it were not *his* territory."

"Gaios, there will be no talk of war," Orrin said.

GHE FIRSG WAVE

"Do you have water in your ears friend, I don't recall saying war... speaking of water," Gaios snapped his fingers, and his servant, a squat boy named Perl, rushed to refill his cup.

"I don't have water between my ears, Gaios, and you speak dangerously about a city with which we are allied."

"And if that city were to kill one of our city's councilors?"

Kyros laughed gruffly, "Polish up your spear my large friend! Even you can't deny that Euripides' death at the blade of a Bouran would mean war!"

Orrin muttered under his breath, although Nic didn't catch his words. Perhaps he was remarking on the irony of Kyros calling anybody else "large."

"I hate to agree with our fat friend, Orrin, but he has the truth of it," the Flat-Nose said.

"Fat," Kyros agreed, "but not flat," gesturing towards Simon's squashed face.

"Fine. Let us send a crew of scouts at first light – see what Boura is doing and how the city is faring. We'll have them look for anything unnatural."

"Perhaps it is time to send one of our Fishermen back upstream?" Gaios suggested.

Nicolaus knew how much Orrin disliked espionage. He'd heard mention of the Fishermen before but had no idea who they were and exactly what they did. As Gaios often said at meetings such as these, "Information is the freshest catch."

Orrin suspected the Fishermen collected far too much of this choice catch and shared only a tiny morsel for the Council.

Gaios chuckled. "A crew and Fishermen. Find me a ship, and maybe we could trade as anglers instead of play as kings."

Chapter 3

Keoki

"Damn the gods!" Keoki muttered, gently tugging on the halter that tethered him to the brown-spotted heifer.

She refused to move. For some reason known only to Zeus himself, the cow had stubbornly planted herself next to an olive tree and would not rise.

"I could kill you right here," Keoki said, glowering.

The heifer mooed angrily.

"You're right, I'm sorry," Keoki said, "That was unfair of me."

Keoki flopped down beside the beast, resting his black curls against its flank.

The heifer mooed again, but this time with appreciation that Keoki had finally given in. Keoki mopped sweat from his brow, relishing the shade the tree provided. This break was much needed.

Maybe the cow is smarter than me.

T.J. VINCENT

The day had begun in frustrating fashion for a farm boy, with the realization that the heifer had meandered off in the night, once more breaching the fenced-in pasture outside Felip and Agnes' farm. Keoki was unsure what the cow's motives were, but she had wandered off twice in the past month, both times inspiring a day-long search.

"Why do you keep leaving?" Keoki asked.

The cow remained silent this time, shallow breathing indicating that she may have fallen asleep.

After finding the heifer at least two leagues from the farm, Keoki had struggled to lead her back. She was much more interested in the wildflowers that bloomed on the surrounding hillsides.

For all the trouble and mischief this particular animal caused, Keoki much liked her. She mooed perceptively, as if responding to Keoki's words. Of course, this was most likely a coincidence – Keoki tended to ramble excessively when nobody was around.

"You need a name, don't you?" Keoki decided.

As the heifer was still asleep, Keoki took her silence for a yes.

"You know that old tale of Io, the woman who got turned into a cow?" Keoki suggested, "How does Io sound?"

More silence.

"Okay, Io it is."

That story had always struck Keoki as strange. His mother and father had told it to him as a boy, and he had always found it curious that the king of the gods felt the need to consort with random mortals. He could have a goddess whenever he pleased. It also seemed unfair that Io got turned into a cow, when she had refused Zeus' advances to begin with.

He had told his father this once.

"Zeus is mean for turning that lady into a cow!"

"Son, you mustn't insult the king of the gods!" he had scolded.

"But Father, Zeus turned her into a cow when she didn't do anything wrong!"

Father had remained insistent, and even gotten his mother to agree. There was just no questioning the gods in their minds.

So here he lay, with Io, the mischievous heifer. The sun had passed its apex and was in the process of descending to the horizon.

Just a few more minutes, and I'll press on home.

Agnes would have his hide if he returned past sunset, even though he was approaching his nineteenth year.

"Let's go, Io," Keoki said, using the olive tree to help him regain his footing.

Io woke as Keoki gave a sharp tug on the rope that looped around her thick neck. She mooed with displeasure, but finally stood.

The two crested the hill by the olive tree and headed down to a narrow footpath that indicated they were only two miles away. Keoki lead his newly named livestock onward, letting Io stop once or twice to graze.

When they finally arrived, Keoki's feet were burning from his trek, and Io fell asleep immediately. Keoki waded past the male and female cattle that paced the fields, patting them as he went.

He had started working with the herd about three years prior, when he finally decided that life as a blacksmith was not for him. Keoki had been an apprentice for Mako, the squarish, burly smith in town. The work had been honest and satisfying, but Keoki hated the people.

Something about the clients he had to deal with – violent, rude, and often in a hurry. His hands grew calloused from hammering flat the iron sheets used for armor, and his forearms were veiny and thick with muscle from sharpening blades. He had been proud at first of his new bulk, but when some foot-soldier had mistaken him for Mako one day, he realized it was time for a change. He didn't want to end up gruff and mean-spirited like Mako.

Perhaps Mako had grown tired of the constant complaining and demands of the Heliken army.

Whatever the reason, it had driven Keoki to Felip and Agnes' farm. Keoki was much more content tending to the livestock and tilling the rocky soil for the grapevines Felip cherished so greatly, his skin growing bronzer the more time he spent in the sun.

"Zeus almighty, Kiki! I thought you'd never get this damned cow back!" a shrill voice called, "What kept you? We're long past done with dinner, and Fil's probably already asleep or in his prayers!"

"Sorry, marm! Io – er, I mean – the cow was halfway to

THE FIRST WAVE

Boura!"

"By all that is holy, why does she keep running off? Whatever. You get inside now, Kiki! I'll fix you a meal."

She whipped around briskly, bustling through the front door back into the kitchen. Keoki loved Agnes. She was the grandmother he had never gotten the privilege to meet and the disciplinarian he had always been able to avoid with his own mother.

She was well past sixty, but one wouldn't know just by looking at her. Agnes' hair was impossibly onyx and fell straight down her wrinkled face. She still looked like she could outrun Keoki himself and was fit enough to walk through the city gates each day, delivering milk, wine, and cheese to the agora. It was uncommon for women to deal in the agora, but Agnes had somehow weaseled her way into tending regular business there. She treated Keoki like a son, meaning she was constantly disappointed in him and made him aware of her displeasure every time he did something stupid.

She yells a lot.

As soon as Keoki got to the kitchen, Agnes shoved him into a chair at their small kitchen table, slamming a bowl of barley down with some goat cheese and olives she must have gathered trading today. Keoki could smell roast quail, too, and his stomach churned. He hadn't realized how hungry hiking around the mountainous countryside between Helike and Boura had made him.

"Thanks, marm," Keoki said, digging into his food immediately.

"Slow down, boy. You look like a pig."

"What's all the noise, Ag? Oh, Keoki!"

It was Felip. He wore his night smock, a long, woolen shirt that Agnes said looked like a, "dress an old lady would wear right before she died of a serious illness." He was lean and fit like his wife, still healthy from years of physical labor under the hot, Achaean sun. Unlike Agnes, his hair had turned wispy white, mingled with smoky grey strands. His face was wrinkled, but smile lines creased his eyes. This revealed the main difference between him and his wife. He had a much more peaceful demeanor, and his deep voice was soothing – soothing enough to calm even Agnes when she raved about the swindling salesmen in the city.

"Did you find the heifer, child?" Felip asked, pulling a chair to seat himself beside Keoki.

"Yessir, she was grazing just past the river."

"Wonderful. What a curious cow, eh? She's got a clever mind to see the world. Touched by the gods, wouldn't you say?"

Everything is touched by the gods in Felip's mind.

"I reckon so," Keoki agreed.

"Ah, well. News from the city today, my love?" he asked Agnes.

Her face reddened slightly, as it always did when they talked. Even now, even forty years after being wed. It was Keoki's favorite thing about the family of which he was now a part.

"Hmm," she began, her voice already less strained, "Well, there's a play this weekend at the theater, but it looks boring. Oh, another little boy got taken last week. I guess that villain isn't finished yet."

"*Another* child?" Felip asked incredulously.

It had been a while since Keoki had heard reports of kids being snatched, but there had been a few too many in the years past. Sure, boys and girls got lost every now and then when they wandered off, but these kids were being plucked right from their homes.

"Yeah, the Council's got no idea who's doing it. Still!"

"Hmph, no surprise there," Felip grumbled.

The ineffectiveness of the Council was one of the only things Felip despised.

"And of course, the whole city is still scared since Euripides got offed."

"The only one who could actually *do* anything, too!"

"And they don't know who did that either?" Keoki clarified.

"Yeah," Felip and Agnes said at the same time.

It had been around two months since one of Helike's five councilors had been assassinated. To Keoki, this really didn't mean much. He'd never met the man, and rarely even went into the city these days. Of course, Euripides *had* been one of the leaders who'd gotten rid of that cult – the Children of the Sea.

"What are you glaring about, Kiki?" Agnes asked, the edge returning to her voice.

"Nothing. Sorry, marm."

He hadn't even realized he'd been doing it. Sort of an involuntary reflex whenever he started thinking of those fanatics.

He unclenched his fist, another thing he hadn't noticed he'd done.

"Sounds like a pretty normal day," Felip said, breaking the silence.

"I suppose so. I'll see if Philomena has anything interesting to say about the poor child tomorrow. She's always collecting rumors."

The excessive sun and Agnes' heavy cooking began to weigh heavily on Keoki's eyelids. He needed to lie down before his head fell to the table and splattered his food.

"Thanks for dinner," Keoki said, rising from his seat and wiping off his face with his jerkin.

"He eats, and leaves," Agnes said, rolling her eyes, "You're naught but a stomach these days, boy."

"Sorry, marm. Tired is all."

"Ah, let the lad sleep!" Felip said, "I must be off as well."

They yawned simultaneously, and Keoki shuffled back to his room.

There were only four rooms in the small farmhouse – a kitchen, two bedrooms, and a common room with a couch. It was comfortable, but Keoki could scarcely find privacy. It was hard when he could still hear Felip and Agnes snoring in two-part harmony while he lay in bed, staring at the blank ceiling above.

Keoki stripped down, enjoying the freedom of removing the dirty clothes from a hard day's work. He sat on his bed, melting into the comfort of the feather mattress. As the twilight morphed into total darkness, the shimmer of stars and moonlight gently

ԵHE FIRST WAVE

guided Keoki into a dreamless sleep.

Chapter 4

Melani

Melani squinted through half-lidded eyes at the sunlight pouring through her bedroom window.

Already?

She shoved her face into the feather pillow at her side, trying to block out the unbearable brightness that greeted her every morning. After wrestling with the notion of going straight back to sleep, Melani rolled out of bed, stretching the fatigue out of her weary muscles. The air blowing gently through her window still had the faintest chill, so Melani draped a light linen robe around her body.

As every morning began for her, Melani loped drowsily into the kitchen and cracked six hen eggs into a pan. She stoked the embers of a dying fire until it began to catch heat and lick the sides of the metal. As breakfast cooked, she returned to the bedroom and sat at the foot of her firm mattress. The smell was usually enough to wake the shape tucked under her woolen blanket.

Sure enough, a quiet voice called shortly after.

"Mel?"

"Breakfast?"

"Please."

They sat in silence as they ate, savoring the food that would hopefully last them until noon. The two lived well enough by Bouran standards. Aside from royalty and noblemen, smiths were a high-regarded trade. Xander had been working metal since he was a child, forging steel and iron into weapons of war, while he himself grew to be a formidable weapon. He was solid as a bull, with sandy hair and skin bronzed from his days in the sun and fire. His axes, swords, and armor were the best that coin could buy throughout the city, and much of Achaea.

Was Melani biased? Perhaps. But her love's skill was enough to feed them well.

"Are you ready?"

"As I'll ever be," Melani responded, gathering her kit and strapping on leather sandals.

"Don't sound so excited," Xander joked, hoisting her up in one arm and carrying her easily through the wooden door of their humble house.

The only blemish on his body was a sunspot on the hand that held her waist.

"Unhand me, monster!" Melani hit Xander's thick shoulders playfully, although she could certainly not muster enough strength to hurt him.

Xander set Melani down on their porch, standing a head above her, and kissed her forehead. Melani was not a tall woman. She was thin, with brown hair hanging loosely past her shoulders. She had deep brown eyes, and skin nearly as bronzed as Xander, although she spent more time under a roof.

"Xan, how many men today?"

Melani detested the soldiers that came by to collect orders from Xander. Usually they were only low-ranking foot-fighters, picking up their officer's armor or getting their first iron blade. Even when more important men came by, it was the same. They always undressed Melani with their eyes or told Xander they would be more than happy to pay extra for the pretty girl.

He hates that more than me, I think.

"Only a couple grunts for shields, and Sir Farlen's new broadsword."

"Ugh... Sir Farlen."

"What about you? How's the river coming along?"

As they talked, Xander heated the forge with burning coals, and began cranking the grindstone to sharpen Sir Farlen's new steel. Melani uncovered the stone on which a beautiful scene lay unfinished.

"I need to add a bit of orange to the sky. It could reflect off the water... what do you think?"

"No idea," Xander admitted.

Melani set to work, hoping Wyrus Warren would give her a

few more days to finish his order. She had been slaving over the image for weeks already, attempting to capture the Bouran river cutting through a sunset landscape with the simple strokes of a paintbrush. Warren was one of her best customers and had an unfathomable wealth. Thankfully, he did not seem to be too particular on the quality of the works he collected. Melani liked being able to experiment with that type of benefactor. Not all her clients were as easy.

The day wore on, and as the sun rose to its zenith, Melani could feel sweat begin to climb across her skin, causing her robe to cling tightly to her body. They lived on a busy street, on the perimeter of Boura's center. Pedestrians plodded along, bidding good day to Melani and Xander. Grey-haired Marlo, from the bakery across the street, brought fresh bread as they toiled, and as always, Melani gave him a swift kiss on the cheek and a smile. Xander nodded his appreciation, and Melani promised to add a new painting to hang wherever he pleased.

Finally, two men approached, bearing spears and leather armor studded with iron plates. "Xander Atsali, our shields."

"Well, it's nice to meet you both, too."

"Did you 'spect us to be nice?" the larger of the two asked gruffly.

"I *expect* manners when I deal in business, sirs. Sorry, not sirs. Forgot I wasn't talking to your betters."

"Watch your tone, boy," the second said menacingly.

"Would you like your shields to work?"

Xander could not help himself. He despised most of the soldiers just as much as Melani. There were so few with honor and gallantry, he claimed.

"Is that a threat?"

"You need shields," Xander explained, "I'm the one with the shields. So, if I were you, I'd pay and get away from my forge."

The bigger one grunted and tossed a pouch to Xander. Coins rattled inside, and Xander caught it deftly.

"Six shields by the anvil. Hard oak and solid, banded iron. They'll do you just fine."

The two grabbed their cargo and huffed back the way they came. As the smaller man passed, he glanced at Melani hungrily, then back at Xander, sneering.

"Did you have to?" Melani asked.

"Oh, come on, Mel. They could've at least asked me how I was doing first."

"Ridiculous," Melani said, shaking her head, but smiling slightly.

It was only minutes later that Melani's first visitor of the day arrived.

"Melani! Melani, Melani, Melani!"

She knew exactly who it was before he even came into view. The sing-song voice belonged to a jolly four-year-old named Thal. He was a plump little boy, with curly red hair and rosy cheeks to match.

"The brave warrior returns!"

GHE FIRSG WAVE

"Where's Xanda?"

"Xan! A little warrior wants some new armor!"

The boy bounced on the balls of his feet, searching with fervor for Xander. Xander hid behind his forge. Suddenly, Thal was whisked into the air with one powerful arm, giggling wildly as Xander plopped him down on Melani's lap.

"Xanda!" he exclaimed.

"Where's your mother?" Melani asked, facing the boy towards her.

"Mama can't catch me!"

"I can see that, little warrior!"

"Thal!"

"There she is! Loren! We seem to have captured a runaway!"

Loren bustled over, the long cloak of a woman practiced in medicine dragging behind her.

"Agh, thank you Melani. He sure loves you and Xander."

"Mama! I want Melani's picture!"

Thal pointed at the stone where the freshly painted sky was drying slowly.

"Melani's *art* is for another, I'm sure, Thal. What would you do with a painting anyway!"

Melani could sense the distaste Loren had for her profession. Loren had been learning to heal since she was scarcely older than ten. When Melani had approached her years ago, she had been more than happy to pass on the trade to a new apprentice. Of course, that was before Melani had met Xander. Before she finally chose to follow her dreams as an artist. The decision had never sat well with Loren.

"Yes, Thal. This painting is for another. I could make one special for you if you wanted! The brave Thal in armor, perhaps!"

"Mama! Please!"

Thal gave his mother his best pleading stare, widening his eyes until he looked like a helpless calf. Loren's face hardened against the attempt.

"Not today, Thal. Melani has, um, *work* to finish."

She visibly struggled to force the word "work" out. Melani gave Loren a tight-lipped smile, the politest expression she could produce.

"Sorry, little warrior. Maybe next time!"

Tears started to well up in Thal's eyes as Loren strutted away with him in her bony arms. He waved good-bye and sniffed loudly.

Melani waved back, and Xander joined at her side.

"Well, she's as fun as ever," he said, still waving.

Melani laughed quietly, wondering what she would do if Thal were hers, instead of Loren's.

Chapter 5

Sapphir

There was water everywhere. It gushed into street shops, through open windows and those shielded by wooden shutters alike. Wooden chairs, empty pots, and other miscellaneous items floated aimlessly atop the current, swept away without discrimination. The columns of the temples were beginning to crumble, and statues toppled down its massive steps. Roofs had already been caved in by the first wave. Sapphir could see her old home, a little annex on the side of the Temple to Poseidon, in ruins.

I can't save it!

Then the worst of it began. From the depths of the growing ocean, bodies rose. They were unmoving and pale, oftentimes bloated with seawater. Salt clung to the hems of their robes, and one man was wrapped tightly in a cocoon of seaweed. It was almost too much for Sapphir to bear. As the bodies emerged, the water level rose unnaturally. It was above her chin now, rushing into her ears and nose... she couldn't breathe!

Sapphir gasped, waking with a start. A thin line of sweat traversed her brow.

A dream. It was all a dream.

Sapphir shuddered and pulled herself out of bed. It was childish to be frightened of dreams, she knew, but Sapphir could not help being terrified of this one. It recurred almost every week. The wave, the dead bodies, the city where she grew up in ruins. Of course, the city meant nothing to her anymore. It was no secret that her kind had been cast out years ago. She could still hear her own cries as her best friend was ripped from her.

And for what?

She knew if she set foot close to that place... she shuddered again.

Sapphir dressed into a loose linen tunic, draping it lightly over her pale shoulders. She preferred the comfort of linens to wool and fancier garments. Training her children often involved chasing them. It was much easier to dress in this way.

The kids were waiting on the cliffside as always. Cy and Ivy were arguing about the type of bird they had just seen, while Celia sat happily drawing pictures in the dirt, and Maya stared at a dragonfly that was hovering over yellow wildflowers. Egan had already taken out his scroll.

"Good morning, children!"

"Morning, ma!" Cy said, while Ivy and Celia echoed.

Egan smiled quickly, then returned to looking sullen. Maya

kept her eyes fixed on the dragonfly but beamed when she heard Sapphir's voice.

"Are you guys ready for your lessons today?"

There was mixed enthusiasm among her audience, but all claimed they were prepared.

"Cy and Ivy, it's time for you two to begin studying transforms! What do you think of that?"

"Oh cool!" Ivy exclaimed.

"Will we get to turn things into animals? I want a pet wolf!"

"Uh, we'll discuss that once we get started," Sapphir said.

She had no intention of allowing Cy to have a pet wolf.

"Egan, can you continue teaching Maya and Celia their letters?" Sapphir asked.

"Yes. May I read one of your scrolls, too?"

"I put one on the table inside for you."

Egan was already very skilled. There was not too much else Sapphir could teach him, he just needed to keep reading and uncovering the knowledge for new charms and spells. Cy and Ivy needed some work. They had tremendous ability. Both possessed deep reserves of untapped potential. But they were also stubborn and seemed to enjoy physical fighting much more than their magical schooling. Celia and Maya were both still learning to read, although Sapphir suspected at times that Maya had discovered her powers and was experimenting with them. She could never quite be sure with that one.

Egan took Celia and Maya by the hands and led them inside,

his bulky frame even more evident next to his younger sisters. This left Sapphir alone with Cy and Ivy. They had already resumed fighting, although this time with the wooden swords Sapphir had fashioned for them against her better judgment.

I should never have armed my children.

"Ivy, Cy, I've brought you both the most basic Scroll of Transforms. You'll need total concentration when you use this type of spell, so let's put those swords down, yes?"

Total concentration was the opposite of what Sapphir currently faced. Ivy had knocked Cy's sword right out of his hand, and now had rested the tip against his chest.

"Ivy!"

"Sorry, Mother!"

Cy shook himself off as he regained his footing, shamefully picking up the wooden stick. His blonde hair was matted down with sweat, and his blue eyes shone with embarrassment.

"She played unfair," Cy said.

"I wasn't being unfair! I'm just better than you!"

"Ivy. Cy. Total concentration!"

"Sorry, Mother," they said in unison, tossing their swords to the side.

Sapphir handed them each a scroll and sat cross-legged in the dirt. The sun peeked out from behind a fluffy white cloud. She could feel its rays rolling warmly across her back. Ivy and Cy sat down in front of her. Cy planted his palm firmly into the ground, making a circular imprint and promptly refilling it with earth.

THE FIRST WAVE

"Let's begin. Who wrote the scroll in front of you?"

"You did."

"You know what I mean Ivy," Sapphir said.

It was true, she had transcribed all the scrolls her children used. However, she made sure they always knew the original maker of each spell. It was key to understanding the incantation and therefore crucial to using it.

"Pythagoras!" Cy offered.

Always his first guess. Why is that always his first guess?

"No, Cy, it's Wallus Marin. Egan told me that yesterday," Ivy said.

"Wallus Marin, that's right. He's a new one for the both of you. A powerful sorcerer, some say even worked with Circe herself."

As Sapphir explained, Cy and Ivy sat with uncharacteristic attention. For all their impudence, they seemed to enjoy learning new spells.

"Read the scroll, children. Learn it, and let the words sit in your mind."

Sapphir made sure to repeat this command before her children began new scrolls. The magic within was contained in the words themselves. In order to use an incantation, all the sorceress had to do was read the words and remember them. If they truly comprehended the scrolls, magic was as simple as recalling the spell in their mind and concentrating on the desired result.

Of course, not just anybody with a scroll could perform its contents. The blood of the Golden Age ran through Sapphir's veins, as it did in Cy and Ivy.

At least... that's what Father told me.

At the world's genesis, the Golden Age of men had been perfect. They possessed no fears, harbored no anger, and reaped rewards without labor. Sapphir had learned that, because of this, they were all imbued with magic – innately capable of the art.

The Golden Age was wiped out in the great flood caused by Zeus and Poseidon. Some believed that as the new ages of men unfolded, descendants of the Golden Age existed. According to her father, Sapphir was one of these lucky few, with the unnatural ability to produce magic as she learned it. Her children had the same talent.

A dangerous gift.

The day stretched onward. Sapphir caught a long silver fish with enough meat to feed them all that night. She offered her children olives, nuts, blackberries, and cheese around midday, and they scarfed it down. All the while, Cy and Ivy studied the scrolls in front of them, reading carefully and repeating the words under their breath. At one point, they took a break to descend to the edge of the water and dip their feet in.

The sun was already creeping towards the horizon by the time Cy and Ivy told Sapphir they were ready to try. She nodded, and they each picked an object to transform.

I tried to turn a tomato into a sparrow the first time.

She vividly remembered throwing the tomato high in the sky, expecting it to fly away. Instead, she had struck her father with a tomato.

And then he struck me.

Hopefully, her children were more gifted.

Ivy stared at the smooth rock she had collected from the seashore. Her face screwed in concentration as she held the rock level with her eyes.

Nothing happened.

"It doesn't work!" she complained after a few minutes.

"Practice and time, child."

Cy was having similar luck, a shell the size of his hand resting on the ground before him.

"Try speaking aloud what you want it to become, it helps to envision the result."

"Sword," Cy said.

"Boat!"

"A boat, Ivy?" Sapphir asked.

"I want to sail around and explore the big land!"

In the distance, only a couple miles by sea, the mainland of Achaea jutted out of the water. Sapphir had never taken her children there – she preferred the security of the island. She made rare journeys back to the city. Ivy had always shown a certain affiliation towards the mountains and landscape that remained a mystery to her.

"Very interesting, Ivy. Maybe try something smaller first, though. Large objects can be particularly hard, especially when you're using something small, like that pebble."

I don't sound like Father, do I?

Sapphir watched as the two continued, closing their eyes and lifting their arms as if they could mold the rock and shell with their bare hands. Suddenly, it happened. Ivy's rock began to shudder, its smooth surface becoming coarser and ridged. There was a sharp popping noise, and a shell lay in the exact spot the rock had been.

Ivy grinned, "I did it!"

Cy looked frustrated, and shut his eyes tighter than ever, his head shaking from the effort. POP! A tiny blade, no bigger than Sapphir's thumb, fell next to Ivy's shell.

"Great work!" Sapphir exclaimed, and both her children bounced with excitement.

"Let's do more!" Cy said, making a circle in the dirt around a beetle that was lounging in the sunlight.

He closed his eyes, and pointed at the beetle, "Snake!"

The beetle waddled away at the noise, unchanged.

"Careful, Cy," Sapphir warned, "Living things are a completely different task. I won't have you changing any animals into teapots, are we clear?"

"Not even bugs?"

"Not even bugs."

Especially not bugs.

Cy and Ivy both looked forlorn at this but changed tack instantly after Ivy pointed at Cy's wooden sword and turned it into a piece of wet clay. They rushed off, wielding the new spell with abandon, failing to make major changes to anything. As Sapphir knew, there was little chance they could transform anything larger than Cy's wooden sword, at least not for a while.

****

Weeks later, Sapphir was preparing herself for sleep. The children had gotten more practice with transforms that day, and she had also taken them to the other side of the island, where they could swim and jump off the rocks into deep water. Celia had taken her bird down to the waterside, and Sapphir could tell it was smitten with her; though perhaps that was due to Celia being her only source of food. She would feed Blackwing bites of fish and meat from the table – basically any food she could smuggle to her bedroom. The osprey's wing seemed to be healing nicely, too. Sapphir wondered if the bird would reach a point when he could fly again. For Celia's sake, part of her hoped he would not. Certainly, Blackwing would fly away as soon as he was capable.

Ivy was becoming rather gifted in transforms, even turning a piece of driftwood into a raft she paddled around by the beach. Sapphir loved to see her abilities progressing, although it worried her slightly as her daughter's independence grew.

She'll want to use these gifts someday.

Sapphir untied the linen robe she had worn that day, stretching her limbs and feeling the cool air settle on her body. She climbed into bed and closed her eyes, breathing deeply.

I can pick up some fruit and fresh vegetables from the village tomorrow, make a nice summer stew.

No sooner had sleep begun to wash over her, then a sharp knock struck the door.

Sapphir wrapped the blanket around her naked body as Celia rushed in. Her hazel hair was a curly, tangled mess, and her face was red from running.

"Mother! I woke up and I had a bad dream and I wanted to tell Ivy about it and–"

"Slow down, dear!"

Celia gulped, "I wanted to tell Ivy, but she's not in the room! She's gone! And I can't find Maya either!"

Chapter 6

Nicolaus

"No, that's quite enough for you," Krassen insisted, wrestling the cup out of Nic's shaking hand.

"Aw, Krass! What's a man supposed to do if he can't trust the barkeep to keep the bar?"

Krassen, the owner of the pub at the bottom of the hill, smiled, "I'm *trying* to keep the bar from being destroyed by the likes of you!"

Nic shook his fist with mock anger. It was hard to stay mad at Krassen. He was even shorter than Nic, with a pudgy face shaped vaguely like a cow. It didn't help that his voice quavered in a low baritone, slurring into something that sounded like a moo to Nic.

"Y-ya know what's hard, Krass?"

"What's hard, Nic?" Krassen answered, humoring his drunk friend.

"Is hard, Krass. It's hard that after your bar is here," Nic slapped the stool beside him, "I have to go up there," he pointed up the hill to the palace walls.

"Nicolaus, if I had a coin for every time you complained about that damn hill, I would be in that palace and not down here!"

"That's funny, Krass! You're funny! I think som- HEY!"

Nic spluttered, spewing water from his mouth and shaking his head in confusion. Krassen had given him his nightly dousing. Nic began to protest furiously.

Krassen shrugged, wiping the surface of the bar with a rough cloth, "If it weren't for that little bath, I'd have to walk you up the damn hill meself! I've got enough to handle down here! You should be thanking me; I don't think our lordly councilors want their attendants stumbling drunk into their quarters!"

Nic sneered, "Fine. Fine, you got me there."

The bucket of water did seem to help Nic organize his thoughts. His mind was still fuzzy from incessant wine, but at least he saw only one Krassen now.

"Alright, give me another few moments to clear my head and I'll get out of here."

"Take your time, lad," Krassen muttered, his voice softening as he began to clean.

Nic sighed. Most nights ended like this. He would be relieved of his duties at the palace by the time Orrin turned in and was free to do as he pleased. That wasn't entirely true – he was expected to return to his quarters before morning. But what was he to do? Most nights, Nic fancied a drink. Opi had come with him once or twice, but she preferred to stay by the castle.

There's nothing to do in the castle, why would she want to stay there?

A sharp draft entered from the nearby window, and Nic shuddered from the chill brought about by his soaked body. He rotated the sturdy cup on the bar. The inside was sticky and stained from tonight's elderberry wine. It was Krassen's homemade vintage, and the only thing Nic could afford in quantity.

Though the bar was empty now, it had been teeming with customers earlier in the night. Krassen's pub was a Heliken favorite. At least, it was a Heliken favorite for common folk, which was the company Nic preferred. Tonight, he'd played Senet with a few swordsmen and the town's baker.

Not many people knew how to play Senet in Helike, but Nic had introduced Krassen's pub to it about a year ago, and the people loved it. The game originated in Egypt, long before Nic was born. His father had mastered it, and some of Nic's fondest memories came from heated competition with his sisters. He remembered how the sand would glow red from the setting sun as they played, and how the pieces would reflect beautiful crimson across the faces he missed so dearly.

I could always win then, too.

Nic shook his head groggily. The wine must have begun to wear off. Rarely would his thoughts have wandered to such dreary recesses otherwise. Nic pulled himself up laboriously from the stool, and pushed the cup towards Krassen, who had returned to a water basin behind the bar and begun washing dishes.

"I should be off," he said, tilting his neck to one side in an effort to stretch.

"Be safe, Nicolaus. Hope I don't see you tomorrow."

Nic smirked and headed to the doors. The Heliken night was warm, but a light wind rolled across the ocean and crept gently between buildings in the town square. Small shops and pubs had closed by this time of night, so there were few candles lit, and the streets were illuminated only by moonlight.

At the first stair he encountered, Nic stumbled and scraped his knee – the wine hadn't yet lost its hold on him. He took in little of the city as he sauntered towards the steps leading up to the castle. Nic was familiar enough with the architecture to know the route even in a totally drunken stupor, which was a threshold he'd managed to avoid tonight. A statue of Poseidon riding a dolphin stood proudly at the center of one of Helike's main squares, his noble trident pointed directly towards the palace, making it especially easy to navigate home.

You're much nicer than the Poseidon in the palace dining room.

A wave crashed to Nic's right, and a shower of sea spray accompanied, providing a pleasant mist. Nic loved the way the ocean seemed to whisper at night when nobody was around, and he wished more than anything, that he could hear what it had to say. He paused, hoping to glean some wisdom from the calming waters.

"No, please!"

Nic raised an eyebrow in confusion.

Am I that drunk?

"No, please! I don't have any, just come to my shop tomorrow morning I promise it's all there!"

"Well we ain't leavin' with nothin' now!" a gruff voice exclaimed.

Ah. Not the ocean.

Nic crouched instinctively, although that didn't help hide him, as there was no cover in the immediate area to hide behind.

I need to stop drinking.

"Wh-wha?" a tremor had set into the first voice.

A woman's voice.

"If'n you don't have money. Then we'll have you," the second voice explained menacingly.

A deep thump sounded, and Nic recognized the sound of a fist hitting flesh. A muffled scream followed, that would have been piercing if not for the hands stifling it.

Bravery set in, that Nic only had after a night of drinking. He charged at full speed towards the voices, still stooped over from his initial crouch, unaware of the disadvantage it gave him.

In the alley between the staircase and the adjacent building, he saw them. Two grown men, average-sized, but hulking when compared to Nic's diminutive stature, stood over the fallen form of a slight woman.

"Grint, take off her dress," the gruff voice suggested, and the larger of the two reached for the thin strip of fabric that covered the woman.

Nic took his opportunity.

"Grint! Hey, you!"

Both men turned to him simultaneously, then laughed. Grint grunted at his compatriot, who nodded approvingly. Then he lunged towards Nic.

"Shit!" Nic yelled, realizing that he had not planned nearly far enough for this situation.

He jumped backwards, falling to the hard ground, and scrambling back towards the staircase. Grint sped forward, grabbing at Nic's legs, as the other one followed with no rush.

Nic kicked out at Grint's outstretched hand and connected with a satisfying crack. Unfortunately, Grint had two hands. An iron grip pulled on Nic's kicking leg, and his head smacked hard against the stone pavement.

The girl was still stuffed under the other figure's arm, as Grint raised a clenched fist and connected with Nic's left ear. A sharp ringing began playing in his head, muddling Nic's thoughts even more. Grint threw him to the ground, and finally spoke.

"Saro, bring the girl here. We can take her in front of the little hero."

The gruff-voiced man, Saro, brought the girl into the open and tossed her on the ground, naked next to Nic. She whimpered and covered her face, curling her legs together in a fruitless effort to shield herself. Nic felt terrible that he couldn't have helped her more. Smacking his head against solid ground had not helped.

And my ear! Who punches a man in the ear?

But for his conscience, he decided he felt terrible more so for the girl lying bare-skinned and bloodied beside him.

Nic's vision was beginning to blur from pain, and he barely noticed as Grint took off his tunic and prepared to mount the girl.

"Stop," he muttered.

Unsurprisingly, Grint showed no signs of stopping.

They're going to kill her.

Nic braced himself for the screams of the poor girl. But he heard nothing. The world went momentarily black, but Nic blinked himself to reality as he heard a deep shout and the crunching of bones. Then, the darkness returned.

✳✳✳✳

Nic woke to dim light and the low murmur of hushed voices. He took in his surroundings woozily – a cozy, stone room, with a feathered mattress and warm fire crackling in the corner. The space was small but decorated with beautiful paintings and ornate vases. Whoever's house he was in, the owner must have been wealthy. On a nearby windowsill, a single candle illuminated the gloom outside.

Good. Still night. I haven't been out too long.

He stood to find himself draped in a white linen robe that certainly didn't belong to him. Nic tried to take a step and immediately regretted the decision. He collapsed back to the bed with a clamor, and heard footsteps moving through the hallway.

"Ah, would you look at that! He lives!"

Nic recognized the woman, but it took him a second to adjust to the weirdness of the situation.

"Oh, er, hello madam."

"Keep your madams and sirs for the castle, child. I never have gotten used to that stuff," the woman said, filling a cup that sat next to Nic's bed with water from a clay pitcher.

She set the pitcher down, and used her only arm to guide herself carefully into a chair beside Nic.

"How do you feel?"

"Uh, I've done better. How did I get here, mad– I mean–"

"Call me Elfie. All my friends do."

"How did I get here, Elfie? If you don't mind me asking."

"Well as it happens, my husband and I were just on an evening walk around the town after everyone went to sleep. He's been so busy recently, what with the talk of war and all. We just wanted some time. Well, some time alone."

Nic nodded, noticing the fatigue and sadness in Elfie's eyes. She was a stout woman, with piercing green eyes and tan skin. Her most defining quality was the scarred left shoulder that accented the absence of her left arm. She'd lost it when she was a young girl, if Nic remembered correctly.

An infection, perhaps?

"Anyways, we're just passing by the beach, I was picking up

shells you know, when Orrin heard a noise. And, well, you know him. He wanted to investigate."

Oh right, and she's married to a Councilor of Helike.

"And that's when we find you isn't it? Totally unconscious, sprawled on the street like a sack of wheat. And those two awful men! Well, as I'm sure you could guess, Orrin dispatched of them. Straight to the ocean for those two! The girl is fine, I'm sure she has to thank you for that mostly. I'll give you her name, she lives just around the corner in a bakery. Oh, she would just love to see you, I'm sure."

"No, madam, er, no Elfie, please. I don't need to see the girl again, but I'm glad she's okay," Nic responded.

He hadn't gotten a good look at the girl in the confusion and blur of events that had left him bruised and broken. But he sure as hell didn't need to see someone who'd witnessed his complete embarrassment at the hands of two random barbarians. Whoever she was, she knew one thing about him – he couldn't protect himself, let alone anyone else.

She would be one more person I could disappoint.

"But you already took her home?" Nic asked.

"She felt better around midday, yes. Then we were able to help her back to the shop," Elfie explained.

"Midday?"

"Yes, dear."

"So, I've... how long have I...?"

"Oh, child. About a day, I suppose!"

"I missed a whole day at the palace! Oh gods, they're going to kill me."

"As it turns out, given that you are currently under the protection and roof of one of those palace residents, I don't think they care. Orrin was so impressed at the bravery you must have shown to fight off those men!"

Bravery? It was the wine.

"Oh," Nic supposed that made sense, "Tell him I say thank you."

"You can tell him yourself! He's here now, like most nights. We hate sleeping in that godsforsaken palace. Orrin! Your servant lives, you can stop making me cook your meals and tend to your clothes," Elfie laughed.

He sleeps here! And I still have to wake him at the palace in the mornings?

The Golden Spear must have been sneaking back into his chambers the same way Nic did every night. Nic was surprised they had never run into each other before.

The hulking figure of Orrin emerged, and he smiled widely at Nic, an expression Nic didn't see the man wear often.

"Uh, hello. Hello, sir," Nic said, correcting his lack of formality quickly.

"Drop the sir, Nicolaus. We aren't in court, eh?"

"Oh. I guess I owe you a thank you. If you hadn't shown up, well, I guess I don't know what would've happened."

"Stroke of luck for the both of us. If you had died, I'd need to find a new servant," Orrin responded, a glint of humor in his eyes.

He's making jokes now?

Nic chuckled, "I guess that's true."

"It was brave of you, taking on two men. Bigger than you, no less. Although perhaps I should teach you a thing or two so it's them on the ground next time, and not you."

"Thanks, but it wasn't bravery I don't think. Just wine."

"Ah, that's not it, Nicolaus. Drunkenness doesn't bring out better qualities in anyone. If you're brave after a few cups of wine, you'll be just as brave without it."

"I'm not sure that's true," Nic retorted.

Orrin shrugged, "You'll be wanting some food I suppose? Rosie made a chicken stew yesterday. It's just delightful. I'll send for a bowl."

Nic's stomach responded. He hadn't realized how starving he was until that moment. It had been over a full day since his last meal, and he rarely went more than a few hours without food. If he was grateful for one thing in his life at the palace, it was the surplus of food. Obviously, the Council ate like Olympians, but the kitchen always cooked too much, perhaps out of fear of disappointing the gluttonous Kyros. He loved enjoying glazed fish or curdled milk drizzled with honey in the courtyard.

Opi eats with me some days. Has she noticed my absence?

Moments later, another woman walked in. She was built like Elfie, although she had both arms. Her green eyes showed the same fierce determination.

"Good morning! You must be Nicolaus. I'm Rosie, here's some stew."

She said all of this in a matter of seconds, with almost no pauses, but her voice had a familiar rich quality and confidence. Nic couldn't help but notice that she was extremely pretty, but for some reason he felt ashamed as the thought passed through his head.

"Nicolaus, this is Rosie, my daughter," Orrin explained, "She lives here with her betrothed, Gerrian."

The fact that she was Orrin's daughter seemed glaringly obvious, and Nic was slightly embarrassed he hadn't come to the conclusion himself. He tried to push down his disappointment that she intended to marry. He didn't want to meet Gerrian.

"Thanks for the stew, Rosie. Lovely to meet you."

She smiled warmly, turned on her heels, and bounced out of the room. Nic looked down at the stew. It smelled amazing, steaming with root vegetables, leeks, and chunks of perfectly browned chicken. Nic took a spoonful and sighed deeply.

"She seems nice."

"Yes, charming girl. We're lucky to have her around the house, it's much more comfortable that way."

"No other children?"

"Hmm. I suppose we've never discussed my family, eh? Well, it's just me and Elfie, of course. And then Rosie and her brother Cerius, but I'm afraid we haven't seen the latter much recently. He went to join the League's Guard in Patras years ago. To be quite honest, I don't even know if he's still alive."

Since waking up, Nic had noticed differences between Orrin in court and at home. He'd certainly dropped some of his usual formality, speaking with the cadence of a commoner. Almost as clear to Nic was the emotion Orrin showed. As he spoke of his son, Nic could see the wistfulness in his eyes. Cerius' leaving hadn't sat well with his family. The League's Guard was a force, mostly composed of noblemen or their sons, that stood watch at the Achaean port cities. The original purpose of the Achaean League was thus upheld, as the coastline was protected from raiding mercenaries and the occasional pirate envoy. However, despite the acclaim that came from success with the League's Guard, Orrin seemed displeased with the choice.

"The League's Guard is a worthy place for any warrior, though, isn't it?" Nic prompted, hoping Orrin would reveal some intriguing secrets of his past.

"Worthy once, yes. Back when pirates raided every week, and the pressures of cities from the North were greater, yes. But the Pellenians have quenched their thirst for power in the East, and our foes from the North would be foolish to tempt the might of Achaea's fully-fledged armies. Now, it's just a folly to please boys who wish to be men."

As Orrin grew angrier, his councilor's tone began to return.

"And to leave after..." Orrin's voice broke momentarily, "Well, I shouldn't let myself get too upset, now. Wouldn't be appropriate I'm afraid."

"After what?" Nic asked, genuinely curious.

"I have three grandchildren, Nicolaus. Had three grandchildren. I don't, we don't... Let's just say I harbor no love for his choice, my friend."

What happened to them?

"I didn't mean to upset you, sir. My apologies, I shouldn't have pressed you."

Orrin mouth twitched weakly, "Not your fault Nicolaus, don't let the teetering mind of an old man cause you any distress."

Nic stayed silent. He wasn't sure what he could say to comfort a man like Orrin. It wasn't often that a world-famous warrior like the Golden Spear almost sheds tears in his presence. Nic had no precedent for the situation.

Orrin patted Nic on the shoulder as he rose and sauntered to the door.

"Get some more sleep Nicolaus and finish up that stew. I'll need you at the Council tomorrow. I've had enough of fetching my own water."

Chapter 7

Keoki

Keoki was done with farming. As he'd left the house that morning, he'd sworn to Fil and Agnes that the next time the cow ran off, he was going to toss away his straw hat and leave for good. Agnes had just scowled and sent him on his way to find Io. Keoki maintained that Io would be better for beef than milk at this point, but he couldn't bring himself to act on that impulse. Fil and Agnes never slaughtered their cattle. They claimed it would be ungodly, even though most high priests would say the exact opposite.

Keoki had to admit that he could never take a knife to Io. She had those big, brown cow eyes that always looked sad and sympathetic.

Stupid cow, with her stupid cow eyes!

Io had chosen a new direction to explore, heading northeast towards an area with more greenery and forest, rather than south downriver. At least he wouldn't have to worry about the cow becoming breakfast for a bunch of Bouran foot-soldiers.

"Io!" he called, with no response, as always.

Keoki was just about to take a break to satiate himself, when he heard a rustling to his left in the woods. He put the loaf of bread back in his pack. The sound was muted at first but grew more deafening by the second. Someone, or something, was running.

Keoki put up his guard immediately, reaching for the stone knife that lay strapped against his outer thigh. He crouched behind a tree, poised to defend himself, when the subjects came into view.

The first girl almost ran directly into Keoki's knife, but he pulled back quickly. She was lithe and lean, with straight black hair cut shorter than Keoki's. Her skin was an olive shade, and she had striking green eyes. Keoki stood about two heads taller than her, and she must have been at least seven years his junior. The second looked almost exactly the same as the first but was at least half her age. She smiled sweetly, as if there was nothing wrong.

"Whoa there, girls," he said, reprimanding himself for using the same tone he would've used on Io.

Keoki decided he needed to spend more time around people.

Eh, perhaps not.

The older girl shook with nervous energy and looked around with panic.

"What's wrong? I'm not going to hurt you. I'm Keoki."

Suddenly, she grabbed Keoki's hand, which he immediately wrenched away, and started to sprint towards the outskirts of the woods.

THE FIRST WAVE

"Girl! I mean, whatever! Why are we running!?"

Keoki was out of breath by the time the two girls stopped. Here, the forest met a steep grassy knoll, covered in wildflowers but too steep to ascend. The girls were very nimble, both darting between trees with ease that Keoki certainly didn't possess. He decided to use his extra size as an excuse for not being able to weave through the forest with such grace.

"What. In the. Name of Hades! Who are you two?"

The older of the two spoke, "I'm Ivy and this is my little sister, Maya."

Ivy turned, watching the trees in anticipation. She still had a frantic air about her, looking in every direction for a way out, but Maya strolled slowly past her and knelt down to inspect a piece of grass with a bright orange beetle on it.

"And why were you running?"

"I accidentally found a bear! It's been chasing us, and I think it wants to kill me!"

Keoki glared back at her, "Did you bother it?"

"I mean, I don't think so... we need to get out!"

"Bears don't just attack little girls; they need something to be angry about first."

"I'm not a little girl!"

"Yes, you are. Trust me, Ivy, I'm a farmer, I know animals. Bears don't just—"

A mighty roar drowned out the rest of Keoki's sentence, and a massive animal charged out of the trees.

"Oh, shit!" Keoki yelled, backing up quickly, before catching Ivy out of the corner of his eye, and realizing with embarrassment that she hadn't been so fast to retreat.

Ivy stood with her fists balled, rooted to the spot, as if she expected to spar with the creature that was now stalking towards her. The bear was enormous, bigger than any Keoki had ever seen. It wasn't uncommon to come across small black bears or even the occasional brown bear, but this beast looked to be at least five times Keoki's weight.

"Ivy get behind me," Keoki demanded, trying to keep his voice to a low rasp.

But she didn't move.

He was well aware that if the bear chose to attack, he'd be torn apart; but this little girl stood even less of a chance.

Maybe the bear will back down at the sight of a large opponent.

Keoki hefted his walking staff and flourished the stone knife in front of him.

"Uh, back off bear! I don't want to hurt you!"

He tried to use a commanding tone, similar to the one he used with the cattle when he wanted them to herd together. The bear was a step away from Ivy, raising itself to its hind legs, just to show off a height over twice hers. It lifted a huge paw, with claws that resembled knives much sharper than the one Keoki held in his right hand.

As it began to swipe down, Keoki tossed aside his staff and

grabbed Ivy with his left hand, pulling her behind him. The little girl screamed and shielded her face. Keoki pushed her aside roughly, hoping she would have enough sense to stay out of the way, then whirled around to face the bear.

The bear seemed to notice Keoki for the first time, leveling its gaze and opening its mouth wide to reveal vicious incisors. It groaned with a deep tone, almost questioning. Keoki's hands were slick with nervous sweat, and his grip on the stone knife was loosening. He tensed his body, prepared for the bear to lunge forward and rip him to pieces.

Yeah, I'm going to die.

"Ivy, RUN!" he yelled.

He didn't turn to see if the girl had fled, but heard no footfalls indicating she had. Keoki could feel the bear's warm breath against his face, and his cheeks flushed with fear.

He accepted his fate.

The animal could take one bite at Keoki and tear the flesh right off his neck. Keoki knew that he would die, alone and far from home, with no witnesses save two girls who would soon be dinner for a bear.

But he was still alive. The bear seemed to be studying Keoki. It pressed its nose against the side of Keoki's head, just above the ear, and then took two steps back as if to take in the entire shape of his body once more.

Keoki was petrified, but finally took time to truly admire the creature. Its fur was a dark brown, the shade of oak bark. Even though the coat was thick and full, Keoki could still make out clear outlines where muscles moved fluidly. It had marble-shaped eyes, that looked too big for its round face. The eyes were a deep brown that Keoki found oddly familiar.

I know those eyes. Why do I know those eyes?

With a grunt, the bear turned away from Keoki, and loped back into the forest.

"W-w-what?"

The voice was not Keoki's, and he whipped around to see Ivy, still on the ground, with a look of shock stamped across her face. Maya was not paying attention. She had picked up the orange beetle and watched extremely carefully as it crawled up her right arm.

"I told you to run, girl."

"Call me Ivy! I hate being called 'girl.'"

"Fine. Ivy, what are you doing so far from home?" Keoki asked, hating how much he sounded like Agnes.

"You don't know I'm far from home!"

Keoki considered this for a second and shrugged, "I guess that's true. Where are you from?"

"I'm from an island."

"So, you are far from home? Where are you two from, Maya?"

He hoped she would give a more precise answer, so he could get them back where they belonged.

Maya's eyes lit up when she heard her name, and she flashed Keoki another brilliant smile. She opened her mouth, and Keoki readied himself for an answer. Then she sneezed. The orange beetle flew away.

"She doesn't talk much," Ivy explained, smirking at Keoki with a smug look on her face.

"Well, where is the rest of your family? Where are your parents?"

"We don't have parents. Just a mother, but she's not here."

Keoki sighed in frustration, "Yes, I have noticed her absence. Did you two run away?"

Maya nodded solemnly, and Ivy glared at her.

"Why? Is your mother abusive? What happened?"

Ivy stuck out her lip, pouting at the interrogation.

"No, Mother is wonderful. We wanted," Maya gave her a quizzical look, "well, *I* wanted to go on an adventure! I've just been on an island with my family for soooo long."

"Aren't there other people on the island?"

"No," Ivy started, then quickly tried to cover up the response, "I mean, there are a few other families, but we don't really like them."

Maya held her concerned gaze on Ivy for a moment, then resumed searching the grass for more insects.

I like this one more.

Keoki was pretty sure Ivy had just lied. Did she really only live alone on an island with Maya and her mother? He decided not to press the subject any further.

"Well, if you don't want me to help escort you home, maybe

I'll just take you back to my farm for dinner."

"Dinner..." Ivy gulped, "You're not going to eat us, are you? That's what they do in the stories."

"That's what who... what? Eat you...? No, I want you to come eat dinner with me, Agnes, and Fil. You had better come up with a better story about where you two come from, otherwise Agnes will be asking you questions all night."

****

The sun dipped below the distant hills as Keoki, Ivy, and Maya approached the farm. He had explained to the two of them why he'd been out so far from home, and how he'd probably lost that heifer for good. Ivy had seemed disturbed by this fact, and Keoki figured she must really love animals. He tried to console her worry by pointing out that Io had an affinity for exploration and was probably having the time of her life. He felt secretly scared, hoping Io didn't have any run-ins with the monster bear they had encountered.

Do bears eat cow meat?

Suddenly, the door to the farmhouse flung open, and Agnes bustled out, reprimanding Keoki as he approached.

"I send you out for a cow, and you come back with two girls? Do these fine young ladies look like a cow to you? We need that heifer's cheese, Keoki! Where'd she go!"

"It's a long story, marm. I was up by the woods a few stadia away when I ran into these girls."

"Oh, and you thought it'd be a good idea to take them home with you? Keoki these girls aren't a day over ten years old! When I say you need to find a woman, I don't mean a daughter!"

"I'm eleven!" Ivy said with indignation.

"Agnes, if you'll just listen! They were about to get attacked by a bear! Biggest one I've ever seen!"

Agnes scoffed, "Oh sure, and you fought it off with that stick of yours, and that toothpick of a knife?"

"Um, well it actually just kind of left…"

"Very brave of you, Kiki."

She's worse than my mother ever would be.

Agnes threw her arms in the air, as if she couldn't believe Keoki's audacity, trying to save those two girls. Just then, Fil emerged, biting happily into an apple.

Thank the gods.

"Ah, Keoki m'boy! I hear you fought off a bear!"

Keoki grinned at Agnes. She rarely retorted so sharply when Fil was around, especially in front of new guests.

"And who are these two lovelies?" he asked, wiping a hand off on his frock, and reaching it out in greeting.

"Hello, mister. I'm Ivy and this is Maya," Ivy said, gesturing towards Maya, who sat serenely at her side, watching the colors of the sky blend from blue to a medley of pink, orange, and red.

"Please," Fil began, shaking Ivy's hand delicately, "call me Fil. You've already had the pleasure of meeting my beautiful flower,

Agnes."

Agnes rolled her eyes, then flashed a polite smile at the two girls and glared back at Keoki. She sighed, as if this anger was not worth her time, and swept back inside.

"I'll have to apologize for her, children," Fil explained warmly, "She's had a long day trying to deal in the market today. One of the bakers who always buys from us was assaulted yesterday, I'm afraid. She's always been most friendly to Agnes, and her father is not nearly as generous with his business. Quite tight with the purse, that one is."

"Is she okay?" Keoki wondered, becoming flustered as soon as he asked.

Agnes had taken Keoki into town to go to the market a few times, and Keoki had always admired the baker. She was very pretty, and one of the only girls around Helike with whom Keoki had ever shared multiple conversations.

Fil chuckled at the redness filling Keoki's face, "I hear the girl is doing okay. Seems a boy from the castle was able to wrestle her out of trouble. He and the Golden Spear, of course."

The Golden Spear.

Keoki had heard stories about the man since he was a child. He'd almost single-handedly saved Helike, and by extension, Achaea, in the battle against Athens years before Keoki was born.

"What was the councilor doing away from the palace?" Keoki wondered aloud.

"Heavens knows, my boy. I dare say the Golden Spear may

find himself restless in these times. He does not bear the proper patience of a politician, I'm afraid. Good man though he may be."

Keoki reflected on the event, wishing he had been the one to save the lady baker. He rarely dreamed of things of this nature. Keoki had become more and more curt over the years and held a general disdain for most individuals he met. The pessimistic outlook had not been one Keoki had held his whole life; but growing up without much wealth in Achaea often meant one grew sterner by the day.

Ivy and Maya still think like that. So carefree.

He looked at Maya, still gazing at the beautiful sunset with wonder.

What island did these two come from? And how will I get them home?

"Well, come inside now, you three! The journey must have left you starving. My dear Agnes made a wonderful vegetable broth, and there may just be enough for all of us."

Ϛhapҭer 8

Ϭelani

"Oh, right!" the squat soldier joked with his much taller armored friend, "As if we'll just roll over to the Heliken gates and march through the city square. The city's twice our size!"

His friend responded, sounding as if snot clogged his nasal passage, "Ucalegon wouldn't send us into that city even if that fat oaf Kyros took a shit in his wine chalice."

The squat soldier cackled at the absurd thought, and their voices began to fade out as they left Xander's forge.

Xander curled his lip and scowled at Melani, "Disgusting, aren't they?"

"The finest the great city of Boura has to offer! I thank Zeus and Poseidon for leaving us with such valiant men to protect our livelihood."

Xander laughed and resumed stoking the flames to his forge. He had three ingots of iron melting slowly in a cauldron, nearly ready to be cast into plated armor for the frontline soldiers.

Xander had worked continuously since word of Helike's mistrust entered the city. Apparently, scouts spotted Heliken soldiers within a league of the Bouran walls, an unnaturally close distance. City folk whispered of the obvious threat this posed and gossiped of the imminent attack. In truth, Melani and Xander believed what most rational citizens agreed – that the soldiers were not but Heliken guards, surveying the land close by their city. However, there would always be discord when another city feels the need to mobilize any number of their force. Lord Ucalegon, the self-proclaimed King of Boura was a suspicious type and roused his army at any sign of quarrel.

Xander and Melani often joked about this, but there was no humor in the results of every panic. It always meant Xander was in high demand from the militants of Boura, and he was hard-pressed to finish his work at the outstanding quality it usually possessed. In times like these, Melani tried her best to help, cooking all the meals and even lending her hand as the smith's assistant. She was admittedly terrible at the latter, but her presence was usually enough to brighten the deeply etched lines under Xander's eyes.

"My love, how many more orders do you need to fill today?"

"Seven breastplates and three more broadswords," he responded without looking up, slowly pouring the molten iron into each respective cast.

"Is there anything you wish for dinner?"

"Fish... yes, fish would be nice."

He stepped back from his work and wiped sweat away with his forearm. Melani watched the sunlight pour through slats in the porch roof, causing Xander's skin to glisten and the mark on his hand to glow red.

He has nice arms.

"I'll run and see if the market has anything extra fresh for you, how does that sound? Yesterday's rainstorm should have brought about some lovely catches."

Xander nodded absentmindedly, setting to work on the leather-clad hilts for the broadswords that were cooling in their molds.

Melani sighed and turned on her heels, heading east up the cobbled road towards the city center. Boura was a bustling town, although not quite as populous as its sister city upriver. Melani had only visited Helike a few times in recent years to sell her artwork, despite the close proximity. Just after she and Xander had met, he took her to eat dinner by the seashore outside Helike's city limits. It had been a beautiful sunset over the countryside that evening. The cities were laid out in similar fashion, their bustling centers crowded with shops, bakeries, and a theater. The Bouran theater was much smaller than Helike's, although Melani found it more comfortable. Only the monstrously wealthy were able to truly experience Heliken theater, as common folk such as Melani would be too far back to make out any of the characters in the shows.

Xander had told her a story once of the time his father had

visited Helike for some event held by the Sons of Poseidon, and there had been a terrible explosion. Thankfully, most people survived the destruction, but Melani always found Xander's retelling strange. Nobody was sure what had caused the commotion.

"MELLLL-A-NEEEE!"

Melani couldn't help but grin as the chubby boy with curly red hair bounced over to her. He and Loren lived close by the marketplace, next to the medicinal school in Boura. Melani saw him most days that she ventured to buy fish and fruit.

"Little warrior!"

She patted his head as he stopped to hug her legs.

"Xanda?"

"He's not here today, little Thal. He's a *really* hard worker."

Thal shrugged, "Making my sword?"

Melani laughed, "I think he'll need you to draw him exactly what you want, so he can make it special for you!"

"As long as you help me draw, Melllllani!"

"Thal!" Loren's called shrilly, "NO SWORDS! What did I tell you about asking Xander Atsali for swords?"

How did she hear us?

"Hello, Loren!" she said, trying to keep a cordial tone.

"Hmmph," Loren responded, bustling out to snatch Thal's hand away from Melani's leg, "Let's get back inside, Thal. Back inside now!"

Thal resisted, but eventually trotted behind Loren back to

their house.

"Goodbye, Thal!"

"Bye, Melani! Bye!!!"

He bumped into Loren's rear end as he turned to wave at Melani, his red hair flopping up and down. Loren cuffed him on the shoulder before sweeping him inside and slamming the door shut.

"Nice to see you, Loren," Melani muttered, before continuing down the road.

Why does it have to be like that with her?

She wished Loren could bring herself to forgive Melani for halting her studies. She and Xander would certainly help with Thal. It must have been exhausting for Loren to try balancing motherhood with her practice.

And Thal loves us!

Finally, Melani arrived at her destination, the sizeable Bouran marketplace. Most days, fishermen ventured to the river delta and into a shallow bay nearby teeming with marine life. They always returned around this time with a plethora of fresh catches – red snapper, grouper, sunfish, and the occasional cutter shark when their luck persisted. The snapper were Xander's favorite, which was great for the both of them, as an entire fish was only a few bronze mares.

The Achaean League had a uniform currency across its twelve city-states and the surrounding municipalities. Each denomination sported the profile of Poseidon, God of the Sea.

GHE FIRSG WAVE

Named for the horse etching on its flip side, bronze mares were abundant and served as the main vehicle for day-to-day purchases. Silver crowns constituted fifty mares. Xander and Melani tended to have almost as many crowns as they did mares, as her art and his armor were priced as luxury items. However, the two of them scarcely saw gold tridents, which themselves were worth a hundred crowns. Only the richest in Achaea got ahold of these. Once, a particularly wealthy customer had bought Melani's first painting on a beautiful ceramic pot for a trident, but luck rarely delivered such an eager collector to her door. Melani had also suspected the man wanted more than just Melani's pot.

"Excuse me, ma'am," Melani tapped an old woman with a flowing red cloak on the shoulder, "Have the fishermen come yet?"

The woman gave Melani a sideways glare before turning away, responding curtly, "No."

Bitch.

"You'll have to forgive Magda."

Melani turned to the sound of the low voice to see a young man with a jingling purse strapped to his light kilt at the hip.

She smiled politely before responding, "Yes, I'm sure she's just had a difficult day."

Melani had no idea if this were the case but possessed no desire to speculate further.

"Difficult few years is more like it," he said, moving closer to Melani, "I'm Tarlen, but my friends call me Tarry. This old coot's forgotten everything she's done every day for the past two years.

She can be a grand bitch most of the time, but she means well. Don't you Magda?"

Melani suspected the woman would snap at Tarlen the same way she'd spoken to her. Instead, Magda cocked her head at Tarry and gave him a toothless grin.

"Forgotten everything, except that I'm a grand bitch," she said, before continuing on to a nearby chair and melting into it.

Melani watched her walk away, then extended her hand to Tarlen, "Sorry, I meant to introduce myself. I'm Melani."

Tarlen took her hand in both of his and kissed it swiftly. Melani did not take fondly to this type of gesture normally, but he seemed to be a well-meaning person, so she tried not to let it bother her. Now that she finally got a good look at him, Melani could not help but notice how handsome Tarlen was. She didn't recognize this in a lustful way, taking in his masculine beauty the same way she would critique her own artwork.

He was tall and dark, with muscular shoulders and a thin waist. He wore no shirt, instead exposing a perfectly chiseled upper body. If he noticed her gaze, he made no mention of it. Melani assumed this was a common occurrence for a man of his stature.

Struggling to find a topic of introduction, Melani began, "How do you know Magda?"

"The old bird is a dear friend of my grandmother's. Never been the kindly sort, especially as she's outlived nearly everyone in the town. Are you a Bouran yourself?"

"Yes, I paint by the smith's shop down the road."

Tarlen's midnight-colored eyes lit up, and he tapped a long finger against his forehead.

"Ah, Xander Atsali? There's a talented smith. I would have enjoyed taking up the art myself, but these hands are meant for much softer talents I'm afraid."

What are softer talents?

"You're familiar with Xander's work? He's my partner, er, we're together."

"A lucky man as well as talented, then."

Tarlen rattled off the compliment without so much as a pause. His voice was smooth and clear, as if he spent most of his time resting it; however, he talked with the experience of one whose trade required it.

"Are you also from here?" Melani asked, assuming the answer was no.

"Born here but raised away. I'm often around the city, though. I trade pelts and fine furs, so I travel quite a lot."

He gestured theatrically, so Melani would understand the extent of his travels. She wondered how he knew of Xander's smith work if he wasn't a true Bouran native. Perhaps he heard talk of it being a tradesman himself.

The two of them were still standing in the middle of the square. Melani presumed the fishermen would be arriving soon by the river, so she decided to take up seating on a bench nearby. She secretly hoped this would signal the end of her conversation with

Tarlen, so that she could enjoy a moment of quiet.

Tarlen decided to join.

Damn.

"You're here for the fish?" he asked.

"Yes, they come every day around this time. Xander's in the mood for some."

"You're a good woman, providing for him."

Melani grew more suspicious the more Tarlen spoke, feeling curious of his intentions. Her mother had often warned about traveling tradesmen.

"What about you? What brings you to Boura today?"

"I've just done a bit of trade at Helike. We received some rare furs and crocodile skins from Egypt and our ship has been doing the rounds at every port. I thought I might take a skiff down to my birth city. With yesterday's rain, it worked nicely to stop here, anyhow."

Helike...

If Tarlen could share any information about the trouble in Helike, Melani could handle a few more minutes of talk. She was curious to know how serious the issue might be.

"Helike," Melani repeated, "How is it there? We've heard rumors. Well, how does it seem?"

Tarlen chuckled, "A diplomatic approach to the question, Melani. You'd make for a decent pelt trader, I believe. I did speak with some soldiers over there. Sold some fine furs for the officers and an extra-large crocodile-skin coat for one of those councilors.

The city is... restless."

"What do you mean?" Melani asked, her interest waxing by the second.

"It would be irresponsible of me to share, I'm afraid."

Melani felt momentarily crestfallen. Then Tarlen smiled at her.

"But we mustn't always be responsible. From what I gather, it began years ago. You've heard of the Children of the Sea?"

Everyone's heard of them.

"Of course, there's a small group of them that preaches in the square most evenings."

"Yes. A historically preachy bunch. Anyway, the Children, as you may know, were an offshoot of the Heliken centerpiece, the Sons of Poseidon. There may be five... well four... councilors of Helike, but the Sons have always had almost equal power in the city. Maybe ten years past, the Children were under some nasty rule – the man's name was Teremos."

"The soldiers told you all of this yesterday?"

Melani already knew all of this information from rumors she'd heard over the years. Teremos had been a radical, and the commoners whispered of his ability to perform dark magic.

"I'm just giving you a little background, Melani. One picks up a lot as a trader. Xander Atsali knows this, I'm sure. Teremos was a magician, or so they say. He and his Children raised chaos within the Sons of Poseidon. Eventually, Euripides and the other councilors ruled an exile for the heretics out of Helike, on pain of execution."

"I've heard of this, but what does it have to do with now?"

"Patience, Melani, it gets there," Tarlen said coyly.

Melani gathered that he had been waiting for a listening ear ever since he'd heard the stories. There was no stopping him now.

"The Children were obviously unhappy with this ruling. Not all of them were villainous of course. Their case was flattened, unfortunately, when Teremos publicly assassinated a group of the Sons' inner circle. There are countless stories of how the killing took place, but us common folk and merchants love the idea that it was magic that killed the Sons."

He chuckled, muttering to himself about the deaths. Melani herself did not love that idea. Tarlen prattled on so easily about murder, but she found the prospect of blood magic, or any magic used for destruction, repulsive.

If magic exists, that is.

"So, now the Children are forcibly removed, you see. Some of them come here, some spread throughout Achaea, and some just fled to distant lands or died, I assume. Euripides was the champion of this motion; it was his crowning achievement."

Melani was beginning to make the connection of Helike's unrest now. Tarlen was on a roll still, and the words were simply flooding out of his mouth.

"The soldiers and officers of Helike are saying, that it was the Children who murdered Euripides; it's the same magic that killed their beloved Sons. And who could've housed them and given the order from such close striking distance? Your Bouran king, that's what they think."

"But it wasn't Ucalegon, was it?" Melani asked.

Tarlen shrugged, raising his arms to the heavens as if expecting the answer to come from Olympus itself.

"Nobody knows for sure! If I had to guess, I'd say that nobody has more to gain from Helike's downfall than their sister city."

Melani was puzzled. She knew Ucalegon only from the stories on the streets, and he was never known to be a brave or tactical man. He certainly wasn't one to start open rebellion against one of the mightiest cities in Achaea.

Unless...

"What are the other port cities saying?"

"Ah, Melani, you ask too much of me now. And not that I wouldn't share with a lovely lady, but because I don't know."

Melani had no response to this, and she hoped Tarlen would allow the conversation to fizzle out. Thankfully, he received the message this time.

He touched her shoulder lightly as he rose, "It's been a pleasure making acquaintance with you, though I must be off. Next time my trade brings me back though, I'd love a meal with you and that blacksmithing prodigy, Xander Atsali, yes?"

Melani was reluctant, and she knew Xander would have no desire.

She nodded anyway, "Yes, nice meeting you, too. I wish you the best of luck with your Egyptian furs!"

T.J. VINCENT

Why'd he feel the need to talk with me?

He flashed one more charming smile, before disappearing into the crowds. Melani stood up, ready to return home and tell Xander everything she'd learned. He usually loved to hear the talk of the city. Perhaps it would cheer him up, even if the gossip could mean war for Boura. She was just about to leave, when she remembered.

The fish!

Wondering if they had simply set up today's catches by the riverbank, instead of hauling them into the city, Melani jogged lightly to the rushing waters. A few people stood around, rinsing out clothes and filling buckets with the clean, fresh water. But Melani saw no fishermen.

Moments later, she spotted a boat paddling up the current, away from the ocean. She hoped for her love's sake that there was a big, juicy red snapper. As it drew closer, Melani sensed something wrong. There were two men, most definitely fishermen she had seen before, waving their hands as they came in, with looks of panic on their faces. Once she could finally see everyone inside, Melani's stomach jumped to her throat.

There were two bodies in addition to the two fishermen, who were now leaping to shore and pulling a tow rope in to tie around the nearest tree. One was clearly dead, pale and gaunt, as if all the blood had drained away, a wicked gash running from his neck to his stomach. The other had two arrows protruding from his body, one from his left thigh, and the other just below his right shoulder.

THE FIRST WAVE

One fisherman raced away immediately, shouting for a healer, while the other pulled his friend ashore. The man was breathing raggedly, eyes rolled back in his sockets, the two arrows sticking up like fishhooks, ready to reel in their newest catch.

Chapter 9

Sapphir

Sapphir flexed her slender fingers, observing the way her nails reflected the warm firelight in the pitch darkness of the forest. She had left the comfort of her remote island as soon as Celia relayed the news that Maya and Ivy were gone, conjuring a small boat from a piece of driftwood. Her stomach fluttered with pride and anguish in that moment, as she knew this must have been the exact way Ivy fled.

A million thoughts raced through Sapphir's mind. She hated leaving her children for any span of time, especially without proper warning. Sure, Egan would have no problem taking care of his younger siblings for a few days, though it would mean he'd need to venture out from the dimly lit study where he spent most of his time; but Sapphir felt forlorn at the mere thought of abandoning them.

And Ivy.

GHE FIRSG WAVE

Sapphir was certain Maya had no part in the plans, merely trundling behind the sister whom she resembled so greatly.

Oh, Ivy!

Sapphir knew the little energetic girl meant no ill will in her departure, but it tore her heart to pieces to think any of her children wished for a different life. Sapphir desired nothing more than to provide a perfect home for them.

The one I never had. What did I do to provoke Ivy to leave?

And what had possessed her second child to take Maya along? She began praying as soon as her boat rolled over the first waves in the open water. How could she know the gods had delivered Ivy and Maya safely to dry land?

After a hard night's journey, sunlight peeked over the mountainous countryside, and Sapphir made shore at a rocky cove on the outskirts of a gnarled forest. Several other boats, ranging from larger fishing skiffs to dinghies like hers, lay sprawled across the beach, either wrecked or untouched. Sapphir prayed one of those was Ivy's creation. For the rest of that day, she scoured every inch of the land, searching for any inkling of the two girls. Yet, she saw no signs.

She finally decided rest would provide her more utility than further pointless searching. Now, Sapphir stoked an adequate fire, roasting a squirrel alongside a few root vegetables. At this point in her life, Sapphir was used to living off the land, though she never needed to in her cozy cave. In the years after the Children's exile from Helike, however, Sapphir had developed excellent hunting and foraging skills.

Every day was a struggle then.

The only fond memory Sapphir possessed of those times was the image of her late husband's soft, brown eyes, looking at her with more fondness than Sapphir could ever hope to see again. Her insides turned.

What would Yusef think of me now?

She was searching for children he'd never truly known, still an exile of the place where they'd fallen in love.

Still an exile.

That's the only thing Yusef would recognize. Occasionally, Sapphir longed to return. She didn't know if the crimes of her family would ever be forgiven, or even whether any Children of the Sea currently resided in Helike. Certainly, Sapphir had never caused as much harm as many other Children, so perhaps they would never notice if she and her family slipped back into the city.

Sapphir brushed this thought aside as always. It wouldn't matter if she hadn't hurt a soul as a Child of the Sea; Helike could never be her family's home.

And I did hurt people.

She had been ten the first time her father had brought her to one of his prisoners. He kept them all in a cave far down the shoreline. Her father had rowed a skiff for almost an hour, saying nothing. Sapphir spun her fingers in her red hair, occasionally sticking a pale hand in the seawater.

When they arrived at the cave, her father moored the boat.

THE FIRST WAVE

The cave floor was sandy, but the walls and ceiling protruded with stalactites, dripping like bloody fangs.

"It smells bad, Father," Sapphir had said, wrinkling her nose.

Her father said nothing until they reached the prisoner. The man was chained to the ground, curled pitifully and shaking.

"Who is he, Father?"

"A bad man, Sapphir."

His voice was honey smooth.

"What did the bad man do?"

Sapphir remembered feeling sad as she looked at the man who was so thin and weak.

"He does not believe in the salvation brought by our Lord Poseidon. And he wants others to think the same way."

"But you want others to think the same way as you," Sapphir had said.

Father had punished her for saying that.

I was always so stupid.

"Do you know what we do with men like this?"

Sapphir hadn't. Not really. But she did have a good idea.

"I want you to do it, Sapphir."

She had stood there, a ten-year-old child who still couldn't pronounce the word 'Hephaestus' properly. She had felt the magical energy stir within her. She didn't want to hurt the thin man. She didn't even understand what he'd done wrong.

"Well, Sapphir... are you strong enough?"

Sapphir waved her hand, extinguishing the fire with a

thought. She lay down, trying to expel these memories. All that mattered right now was getting a few hours of rest. She needed to revitalize before her journey could continue. Sapphir sensed in her bones that she wasn't close to her missing children. She could try a detection spell to confirm her suspicions, but Sapphir figured it was best to let her magical energy reserves rest along with her body – such a spell merely revealed life, and the forest was most likely teeming with wild animals.

Her eyes had scarcely begun to close when a twig snapped. Sapphir's tired brain stirred. Before she could fully rouse herself, however, they were all around. Sapphir felt her body tugged roughly, as thick, coarse hands grabbed her by her thin ankles. Another pair of hands grabbed her by the shoulders, and she was bound before she could begin to fight back.

By this point, Sapphir was fully awake, berating herself inwardly that she hadn't used the detection spell moments ago. She took stock of the situation in a heartbeat. Her legs were tied together with a strong rope, and her arms were pinned firmly to her sides. Two ragged men held her upright with ease, and three more scavenged her supply pack. They were all dressed in torn clothing, with miscellaneous pelts and jewelry, most likely stolen property, loosely adorning their wrists and necks.

"Nothin', she's got no crowns and no tridents. Not even a mare!"

"She *is* wearing some fine linen. Why you got fine linen but no gold, woman?"

ᏚᎻᎬ FIRST WAVE

Sapphir pursed her lips defiantly. Gods, how could she have been so stupid. She looked at the sky and cursed under her breath. It was true, Sapphir traveled with no coins in her purse. She kept a smaller bag tucked within her robes, to avoid pickpockets and petty thieves. How the bandits hadn't felt it when they tied her up, Sapphir had no idea. They must have been as idiotic as they appeared.

"Speak, bitch! Or we'll cut your tongue out!" the shortest and roundest of the bunch spat.

A woman. This one's a woman.

Not many women ranged in bandit clans such as these.

"How's she s'pposed to speak if she's got no tongue?" a thin man with an untidy, pointed beard wondered.

The rotund thief paused, "I don't know, do I? We can cut out one of her eyeballs, then!"

Finally, the man who Sapphir assumed was the leader of the group stepped forward. He was the cleanest of the bunch, wearing thick braids adorned with gold loops.

"We'll have no murder today. What's your name, woman?"

Sapphir blew a strand of red hair away from her face, feeling a trickle of blood roll over her lip. She glared back calmly at the men and woman, taking their measure and reading their emotions in a heartbeat. It had been years since Sapphir last fought. Ever since Maya came along, her family lived a peaceful life on the island, with plenty of sights to see and scrolls to learn. The closest Sapphir ever got to a mere argument was when she haggled for prices with local farmers and fisherfolk on the nearby shores. She led a relaxed and happy life, seldom haunted by the memories of her past. However, this moment, the seconds just before a fight, brought about a feeling Sapphir would reluctantly admit she missed.

Three of the four men standing before her suspected no danger in their current situation. The fat woman sweated profusely, most likely from the effort it took her to support her own weight. Sapphir felt fury that an evil fool like her was more well-fed than most peaceful commoners. The man with the pointed beard twisted his finger through it casually, as if the prospect of killing yet another helpless woman would not lose him a wink of sleep. The other two were splitting a hard piece of crusty bread Sapphir had brought along for nourishment; they seemed less interested in their captive than they were in finding a bite to eat.

The leader wore a different expression. His hand rested at the knife thrust through his belt, and his eyes studied Sapphir with a mixture of malice and interest. He certainly wouldn't hesitate to gut her if it meant profit for him. Yet, somehow, he suspected this was not the case. He wanted to know more, needed to learn Sapphir's nature before making any decisions. It was obvious that the others awaited his signal.

Sapphir hated that she loved the confidence rushing through her, the knowledge that she knew something all five of them did not. She closed her eyes, letting her mind fracture into three strands of consciousness. The first sent energy coursing through her body, searing the fibers that wove the rope binding her. The second found the words of a deadly animation spell, one that morphed loose pebbles and stones into sharpened arrowheads. The third allowed her to focus on the sounds and motion of her quarries.

Her eyes snapped open. In an instant the rope burned away, leaving only minor abrasions where rips in her robe left pale skin exposed. The bandit leader jumped backwards in surprise, drawing his blade instinctively. The two men enjoying Sapphir's bread yelled, letting crumbs rain down as they struggled to retrieve their respective weapons. For them, and the thin man with the pointed beard, there was no time to react properly. The pointed stones Sapphir sent flying found their mark, opening the throat of one, and bombarding the chests of two others.

Meanwhile, the fat bandit turned tail and fled. She made it six steps before Sapphir turned the ground at her feet to sludge, and her feet began to sink into the Earth. She had no time to scream before Sapphir closed her hand, and the woman's voice was silenced forever.

Sapphir stretched casually, massaging her hands and rolling her shoulders in circles to relieve her aching back. Ten years ago, being tied up would not have felt so uncomfortable. The leader steadied his blade at Sapphir, poised to strike if she dared to come any closer. However, the malice had left his eyes, leaving only fear with a hint of curiosity and admiration.

"You're one of them, aren't you? One of those Children.

Magicians."

Sapphir responded for the first time, "What does it matter who I am? I know what you are. I know you kill, rape, and steal whatever you like. You're a murderer!"

The man stood up straight, raised his arms in surrender, and laughed, "My lady, these men were no friends of mine, their deaths are nothing to me. But look around you!"

The man with the pointed beard sputtered loudly, spitting blood unconsciously as he drowned upon it. Sapphir cringed inwardly, the adrenaline from the battle wearing off, evolving into the remorse that always followed.

"You stand here, calling me a raper, thief, and murderer... You're just like all of your kind."

Sapphir balled her fists; she didn't have to listen. At any moment, he could be dead.

"I've killed for one year. One year after my daughter died because I couldn't feed her. I won't let that happen to my son. But your kind, your people, have killed more and stolen more from us all! I remember them. I was still in the city then. Evil – all of them."

Sapphir knew he was playing with her. He wanted to throw her off, try to get a rise out of her so she'd make a mistake.

"So, kill me, witch! Kill me and prove me right."

He is right.

She took a step forward.

"I don't want to kill you; I'm just looking for my children. Drop the knife and run – run and never look back."

THE FIRST WAVE

The bandit lowered his arms, and Sapphir knew without a doubt that he had already made his decision. She knew he'd committed crimes worthy of the fate about to befall him, but it did not make her feel better. She began one of the most complex spells she knew.

As quick as the eye could register, he threw the knife. Sapphir finished the spell, and everything slowed. The bandit's eyes followed the blade as it seemed to move through molasses towards Sapphir. She stepped easily to one side and plucked the knife from midair as it moved past. Time resumed its normal speed, and the bandit's eyes widened with shock as Sapphir stepped forward and plunged his own blade into his chest.

He collapsed to the ground, eyes fixed sightlessly on Sapphir as she dropped to her knees. Around her, four men and one woman lay in pools of their own blood, growing colder by the minute. It was a grotesque scene, and the smell of death hung heavy to the air. Sapphir looked at her pale hands with horror, spattered with red that was not hers. She looked up to the sky, pleading silently with the gods to forgive.

"Yusef," she whispered, with no response, "Yusef, what would you have done? What should I have done?"

Sapphir shuddered as his face flashed before hers. He looked at her with such love, such fierce protection – nothing could stand in the way of the two of them. Sapphir blinked and the four men still lay motionless, with holes in their bodies where Sapphir had cut them all down. As she watched, the world shifted, and all the men were Yusef, lying dead at the foot of Poseidon's statue in Helike's city center.

Yusef... no they aren't Yusef. They're not Yusef. Not. Yusef.

Then, her mind steadied. Sapphir saw her children, all five of them back on the island with her. She needed to find Maya and Ivy, needed to protect them the way Yusef had protected her. The dead men before her had tried to stop her from finding them – from making sure they were okay. They deserved their fate.

Sapphir stood, after what seemed like ages. The trees rustled steadily as the wind drifted past. A brittle leaf landed on Sapphir's hair, and she brushed it away.

In a way, she was thankful for the thieves. She had her lead now, had a path to pursue that might lead her to Ivy and Maya. If the bandits hailed from a central camp, maybe she would find more captives just like her. Younger, female captives that could be sold for a healthy price.

Chapter 10

Nicolaus

Nicolaus flicked idly at a candle flame, watching the shadows on his wall dance merrily to the rhythm of his movements. Dawn was beginning to break in Helike, and Nic wished he could see the sprawl of the city, the arid mountains in the East, or patchy forested hills to the West. Instead, his window revealed only the palace courtyards – a smattering of statues and palm trees with a marble fountain as its focal point.

He had returned to the palace two days after waking in Orrin's home. Though he missed having no responsibilities, Nic felt relieved he didn't have Elfie catering to his every need.

Servants feel uncomfortable being served.

At least, that was his experience. The Council meant to meet today – a debriefing called by Gaios. From what Nic understood, the Fishermen had made their catch.

Stupid Fishermen.

Nic lurched out of bed, steadying himself against the foot of the mattress. His leg still ached from the bruising he'd received. He donned the dark blue tunic of a Heliken steward, fastened it with his stiff leather belt, and strapped on his sandals.

He needed a new pair of sandals. The material had worn thin, especially towards the back, leaving him with scarce support in the ankles. This made walking increasingly difficult and did no favors for his handicapped leg.

Grey light began to fill the corridors as Nic made his way to Orrin's chambers. Rainclouds cloaked the sky outside. Nic always appreciated the rain. It made him less depressed that he was trapped inside all day.

Nic felt short of breath by the time he made it to the heavy, wooden door. His days of immobility had left him weaker than he'd ever been. He watched his skinny arm extend to the handle, his heart sinking with embarrassment that the door posed such an obstacle.

Before he could heave, Orrin emerged, fully dressed in his formal himation.

"Good morning, Nicolaus."

"Hello, sir."

Ever since calling Orrin by his true name at his home, Nic found himself stumbling over previously trivial courtesies.

"Please, let us go. I would like very much to make this a quick meeting."

"Of course, sir," Nic responded, taking the lead down the

staircase, so Orrin wouldn't be inconvenienced by opening his own doors.

The two descended to the courtroom, where Gaios and Simon awaited in their velvet thrones. Euripides' empty chair still occupied a spot at the table, a constant reminder to the other four councilors of the danger of their position.

"Lovely of you to join us, dear Orrin," Gaios said.

"Greetings Lord Gaios, Lord Simon."

The Flat-Nose nodded, his gaunt cheekbones defining dark circles around his eyes. Nicolaus wondered what kept a man like Simon the Flat-Nose awake at night.

Nic took his place next to Opi. He was happy to see her after being away and stupidly wondered if she felt the same.

She probably didn't notice I was gone.

"Hello, Nicolaus," Opi muttered, tilting her head towards him.

"Oh, hi. Hi, Opi."

They both straightened, and Nic stole a sideways glance to see Opi's face.

Is she smiling?

Opi was the only attendant Nic knew. Euripides' servant, whose name Nic couldn't recall, had been dismissed after the councilor's death. Gaios never kept the same steward for more than a moon's turn, so Nic never bothered to learn their names. Similarly, Kyros rarely kept servants for the long-term. They came and left more sporadically, however, and were almost always female. Nic suspected the girls were instruments for Kyros' sexual pleasure.

Kyros entered moments later, following a pretty maid who took her place on the other side of Opi. He wore a massive crocodile-skin coat over his himation.

He looks like an oversized gorgon.

"Right on schedule," Simon chided, smirking as he took a sip of berry wine.

"Our next meeting is going to be in my chambers," he huffed, "If I have to walk another flight of stairs, I may follow Euripides to an early grave."

"I think the grave might be the only thing you'll ever arrive early to."

"Lord Kyros, Lord Simon. Please keep the japes to a minimum today. Lord Gaios claims to have important information."

Nic's back felt sweaty. The oncoming storm seemed to have brought with it an uncomfortable humidity that settled in the courtroom. He wondered sometimes why the councilors allowed him and the others to be in the room during meetings. Of course, they weren't always allowed. Every now and then, the councilors would dismiss them to discuss the most confidential topics.

He guessed they felt no need to fear a few low-class individuals like Opi and Nic walking around with information that would soon become common knowledge across Helike.

"Yes, thank you, Lord Orrin," Gaios began, "It seems our Fishermen stumbled upon someone very interesting in Boura."

"Just tell us who it is, please," Kyros said.

THE FIRST WAVE

"Boy," Gaios pointed to his steward, "Go fetch the guards."

A boy younger than Nic dashed out of the room, and Gaios continued.

"Kyros, your eagerness is pleasing. It would seem our plan bore fruit much faster than we could have expected."

"Our plan. You mean hiring the most skilled men in Achaea at great expense to the Council?" Simon clarified with distaste, glaring at Gaios.

Gaios returned his look with a queer hunger, "Yes, Flat-Nose. My plan being to utilize a valuable resource for our city's safety. The murder of Euripides was a tragedy and has put Helike in its most vulnerable position since the Children of the Sea were exiled. If magic was truly the cause for his death, we would all be in danger. Thankfully, it would seem our Fishermen have other news."

The doors burst open, and two burly Heliken soldiers walked into the courtroom, a shackled prisoner shepherded between them. Nic raised his eyebrows at Opi. Rarely did anything besides idle talk and unnecessary rapport happen during these meetings.

"May I present, for your enjoyment, Rizon Atsali," a smug look crossed Gaios' face as he gestured dramatically to the chained man, then at Nic and the other three servants, "And you four, fetch us some wine, then return to your quarters. You are dismissed."

✶✶✶✶

Nicolaus paced his room in frustration. For once, he had been intrigued by a Council meeting, and now, he was left wondering who Rizon Atsali was and what he might have done. Rain fell outside Nic's window, a monotonous tapping of water droplets causing time to pass ever slower.

And the Flat-Nose even seemed to be challenging Gaios today. What's going on?

A sharp knock pulled Nic out of his thoughts.

"Nicolaus," Orrin's deep voice echoed through the room as he cracked the door open.

"Sir! Hello, sir," Nic called clamoring to swing the door open.

The Golden Spear never came to Nic's room, yet, here he stood, towering over Nic in his sea-green himation. He filled the chamber, squashed between the foot of Nic's bed and the door.

"There isn't much room in here, sir. What do you need from me?"

Orrin tried to enter further, bumping into a candle before twisting to catch it.

"A favor, son. That's all. But you are correct, of course. Let us return to my chambers before I break your bedframe trying to sit down."

Nic followed the huge man from his room through the great dining hall, past the atrium, and up the spiral steps that led to Orrin's high tower. He had no idea why Orrin needed him. There was a gravity in the Golden Spear's voice that Nic rarely heard.

What happened in the Council chambers?

GHE FIRSG WAVE

"Nicolaus," Orrin started, closing the hefty door easily with one hand, "I have a task for you."

"What would that be, sir?"

"You saw the man they captured? The one the Fishermen brought to Gaios?"

"Yes."

"They say he was Euripides' killer."

Nic's intrigue rose, and his heart thumped slightly faster. He was oddly disappointed he had to hear the information second-hand from Orrin.

"Is that true? Why did he...? How do they know?"

"Nobody ever knows how they know anything. The Fishermen are a mysterious group. Unfortunately, Gaios and Kyros feel we must assume it to be true, and the Flat-Nose agrees."

The Flat-Nose and Kyros agree on something?

"And what do you want me to do?"

Orrin sat in the chair behind his mahogany desk, folding his arms calmly, though his foot tapped softly against the floor.

"Nicolaus, we have reason to believe that a non-magical Bouran assassin such as him *must* be working directly for Ucalegon. If this is true, as the Council believes, action must be taken."

The King of Boura might not be as spineless as they all thought.

The Golden Spear's voice was somehow steady yet layered with a thick tone of displeasure. His eyes bore straight through

Nic's.

"What sort of action?"

"We are blocking Boura's access to the sea. Gaios believes cutting trade will force Ucalegon's hand – a fitting response for a man like Gaios. The other councilors see war as the only solution to Euripides' killing."

So, the common people must go hungry.

That didn't seem right to Nic, but he guessed Orrin agreed with him and didn't mention it.

And war... what would war mean for me?

"My lord, sir, will they execute the killer?"

"Yes, the man will be executed. Almost certainly. Nicolaus, I have lived a very long life. I've seen all manner of people do all manner of things. But this... this is strange to me. We know not *why* he did what he did. Why would he put his life at risk to take Euripides' life? He is not a man of the Bouran army, not a member of Ucalegon's court. Why would the King have thought to use him? And who could he be working for if *not* Ucalegon? Nicolaus, we need you... well, *I* need you to discover this for me."

"Sir, what do you mean?"

"Rizon Atsali sits in the cell beneath the palace. I need you to figure out who he is, and why he would have need to murder one of the councilors of Helike. If he's not working for Ucalegon, then maybe... Nicolaus, we need a better solution than war. Helike needn't bleed for this. The League needn't bleed."

Nic looked at him with shock. Why was the Golden Spear

trusting him? There must have been more qualified people than his servant for something like this. His mind raced with confusion, and his fingers twitched.

"Sir, I don't want to be a disappointment. But what am I – how would I even do this? Why should it be me?"

Orrin returned Nic's gaze, his deep green eyes meeting Nic's brown ones. Nic felt the sweat beginning to moisten his dark skin. He couldn't find a reason to turn down the task. He also felt he had no choice.

But I need to know why. Why me?

"Nicolaus, who else could I ask that the other councilors don't have political sway over? They are cleverer than I am. It must be you. *You* are all I have."

Orrin rubbed his bald head with a massive hand, sighing with exasperation at his situation. Nic wasn't used to Orrin showing such weakness. He always considered the man to be a legend – everyone in Achaea did. Yet, the person he saw before him seemed vulnerable, grasping for anything to keep the League at peace. Nic's resolution stiffened.

He needs me.

"I... I can try."

"Rizon will never share his motives with me. Not to mention, the other councilors would question why I felt the need to go behind their back for answers. Go to the cells and talk to him, that is all you must do. I will protect you if anything should go wrong."

When everything goes wrong.

But what choice did Nic have?

He nodded firmly, and Orrin's eyes shone with pride and gratitude.

"Thank you, Nicolaus."

He opened his hefty bedchamber doors, gesturing for Nic to return to his quarters. However, the doorway was already occupied by another.

"Might I enter, dear councilor?" Gaios asked, flashing perfect teeth and swiping aside his well-groomed hair, "I fear we have more to discuss, just the two of us."

Gaios was a tall man, but Orrin still stood well over him. Unfortunately, it was clear to Nicolaus who had control in this situation.

Orrin regained his composure, brushing Nic to the side and beckoning for Gaios to enter. Gaios looked Nic directly in the eyes, his mouth twitching into the ghost of a smirk.

He knows. How can he know?

"It seems we have plenty of refreshments here, boy. You are free to see yourself out."

Orrin said nothing, averting his eyes from Nic's. Gaios took a seat in the chair at Orrin's mahogany desk, forcing the Golden Spear to sit at the foot of his bed like a young maid.

He doesn't know what to do around Gaios.

Nic prayed Gaios had not heard any of the discussion moments before, trying to convince himself that the door was too thick for sound to escape. He exited, one foot in front of the other, bowing under the weight of thousands on his narrow shoulders.

Chapter 11

Keoki

The girls were bothering him. Well, Ivy was bothering him. She asked relentless questions, about anything and everything. After Fil and Agnes had finished feeding the three weary travelers, Keoki had imagined Maya and Ivy would be ready for a good night's rest. However, the food seemed only to energize the two.

"Have you got a sword?" Ivy wondered, tapping Keoki sharply on the shoulder as he pretended not to hear, "A sword, Keoki! Have you got one?"

"No. I'm a farmer, why would I need a sword?"

He let the question hang, but Ivy showed no interest in grabbing ahold of it.

"Today we saw a bear."

"Yes, we did."

"Well, maybe you could have used a sword to kill the bear."

"The bear wasn't doing anything wrong."

"Yeah, but if it had attacked you, you could have used a sword. Have you ever held a sword?"

"Yes, Ivy. I worked as a smith for a few years, so I've held a few swords."

"I like swords! I tried to make a sword yesterday," Ivy explained, dancing around Keoki with a stick she'd found on the walk from the woods.

"Is that so? What did you use to make this sword?"

Ivy paused momentarily, glancing at Maya nervously before quickly responding, "Er, I made one with wood. I tried to make one with wood."

Her hesitation hadn't escaped Keoki, but he decided not to pursue any further.

"Doesn't sound like a very good sword."

Ivy screwed her face in agitation. After a few swings of her stick, however, her good mood returned. Maya watched this entire exchange without saying a word. She had taken a piece of celery from Agnes at dinner and was enjoying the way firelight glowed green through the translucent vegetable. Keoki got the sense that her mind worked in ways he wouldn't be able to comprehend. She seemed extraordinarily thoughtful for a girl of her age.

THWACK!

"What in the name of Hades! Ivy!" Keoki yelped, feeling a sting in his left calf.

I will never have children.

She wound up to deal another blow, this time to Keoki's

midriff. He snatched the stick from Ivy, snapping it in half with one hand.

"Why? Ivy, why!"

"You said my wooden sword wouldn't have been a good sword! Well, did that hurt?"

Keoki grumbled, stalking away towards a chair by the dining table. Felip and Agnes were finished cleaning up from dinner and sat, privately discussing Agnes' day in the city.

"Yes, and Philomena says her boys are already snatching themselves up some fine leather armor from one of Mako's shops."

Felip grunted.

"Hmmph, I'm not keen on any trouble with Boura. What's the need for the violence anyway?"

"Ha! If this had been thirty years ago you would be strapping up that little dagger of yours and filling your quiver."

Keoki raised an eyebrow, "Fil, I didn't know you could use a bow."

Felip smiled ruefully, spinning a spoon on his thumb easily. "You didn't think the old man was always a farmer, eh? Well, I suppose I was still a farmer then, but I could handle myself just fine."

"Handle yourself just fine? When I first met Felip he was Helike's best archer!"

"You might be a little biased there, my dear. That life is long behind me now, Keoki. And you'll consider yourself lucky if Helike doesn't recruit farm boys for the battles if they come. Though I've no doubt you'd do just fine."

Keoki shrugged. He felt no longing to be on the battlefield like so many young men his age. The prospect of running a blade through a man's flesh, seeing the blood spill until his body paled...

No, much better to stay on the farm.

"There's gonna be a big fight?" Ivy skipped into the room, twirling lightly as she passed Keoki, then crouching into a swordsman's stance.

"Yes, and I'm sure a fearsome maiden like yourself would send shivers down the spines of any foe!" Felip laughed, batting her play sword away with his spoon.

"Felip," Agnes scolded, "That's no way to teach a little lady."

"I'm not a little lady!" Ivy protested.

Maya waltzed into the room at that moment. She reached her hand towards Keoki, and for a second, he could swear flames leapt between her fingers. He blinked, and the fire vanished. He accepted Maya's hand, lifting her onto his shoulders, where she began examining a strand of his curly, dark hair.

"If there's to be trouble in the city, would it be best to take these two travelers back home?" Keoki asked, hoping Ivy wouldn't protest.

"Afraid so. Would you know how to get back home, dear?" Felip asked.

"Of course," Ivy said quickly, "But, um, do we have to go now?"

"Well, let's get a good night's rest first! But then, yes, I'm sure your mother and father are fiercely worried about you."

Maya nodded. Ivy bit her lip.

What are they nervous about?

"Yeah, Mother will be... worried."

"No fear, girls, Keoki will get you back to her swiftly as he can. You'll be back before she can even begin looking for you!"

✳✳✳✳

Grey enveloped the skies the next morning, and the crisp scent of rain cut through the air. The temperature would drop at the very least, but rain would bring about a difficult day hiking back to the ocean and the girls' home. Agnes prepared a fresh pot of boiled oats for breakfast, and there were plump blueberries to accompany. Keoki ate in silence, while Ivy chattered on about how much she wanted to see the cows. Keoki felt a pang of guilt that Io was still lost in the woods somewhere. He prayed for her safety, and a piece of him hoped to run into her today.

He closed his eyes momentarily, as the image of the massive bear with familiar brown eyes popped into his mind. Surely, the bear would avoid Io for easier prey.

Keoki gathered his pack, stuffing the stone knife into his belt and gripping his walking staff tightly. He had bread, cheese, and apples for the road – hopefully enough to sustain them through a day's journey.

The girls followed Keoki down the winding road that led towards the hills below, and they struck off northeast towards the ocean. A light drizzle began falling just as the three left, but Keoki was undeterred as it slowly gained momentum, until most of his hair sopped with rainwater. Maya closed her eyes as they walked, letting droplets splash off her shoulders. She appeared perfectly comfortable.

"Does it have to rain?" Ivy wondered.

Her hair was soaked like Keoki's, and he realized Maya's hadn't absorbed anything. The water seemed to bead onto her hair, sliding off as if it were made of metal.

"Uh, I'm not sure why it rains. It has to for the plants to grow, so maybe the gods give it to us for that reason."

"But then, why don't the gods just make the plants not need rain? Then it wouldn't have to rain."

"Fair point," Keoki muttered, choosing to ignore the peculiarity of Maya's dry hair.

"Are Felip and Agnes your mother and father? They're so old."

"No, they're not."

"Grandparents?"

"No."

"Why do you live with two old people?"

Keoki glared at Ivy, silently lamenting at her unabated curiosity.

"Do you really need to know?"

Ivy considered, then spun around and began walking backwards, "No. But I *want* to know."

"Well, if *you* tell me why you ran away from home, *I'll* tell you why I live with two old people, deal?"

Ivy smiled, turning on her heels and continuing forward.

"You first," he said.

"I didn't want to run away. I wasn't trying to leave my mother and my brothers and my sister, Celia. I just wanted to explore. Do you get it? Do you ever want to just see all the world?"

"No, I've seen enough of the world already, I think," Keoki responded.

"What parts of the world?"

She's trying to avoid the question.

"You first."

"I just have been on the island for so many years now, and it's fun to live there with my family, but I've learned all these, uh, things, and I want to go use them!"

"What, so you've read a few stories, and now you want to see all the things from them?"

"Yeah, stories. And scrolls also. And I want to see what's on the mainland. What's north and what's south?"

"Well, I don't want to disappoint you, Ivy, but this is the mainland. It's farms, and cities, and scattered forests. And people. People are shit, mostly. If I were you, on an island all alone..."

All alone.

Keoki's voice trailed. He would love to be alone on an island, with nobody around and the constant rhythm of the waves crashing against rock. Ivy didn't know how lucky she was.

The corners of Ivy's mouth curved down.

"Oh. Well, that's what I wanted to see, I guess. There really isn't more?"

She looked positively crestfallen. Keoki immediately felt ashamed. He couldn't tear down a little girl like this, just because she wanted to see the world, and he hated the world.

Well, parts of it.

He did like the trees and the animals, the way the sky burst with colors to usher in each morning and night.

Somewhere, it's that beautiful all the time.

"Ivy, I guess I haven't seen the whole world. Maybe one day your whole family can travel it together! Then you would get to see it and be with them."

"Mother would never leave the island," Ivy said, "Unless she's getting food from the traders, she doesn't leave. She won't say why exactly. I know she's from the big city, but she doesn't want to take us there."

For a minute, the three of them walked without speaking. Keoki never considered what Ivy's life was truly like. He saw a zealous, energetic girl without any sense. Someone who left home without any purpose.

But I left home without any purpose.

That was different, of course. Where should he have gone? Certainly, he could not have stayed.

"Is your mother kind?" Keoki wondered.

"Yes, she is lovely to us. She always has been. Well, as long as I can remember. I don't remember anything too long ago. I think

I've always been that way. She's lonely without Father though, I think."

"What happened to your father?"

"I don't know. I don't remember him, but Mother always says he was lovely, too."

"You know, I don't have a father, either. Or a mother."

"Your turn?"

Keoki chuckled, "I guess so."

They walked a few more paces. The rain had died down as they neared the woodlands. The ocean was only an hour or two from here. Once they arrived, Keoki would pay some tradesman to boat them out. He wondered how they would locate Ivy and Maya's island from the sea. He hoped they knew some landscape that would mark home.

"So, what happened to your father and mother?" Ivy prompted.

"I grew up in Helike, you see. In the city. My father was a priest for the Sons of Poseidon. We lived in the main temple. My mother took care of me while my father preached and taught people all about Poseidon and the gods. I was happy."

"Why did you leave?"

"They, uh. I–" Keoki paused.

He smelled them before seeing anything; the rank odor of unwashed men was compounded by the size of the group. Agnes shared plenty of tales warning Keoki about the guilds around the Achaean countryside. Tribesmen and thieves, either protective of their territories or on a constant hunt for valuables. Fil insisted there was a market in the East, near Ionia, that bought all sorts of stolen goods. He should have stayed to the road, taken the longer route to a Heliken port, rather than heading for the closer trading hub in a village east of the city.

"Maya, Ivy, stay close," he whispered sharply, knowing it was too late.

Two men slipped out from trees nearby. Their faces were rough, scarred maps of facial topography. Each were loosely bejeweled, contrasting to the unmatched clothing they wore. Neither was as muscular as Keoki, which he hoped would discourage any physical confrontation.

These wishful thoughts were dashed moments later, when four more men emerged. Each was uglier than the last, speckled with dust and dirt, burnt to a crisp from days spent roving in sunlight. Keoki felt his stomach sink as they approached, one slipping a steel dagger from his tunic.

Maya whimpered, twisting herself into the folds of Keoki's robes. Ivy set her jaw, stepping next to Maya and clutching her shoulders protectively. Keoki could see panic shimmering in her green eyes.

"Hello, gentlemen," Keoki said, deepening his voice as much as possible.

Gentlemen? Why in Hades did I call them gentlemen?

"Hear that, big man called us gentle!" one of the men jeered, twirling a spear enthusiastically.

The others cackled. Each man was armed with some weapon, ranging from knives to spears, with one axe to complete the picture.

"Uh, how can I help you?"

"How can he help us, he asked!" the same man japed, leveling his spear at Keoki.

"We all heard him, Dil," the man with the axe scolded, looking at the others in disbelief.

"Yeah, Dil. You do this every time!"

Dil attempted to cover his embarrassment with a scowl.

"We don't have to fight. Give us what we want, and you're free to go."

"I have some mares and crowns," Keoki offered, pulling a handful of coins out of his pack.

"Hmm, I'm afraid that won't do big man. Those girls are worth tridents."

"You won't be taking the girls," Keoki said with resolution.

Ivy and Maya huddled closer to Keoki as they realized the situation. Stolen jewels and furs weren't the only valuables sold in Ionia. Strong men were often taken and sold to slavery, but young girls were coveted above even that. Wealthy men would give almost anything for servants and slaves for more unseemly activities.

"And what you gonna do to stop us?"

One man pointed his spear towards Ivy and Maya, "Get the girls."

ᲚᲮᎬ ᲤᏆᏒᏚᲚ ᏔᎪᏙᎬ

The six men closed in on Keoki, Ivy, and Maya. Keoki hefted his staff and drew his stone knife.

"Capture the big man, too if you can. Or just kill him."

The man with the axe made the first move, slashing wildly at Keoki's chest, as one of the others lunged forward with his spear. He barely had time to swing his staff in front, catching the handle of the axe and knocking it sideways. He was too slow to stop the spear, however. Hot, sticky blood bubbled from Keoki's shoulder before he felt any pain. Then, his arm caught fire. His entire left side went numb as the bandit withdrew his spear from Keoki's body.

Keoki yelled in pain, falling to one knee.

"Keoki!"

Ivy's voice seemed garbled in Keoki's head, as if he were underwater.

Run.

He pleaded inwardly that the girls would escape, the same way they'd dashed from the bear yesterday.

Keoki could hear Ivy shouting but couldn't recognize any of the words. Light blinded Keoki's already blurred vision and he heard an inhuman shriek.

As he slipped in and out of consciousness, faces flashed in Keoki's mind. Familiar faces – ones he hadn't seen in years.

Am I dying?

The warm, brown eyes that stood out on the woman's angular face glistened with love and humor.

"Afraid you aren't, darling. I'll have to miss you many more years before you're with us again."

But I want to come with you!

Keoki was frustrated. His clouded mind saw two people he loved, people he missed and wanted to be with. The pain would go away if he died.

A deeper voice responded to Keoki this time.

"Think of those two little girls. You have a duty. You have to get them home."

The faces swirled and disappeared. Keoki's vision began to clear and he remained propped in a stunted kneeling position, leaning heavily against his staff. How long had it been since the fight began? Minutes? Seconds?

Two men lay dead on the ground. A third stood, dagger millimeters from Keoki's neck. Somehow, Keoki still clutched his stone knife. His body took control, swinging his arm sideways to bury the knife deep in the man holding him at dagger-point. The man stared blankly in confusion, shocked at Keoki's sudden movement, and the blood that spurted from his stomach.

He collapsed next to Keoki, unable to finish the job that seemed like a simple task moments ago.

Keoki staggered to his feet, using his staff as a crutch to steady himself. It was then that he finally noticed Ivy and Maya, bound back-to-back to each other, gagged with thick, oily cloth. The girls stared at Keoki in terror, and he wondered if he'd added to their fear by killing the third man.

THE FIRST WAVE

How did the other two die?

Keoki had never killed a man before. He was shocked at how simple it had been. One second later, and the man would have sliced open his neck without pause. So, Keoki stabbed him first. He did not feel any remorse. Especially now, seeing two young girls treated no better than animals on a hunt.

Two men stood before him, both brandishing swords. Their expressions were uneasy, however, as their three companions lay dead before them.

Too late Keoki began to wonder where the sixth had disappeared to. A crunch of dead leaves behind him stimulated Keoki's instincts, but he seemed to move in slow-motion, impeded by the intense agony of his spear wound. Out of the corner of his eye, Keoki saw a muscular arm swinging towards his head.

The world went black.

Chapter 12

Melani

"By the gods!" an old man yelled, scrambling up so hastily that he dropped the roughspun tunic he was cleaning into the river.

Melani felt herself rooted to the spot. The fishermen had arrived so quickly, leaping to shore with a dead man and his wounded companion, who certainly would follow suit. In desperation, the third man, unharmed but visibly shaken, fell to his friend's side, while another dashed to retrieve a healer. The third man placed his hands by the arrows, pleading in a rapid tone.

"Athena! Zeus, Poseidon, oh gods! The god of healing, what's his name... Escl– agh! If there's any justice on Olympus, gods! Apollo!"

He began to sob, unable to find the words he needed to save his friend. Melani knew words would not save the man, even if a proper prayer was carried out. She was a student of medicine, having studied for four years before deciding to turn to painting.

No, words alone would not do.

Melani steadied her breath, approaching the wheezing man, slower than she wanted. His friend looked up, hair matted down by river water and sweat.

"Find someone, please! We need a healer! Forgive me, Aggio!"

The dying man, presumably Aggio, spat up blood, the corners of his mouth foaming.

"Prop his head up," Melani demanded, "Prop him up or he'll drown on his own blood."

She spoke firmly, trying to keep a kind tone. The fisherman did as she instructed, resting Aggio's back against his leg as he knelt. Aggio's head lolled forward, dripping blood onto his torn cloth tunic.

"Do you have a knife?"

"Yes, ma'am, I do," he responded, pulling a serrated blade from the leather bag nearby.

Fishermen always carried knives, Melani supposed.

She took the hilt of the blade, carefully cutting open Aggio's tunic, ripping away the cloth to reveal his bare body. Two arrows stuck out of Aggio. One mangled his thigh, but the more pressing concern was the arrow buried deep into his right shoulder.

"A few more inches and his throat would've been torn out," Melani muttered.

She studied the wound. Certainly, the arrow could not be left in, but much of the blood had dried, plugging the hole that would soon gush blood if Melani removed it. However, the shot had probably broken Aggio's collarbone, as well, which would never heal properly if any bit of arrowhead was left in.

"And if it's poison-tipped..."

Yes, the arrow must be removed now.

Melani slid the knife beside the arrowhead, which was coarse stone, sharpened into a wicked point. There was space between the wound and the stone – enough for Melani to carve in a complete circle.

Thank the gods she still had her steady hand.

Due to blood loss, Aggio did not react as Melani extracted the first arrow gently. She tied strips of cloth from his tunic in a tight knot around his shoulder and neck, praying that it would slow the bleeding. As she worked, Melani was shocked to find that her heart was beating steadily. She made each movement with careful efficiency.

Unfortunately, the process still took over ten minutes. By the time she began working on his leg, Aggio awoke.

He gasped in pain, twitching violently just as Melani lowered the knife to his thigh. Thankfully, Melani pulled back in time and didn't run him through.

"Mari! What, what's going on, I'm–" he punctuated his first words with a shriek.

Melani wished he were still unconscious.

"Aggio. That's your name, right? Aggio?"

"Yes," he said, gritting his teeth.

ᏉᎻᎬ ᎦᏆᎡᏚᏆ ᏯᎪᏙᎬ

"Aggio, I'm going to need you to be strong for me now, this will take only a few minutes."

Aggio nodded, tight-lipped and determined, tears wetting his dirt-stained face.

As she dug the blade into his leg, carefully extricating the rough tip, Aggio let out a strained yelp. She could see muscle tissue tearing as she pulled slowly. A fountain of blood burst forth as she unveiled a ruptured vein. Melani felt her stomach tighten at the sight; she counted her blessings that this wasn't the work that occupied her daily life.

"He's bleeding lots, marm!" Mari exclaimed.

"Yes, Mari, I've noticed," Melani said, her voice barely audible under Aggio's howls.

She placed the arrow carefully to one side, staunching the blood-flow with more of Aggio's shirt before tightly tying off the area above and below the wound.

He'll be lucky if they don't cut the leg.

She chose not to frighten Aggio any more than needed.

"How are you feeling, Aggio?"

No response.

"Aggio?"

"He's passed out, marm," Mari said, placing his hand on his friend's forehead, "He's awful hot, too. Feverish."

"The pain may have been too much, but if he's breathing... well, he's survived this long."

Aggio's chest rose and fell steadily, though it seemed to be a

134

difficulty for his lungs. He looked to be a few years younger than Melani. A doughy boy, she figured the extra fat may have saved him. Mari was leaner and older, perhaps a brother? Now that she was able to examine their faces, they had the same eyes and hair color.

Mari rested his head gently on Aggio's, lips moving quickly, most likely in prayer. She felt uncomfortable, suddenly, her frantic fear dissipating to a mild discomfort. Had she done enough to save Aggio? Should she have waited for a real healer to arrive? The rough removal she'd performed seemed effective enough, but the cloth on his shoulder was already soaked red and dripping.

"How did this happen, Mari?"

"Helikens. Soldiers upriver. They wouldn't let us pass to the ocean, said they had strict orders not to. No trade, they said. We tried to move past, and... they shot."

Melani did not like the sounds of that. Her concerns heightened when Loren arrived several minutes later.

Of all the healers in Boura, it has to be Loren.

In the four years that Melani practiced medicine, Loren had been her mentor, her teacher. She'd showed Melani how to handle a scalpel, amputations, winter fevers, and so much more. Melani would always be thankful, and Loren would always be cold. She despised Melani's decision to turn to art, claiming her talent was wasted on trivial entertainment when lives were at stake.

And the worst part? Melani agreed. She felt twinges of guilt every time someone coughed, every time she saw a guard with a nasty gash on his arm. Every time a child died. But she was happy most always. Happy with Xander, happy with the silver crowns and bronze mares and golds tridents.

Happy.

"Where is he? The boy with the arrows?"

Loren wore her long, linen cloak, the mark of a healer. She spoke with a commanding tone, as always, carrying a leather pack full of poultices, bandages, and medical instruments.

Mari looked up, "Aggio's here, m'lady. The pretty girl there took the arrows out."

The pretty girl there. That's all they think of me. All anyone thinks of me.

"Hello, Loren," Melani said, "He had arrows in his shoulder and thigh. I cut them out and bandaged them, as best as I could."

"Cut them out? Always too impatient, Melani, you always have been."

Loren rummaged through her bag, taking out a cask with a familiar mix of water and herbs.

"Did you think to clean the wounds?"

"He was losing too much blood in his leg, Loren. And the arrows may be poison. I was here first, and I did my best to salvage his life."

"And if he dies of infection, what then?"

"If we'd waited for you, he wouldn't have to worry about infection, he'd already be dead."

Loren wrinkled her nose, carefully removing the dirty strips of cloth from Aggio before methodically cleaning and bandaging them. She smirked at the jagged cuts the serrated blade left.

"Tried to cut him to pieces yourself, I see."

She always spoke this way. This was half the reason Melani hadn't kept the desire to become a healer! How could she work with haughty bitches like Loren?

She knows I'm right, and she doesn't care.

"M'lady, the Lady Melani saved his life," Mari ensured.

"Yes, you and your unconscious friend were all too lucky a talented *lady* like Melani was here to save him."

They were.

"I. Yes, we are thanking the Lady Melani," Mari said, smiling at Melani.

The familiar lust shone in his eyes. The look every man gave Melani. The look only Xander didn't give her. His was a look of love. Well, Xander and Tarlen. The mysterious Tarlen who'd left moments before Aggio lay dying on the riverside. Her gut told her Tarlen's visit could not be coincidental.

"I'm no lady, Mari. But thank you. I'm sure Aggio is in much more practiced hands with Loren, so I'll be going now."

She was not a lady. She was just a painter, and the darkening sky meant she needed to return home. If only she had fish to cook Xander for dinner. Loren gave Melani an eyeroll.

"Yes, you've done enough here, Lady Melani. Give my best to Xander Atsali."

THE FIRST WAVE

****

By the time Melani arrived home, night had swept day out of the sky for good. She could scarcely see her own hand as she reached for the door. Curtains were drawn at her house, and the fires of Xander's forge were quenched for the evening. Her stomach growled fiercely.

She lamented at the absence of fish at today's market. Perhaps it would be boiled vegetables and some eggs, previously earmarked for the next morning.

When she stepped inside, however, Melani was delighted at the mouth-watering smell of perfectly cooked sausage. She could hear crackling as oil seeped onto the pan.

Where did he find sausage?

No matter where one lived in Achaea, sausage was a rare treat, reserved for the wealthiest.

"Xander?" Melani called, her heart already rising, despite the day's turmoil.

"Mel! Come in!"

As soon as she entered the kitchen, Xander wrapped her in a hug, kissing the top of her head. She saw a pot overflowing with carrots, cabbage, and steamed leeks. The fragrance of the pork sausage wafted past once more, and Melani relished the sight of the browning meat. She never realized the intensity of her hunger until food was nearby.

"Xander! Look at you, cooking for your lady."

She only felt like a lady around Xander.

"Ah, I was just hungry. You never came back with fish, so I thought I'd replace you with sausage."

"Mmm, I wouldn't blame you."

"What would I be, if you were having a food instead of me?"

"Something boring," Melani laughed, "Like a cabbage."

Xander frowned in mock displeasure, "Sausage and cabbage is a tasty meal if you prepare it correctly."

Melani kissed him lightly, standing on her toes to reach.

"Did you finish all the orders today?"

"Yes. Well, mostly. I finished the seven breastplates and the three broadswords, but *King* Ucalegon would like a special battle-axe done just for his personal guard."

"Parex the Hammer? Why don't you make him a hammer?"

"I guess a battle-axe could be a hammer if you turned it sideways," Xander offered, pondering.

Parex the Hammer was easily the most skilled fighter in Achaea. That is, if you believed Parex the Hammer. There was no doubt he was a transcendent talent, wielding any weapon with wolfish ferocity and the experience of a man thrice his age. He was a boastful sot but loyal to a fault, never leaving Ucalegon's side and welcoming any would-be attacker with steel.

"Are you busy tomorrow, as well?"

"Of course."

They paused for a minute, piling plates with sausage and vegetables and ravaging them in earnest. The sausage was delicious, well-spiced with peppers and a hot chili from Ionia. The carrots and leeks were vegetables, necessary but unremarkable.

"Where did you get sausage?"

"Parex. He said I could have a gold trident or a sausage. I think you know how easy that decision was for me."

Melani had never been so thankful for Xander's appetite.

"And how was your day?"

"It was fine. I pulled two arrows out of a man."

"What!? Who?"

"A fisherman named Aggio. Maybe sixteen years old. He and his friends were held up on the river by Heliken soldiers. Two were shot; one died. Aggio barely held on to his life."

Xander took her hand from across the table, beaming with pride, "Mel, that was so brave! You saved his life!"

His face fell slightly.

"But the other. He was dead when he arrived? And you said soldiers shot them... this is exactly what they've been talking about. The Helikens... they're actually attacking, aren't they?"

"Why would they stop a few fisherfolk from getting to the sea? Do they mean to stop us from having red snapper?" Melani exclaimed, chuckling at the absurdity.

Xander's chin stuck out, "I don't know Mel," he said, trepidation creeping into his voice, "Fish is one thing. If they aren't letting anyone upriver, they may be trying to cut off our trade altogether. The sea is our ticket to all the other cities in Achaea."

"Mari said the Helikens mentioned that! No trade, he said."

"Mari? Was he one of the other fishermen?"

"Yeah, he was."

A disturbing thought itched in the back of Melani's mind.

"And I met someone else. A guy named Tarlen. He talked my ear off about the Children of the Sea."

"The *magic* people from the Sons of Poseidon? Why'd he bring that up?" Xander asked, leaning forward with curiosity.

"He said the Helikens think they might have been Euripides' murderer. You know, that councilor in Helike."

"Yeah, I remember him. But what would that have to do with Boura?"

"Maybe they think Ucalegon hired the magicians. A lot of Children came here after they were exiled. I don't know, this is just what Tarlen said."

"Who is this Tarlen guy?

"That's what I wanted to tell you! He was a tradesman! Said he came down from Helike. But how did he do that if they've blocked trade?"

Xander bit his lip, "Maybe he got past them somehow?"

"He knew your name. Xander Atsali, he kept saying."

"That *is* my name," Xander confirmed, "I suppose I'm a popular Achaean. Doesn't everybody love Xander Atsali?"

"Oh stop, I just thought he was weird!"

Xander nodded, putting dishes on the countertop.

"The drama of the town! Not much we can do about it. If Helike presses, and it comes to war, I'll have to fight, you know."

Melani knew. She dreaded the possibility of being abandoned. Dreaded even more that Xander might not come home if he left.

"I'll come with you."

"And do what?" Xander looked incredulous, "I don't want you in danger any more than I want to go, my love."

"I can't sit around waiting for you to come back if that happens. I can be a healer, I did it today. I would do it again to stay with you."

Xander smiled, "Let's just pray to the gods it doesn't come to that."

Melani felt frustrated. She knew Xander didn't want to talk about these kinds of things, but there was no way she would let him leave for battle alone. She couldn't. Her mother never went with her father when he'd gone off to fight. She would not make that same mistake. Father and Mother were lucky to have their lives, blessed to live in Patras with her grandparents and sister. But this was the life she had chosen – just Xander. She would not allow him to escape her.

"Do you plan on washing those plates?" she asked, letting hardness edge her tone.

Xander winked, "Always for you. But I don't think the plates are going anywhere."

"Some animal will smell the sausage and try to get in our house, you know."

Xander picked her up, "And *you* know I've always wanted a pet!"

Melani giggled, "What are you doing?"

She already knew the answer. She knew it from the way he was looking at her. Not lustfully like Mari and so many others did, but with love and affection, protectiveness. He saw the sadness in her eyes, the worry that came with talk of war, and he wanted to fix that.

When he kissed her, she did nothing at first. She still wanted to talk. But it was only seconds before she responded, feeling his tongue with hers and delighting in the softness of his lips. The worry began to melt away, as he pulled her in tighter, and her legs wrapped around his waist. She could feel the definition of his muscles as her hands ran across his back. Her left hand stopped to rest at his neck, while her right reached for the fastenings of his tunic. As he undid her robe, his hand brushed against the small of her back in a way that sent shivers down her spine. Soon they were in their bed, bodies intertwined as a cool wind whispered lazily to the tree branches outside.

Chapter 13

Sapphir

Sapphir concentrated, arms akimbo, running the words over in her mind.

And the flames ignite, powerful and... and... and what?

She could not remember. She huffed, pushing her red hair aside as she felt the energy within her quelling. Fear took its place. She had failed once again, and Father would not appreciate that.

He said nothing. His blue eyes, flecked with purple and yellow spots, merely observed. Father was much taller than her, almost twice her height, though she was tall for a girl of eight. His slenderness disguised immense strength – she knew this all too well.

"You broke concentration."

Father spoke with a soft, rich tone, and his honeyed words pleased most with whom he spoke. Sapphir and her mother were not fooled. Mother knew that behind every phrase was only a sliver of the truth.

"I'm sorry, Father. I couldn't remember the words."

"Could not remember."

He said the words slowly, letting disapproval seep into each one.

"Tell me, child, if you do not remember your words, can you become a sorceress? Will you be able to serve the God of the Sea as faithfully as other Children?"

Sapphir felt the urge to cry. Angry tears, frustrated tears. She could not simply remember every word of every scroll! How would she ever serve the gods properly. And she wanted so badly to perform magic like Father and Mother.

"I cannot be a sorceress if I do not remember."

"So why have you forgotten?"

"It's hard, Father!"

"Of course, it is difficult. If it were not, every child with the blood of the Golden Age would be a mage. But only us, only the Children of the Sea, remain in Achaea. Sapphir, do you wish to be a Child of the Sea?"

"I... Father, I..."

She never saw his hand move. Just felt the crack of his thin fingers against her jaw. She should not have hesitated. Tears welled up in her eyes, but she could not let them fall. She felt her face begin to moisten.

Sapphir blinked, wiping the rainwater off her face. She must have fallen asleep. Briefly, of course. Her pursuit lasted through the night, until she made the fateful error of sitting down on a fallen tree. Perhaps two hours had passed since she had drifted off. Where the sun should have been, stony grey clouds cried a misty blanket across the sky.

Sapphir stood, stretching the fatigue out of her muscles. She ate some bread and cheese taken from the packs of the deceased bandits. She had not planned to sleep, but it seemed already beneficial. If she performed any more magic without rest, the consequences could be dire. As it was, Sapphir could feel energy circulating from her fingers to her toes.

She sighed, setting off in the same direction she began following the night before. Wherever the bandits had come from, there were probably more. She dreaded that Ivy and Maya were already out of her reach, but if outlaws found Sapphir, perhaps they captured the two girls as well. The idea filled Sapphir simultaneously with fear and hope.

Only a couple hours passed before Sapphir neared the edge of the woods. There was a peculiar, yet familiar scent in the air. The stench of blood and death. Sapphir tensed, expecting to be set upon for the second time. This time she would be ready. Sparks flitted across her fingertips, and her eyes sharpened.

But there was nobody.

Well, nobody that would pose her any threat.

Three men sprawled dead across the ground. Red splotches pooled in divots throughout the earth that surrounded them. She studied the bodies, stepping closer to better examine their faces.

An axe lay across one corpse, though she could tell it was not the murder instrument. Another man still clutched a dagger, a look of surprise permanently etched on his comatose features. His stomach was mangled. The blade that killed him could not have been exceedingly sharp.

Of the three men, two wore no visible wounds.

When she touched the man with the axe, she gasped. His body burned. She could feel unnatural textures in his midriff, as if his organs were not ordered properly.

This was no ordinary killing.

Sapphir knew instinctively that her girls were close. The gutted man puzzled her, but the other two lives had ended with magic. If it were not Ivy and Maya, other Children ranged the woods, and hers were in more danger than any number of bandits could have caused.

Sapphir silently thanked Poseidon for the rain. Weeks had passed since the last proper storm, and she would appreciate the extra help that mud provided. She circled the perimeter of the scene. Footsteps too large to be Maya or Ivy trailed away from the spot.

They must have carried my girls. I need to move quickly.

If she did not act swiftly, the girls would more than likely be sold in the Ionian markets. Slave girls were coveted above all. She shuddered at the thought of little Maya's body belonging to some rich folk in the East. The disparity between Ionian opulence and the barbarism of Helike's neighboring territories was shocking, but their treatment of young women mirrored each other all too well.

Sapphir quickened her pace in pursuit. The rain continued at a steady downpour. She worried that the tracks would be covered by too much muck but felt certain she could not be far behind. A winding path emerged, recognizable in contrast to the untamed wild she had traversed all day.

The end must be close.

She felt the grade of the Earth begin to rise, sloping up towards a rocky mountainside. Of course, such a place would be perfect for a clan of bandits. The higher elevation made them less susceptible to ambush from other outlaws and wild men. Achaean guardsmen dare not take on foes with such a geographic disadvantage as well. They had chosen their home well.

Sapphir clung to the treeline a while longer, not wanting to reveal herself to onlookers from above. She could see caves dimpled into the stony mountain. Surely, her children were in one of those. As she focused harder, Sapphir began noting figures standing outside each cave.

Watchmen. These men are disciplined, for a bandit clan.

She wondered how many stood between her, Maya, and Ivy. She felt no qualms destroying the entire encampment. If only she could do so without harming Maya and Ivy.

I need to get a closer look.

Sapphir shut her eyes, staying absolutely still, finding the words for a spell she had learned years ago. The veil would last just long enough, but Sapphir knew it required continuous concentration and deliberate movements. When she held out her arms to look at them, she saw only the rocky slope ahead. She approached and began to make her way up towards the caves.

Sapphir's mind was working double now, maintaining a grasp on her camouflage charm while searching each cave for her children. She passed the first guard carefully, ready to defend herself at any instant; but the fighting never began. They could not see her.

Sapphir grew more and more anxious as the minutes passed, finding it increasingly difficult to sustain her invisibility. She noticed unusual things about the encampment, as well.

Women and children. The occasional chicken. Weaving stations, even a dog. This was no simple bandit clan; this was a tribe with families and livelihoods.

They have my girls. This is all blood money, stolen money.

She needed to remind herself of that. The lives these outlaws had built were not deserved, not morally achieved under the grace of the Olympians.

Yet, I have killed them.

How was she any better?

She was so distracted, she almost meandered right past a small cave, tucked behind a ridge within the mountain. More guards stood outside this entrance. Not true guards, of course — sentinels of the bandit tribe, bejeweled, yet ragged, with rough swords and spears.

ᏖᏂᎬ ᖴᏆᎡᏕᏖ ᎳᎪᏙᎬ

Inside the cave, someone had lit a cookfire. Three men sat inside, more well-kept than many of the others, sharper blades and bigger jewels adorning their torn clothes. Beside them, a younger man slumped, tied tightly to a staff that jutted from the ground. Shaggy curls hung down, covering his face. He wore a farmer's outfit, with a loose-fitting chiton covering his body. The garment hung over only one arm, and Sapphir noticed his bronzed shoulders, chiseled from working outdoors.

As she scanned the rest of the cave, she almost let out a yelp. Huddled in a corner, two young girls sat, bound together, with gags stuffed unceremoniously into their mouths.

These men must have noticed the dangers of letting young magicians speak.

Any pride she felt turned instantly to discomfort, as she knew the men lying dead in the woods outside had perished at the hands of one, or both, of her daughters. They must have had no choice, but Sapphir feared above all that her children would one day grow to be like her. She could not let them fall into that pattern.

Sapphir could sense her spell waning. She slipped into the cave, unseen and unheard by any of the guards. As soon as she started a new spell, her form would return to normal.

She took three shallow breaths, letting herself calm.

One. Two. Three.

Chapter 14

Nicolaus

Two days had passed since the Fishermen brought Rizon Atsali to the Council. Orrin had delivered no further instructions for Nic regarding his new task. He decided tonight would be his first attempt. Two Heliken guards were stationed by the stairs leading down to the cells below — every minute of every day.

They needed no more manpower. Nic had explored the prison before. The bars of hardened iron were strong and unmoving, with unbreakable locks that provided a last barrier if anyone could free themselves from their chains. It was pitch dark at all hours, save for a few torches. Rats dashed about in the shadows; the scratching of their claws was the only music for the captives. Without functional outhouses, the stench of urine and shit clung to the air.

Nic possessed no desire to return. With Orrin's claim that the fate of Helike and Achaea hung in the balance, however, Nic was obligated. He owed Orrin his life, after all. He'd slept fitfully the past two nights, as he grappled with his newfound directive. Nic was not attached to Helike – he loved his home in Memphis much more and only had one true friend in the city. If Krassen could even be counted as a true friend, that is. Would the barkeep care if Nic never returned for a cup of wine? Before two days ago, he felt no inspiration to be more than a servant. He always figured that he would serve in the palace his whole life. Then one day, he would die.

Yet, a part of him wanted more. The sliver of his brain that had come alive the night he saved the bakery girl. Or at least bought her enough time to be rescued by Orrin. It compelled him to agree to Orrin's proposal, lit a spark within him when he imagined saving Helike from certain war.

Most of him just wanted a drink.

He strolled the windowed corridors, which revealed a starry night over the city of Helike. From here, he could see all the way down to Krassen's bar, one of the few buildings that remained lit in the darkness.

Maybe just one cup, then back to my duty.

Nic resisted the urge. His mind needed to be sharp if he wished to pass the guards and deal with Rizon Atsali properly. The staircase by which the guards stood was located at the far corner of the palace on the side facing the city. The prison itself descended into the palace hillside. Nic had searched the outside of the palace walls the first day, looking for any sort of indication of a secret tunnel. The effort proved fruitless – of course, a secret tunnel wouldn't be visible to the casual observer.

Instead, Nic stood in view of the staircase, watching the two guards from behind a statue of Poseidon.

There are too many of these damned things!

But Nic thanked the overly pious Helikens for placing this one. His only hope seemed to be to wait until the current guards simply abandoned their post or left to exchange with new guards. If that is what it would take, Nic decided, he would stand and wait.

Hours passed. Or perhaps, mere minutes. Nic's thoughts meandered without direction. Poseidon's hands were rougher than the rest of his body, appearing calloused in the marble. Nic's hands were not as worn. Months inside the castle walls left no real need for tough skin. He wanted someone to talk to – maybe Krassen.

Or Opi. She can be fun to talk to.

Pit, pat, pit, pat.

The sound of light feet on a hard floor caught Nic's attention, and he shrunk quickly behind the statue, melting into the wall's shadow. The walking subsided.

"Good soldiers, how long has it been since your watch began?"

With a start, Nic realized he recognized the voice. The nasal buzz could belong to only one man in Helike – the Flat-Nose.

What is the councilor doing awake? Do he and Gaios know about my mission?

"It's been four hours, sir," the larger of the two guards responded, his reedy voice a curious dissonance from his size.

"A tiresome duty, yet you two bear it boldly, as always. How does a cup of wine sound? Walk with me a minute, and we shall pick out a worthy vintage."

"I'd be a liar if I said that didn't sound nice. Let's be quick about it, then I'll come back to me post. Wait here, Bates."

"Ah, why not join us Bates? Surely, no prisoner will escape in the minutes we're gone."

Steps receded down the hallway. Nic could not believe his luck. He poked his head around the statue. Indeed, both guards and the Flat-Nose had rounded the corner to enjoy a quick cup of wine. Nic wondered why Simon concerned himself with the castle guard. He figured there was more to it than the camaraderie of a few lowly soldiers. The Flat-Nose rarely did anything solely for entertainment, so far as Nic knew.

Nic raced for the stairs, stumbling as his foot clipped the side of Poseidon's statue. He regained his balance and padded down to the dungeon. Like every staircase in Helike's palace, it spiraled excessively. He could feel the air dampen and cool as he descended, the smell of shit thickening. As he remembered, only a few torches lit the cells. A maze of iron bars and disheveled men sprawled in front of him. Sure enough, every cell was sturdily built, with thick iron bars. There truly was no need for guards above.

Some cells held only one prisoner; some were vacant. Three that Nic passed had more than one man inside, spread as far apart as the close confines permitted. The men were scarred and caked with dirt. He saw no women, save for a hulking figure with breasts too large to be a man. Her jaw stuck out when he noticed, and she bared her teeth, rotting and yellow.

Nic was thankful the light was so low.

He wondered if this fate had been in store for him if the councilors had decided they needed no more serving men when the raiders had found him. He'd been with his younger sisters that day. Gabrielle played in the river, splashing Nic with muddy water as he ducked behind the reeds with Ibbie. Ibbie was only a baby then, maybe three years of age. She giggled every time droplets sprayed her face, clinging to Nic's leg.

As the sun set, painting distant sands red, the children had regrouped with Mother and Father. Ibbie started to cry just as they began to eat. She'd forgotten her doll by the riverside. Nic comforted her. He would get it.

The men had found him cleaning mud off Ibbie's doll. He did not speak their language, could not explain why he was at the river by night. Six boys around his age were already on their boat, so they decided to add a seventh. From there, Helike was only a short journey by sea, and Nicolaus was given his new home. He often longed for Memphis but had no means to return. If he could pass the city limits, he would be an outsider wandering aimlessly through Northern Greece, still thousands of miles from home. He was safe here.

Nic wondered what his two sisters were up to now. Gabrielle would be nearing thirteen years, and Ibbie nine. His two older brothers were grown men now, a scribe and a warrior. Nic had just begun training as a scribe before he was brought to Helike.

THE FIRST WAVE

Stolen.

Taken to this place. This damn city. Yet, he wanted to help protect it.

Why is that?

He finally reached the last cell – the furthest corner from the stairs, where an entire section of surrounding cells stood vacant. A single torch bathed the inhabitant in an orange glow.

Nic recognized him immediately. His beard was well-groomed, though days in the prison had darkened it with grime. The man's body was lean and fit, giving him the look of a hunting dog. His eyes were hawkish and perceptive; the rest of his face yielded no emotion. He sat with his back to the wall, glowering at his new company.

"Rizon Atsali?"

The man nodded.

"Hi," Nic said nervously, "I'm Nicolaus, attendant to the Golden Spear, Orrin of the Heliken Council."

Rizon arched an eyebrow, "Long name for a slave."

"I suppose that's true. Call me Nic, then."

Rizon suddenly took a deep interest in a fly buzzing by his chamber pot.

"So, did you murder Euripides?"

Nic had no idea what else to say. He knew that this was not the best way to find the answers Orrin desired, but how else?

Rizon grunted sharply in what may have been a laugh, "You're a diplomatic man. I can see why they've chosen you to unpuzzle the mysteries of your councilor's death."

"Apologies, sir."

"Sir? How very kind of you."

Nic closed his eyes in frustration. He was not used to this. He usually listened to politicians quip with each other, not doing much of the thinking for himself.

"You're right. I have no idea what I'm doing, does that make you happy?"

"It certainly doesn't hurt my mood, knowing they sent their best and brightest to pick my brain."

Nic disliked the man. Though, he supposed he would have a similar stubbornness in Rizon's situation. However, he found it difficult to sympathize with him. He would need to employ a different tactic to get the information.

"Where did they catch you?"

Rizon continued to look down, paying no attention to Nic's question.

"Listen, I'm trying to help you! They'll execute you if you stay quiet. Tomorrow. Or the next day, they'll hang you or cut your head off in the middle of Helike. Do you want that?"

Rizon snapped his gaze to Nicolaus, the whites of his eyes reflecting menacingly in the torchlight, "You think I don't know this? Do you believe that you're the first person to come down here and speak with me?"

Nic considered this. He studied Rizon more closely now, noticing burn marks and whip lashes where he hadn't before; there were cuts around his eyes that were too clean to be from anything but a honed blade.

"They're torturing you."

Rizon grinned yellow-tinted teeth at Nic, "And this surprises you? Let me make this easy for you, Nicolaus. I did kill Euripides. Cut his throat as he slept in his bedchambers in the Eastern Wing of this very castle. And I'd do it again."

"Why though? Were you hired by Ucalegon?"

"Ucalegon? You think that cowardly shit would move against the most powerful city in Achaea?"

Nic leaned against the wall in an attempt to appear more casual, then recoiled. It was slimy, and he didn't want to know why. He hoped Rizon hadn't noticed.

"So, who sent you? Why would you risk your life like that?"

"Helike's heroic leader overstepped his boundaries more than he realized. He made decisions that upset some powerful people."

"The Children of the Sea? The mages he exiled, right?"

Rizon scoffed, "A mage wouldn't need a man to sneak into Euripides' chambers at night to kill him."

"Maybe if they didn't want people to think it was their doing," Nic suggested, feeling confident in his theory.

"If mages were involved, I knew nothing of it. I wish I could tell you differently, because perhaps we wouldn't be having this conversation then."

What does he mean?

"You see, Nicolaus, they left me with no option. The

Fishermen told your Council everything they need to know. Everything I can tell you all, I already have."

"I have to know who you're working for! Orrin thinks... well... there will be war unless they have reason to believe Ucalegon didn't send you!"

"Orrin the Golden Spear says, eh? Why do you care if Helike and Boura go to war? You speak as if our tongue isn't your first language, and you certainly don't look like a native Heliken."

"I care if common people die for no reason, other than the death of one man. Why should innocent people give their lives for Euripides? Because you're too stubborn to say why you killed him, and who you killed him for?"

As he spoke, Nic could feel the truth in his words. He didn't care about Euripides, cared nothing for the Council, and their petty power struggles. But should thousands die because one man cut another's throat? Surely, there was a better solution.

"You're a noble slave," Rizon said, "You have any family?"

"Sisters. Brothers. A mother and father, yes. They're leagues away, though."

"Say you had to choose between the life of a man you didn't know and the lives of your sisters."

I'd choose Gabrielle and Ibbie.

"I'll tell you... for me, a man without nobility, the decision was simple. I would cut Euripides' throat every time. And hang. Every time."

Nic stood without speaking for minutes, staring at the lithe man as he curled up, facing away from the light. He had gathered no new information for Orrin. He had failed. Yet, he felt Rizon Atsali – a man who chose his own death above that of his family – deserved more. He needed to convince Orrin to stall the execution and cease the torture. Rizon Atsali was not a true enemy of Helike.

He spoke with his back to Nic.

"If you'd like an easier exit than the one you came down, I suggest you check the wall two cells to my left. That's how he leaves every time."

"Who?" Nic wondered aloud, with no answer.

He tested the cell door, finding it unlocked as Rizon suggested. The back of the cell seemed the same to Nic as any other, made of solid stone and covered with mud, shit, and spider webs. When he pushed gingerly, however, he felt the stones budge.

A hidden door!

He knew there would be some in the ancient castle.

Nic paused, looking back at Rizon with pity. He certainly *had* committed a terrible crime, but something still felt wrong to Nic.

He crawled through the tunnel, which smelled of must and dripped steadily from the ceiling. It was entirely dark inside, and Nic could feel himself clenching in fear. If he could not fit at any point, or the passage came to a stop, there was no room to turn around. Nic would have to back out painstakingly the way he'd come. It could take hours even if he could navigate all the curves.

After what seemed like a century passed, Nic finally saw a sliver of light. Gingerly, he slid the stone sideways. Nic pulled himself out, praying to gods he did not believe in that there were no guards lurking on the other side.

Nic took a deep sigh of relief as he surveyed the surroundings. He'd emerged next to a statue of Athena, gripping her aegis and a stout spear. He brushed dirt lightly off his robes, ready to make a dash back to his chambers, when a nasally voice stopped him.

"Ah, Orrin's little steward. I had hoped you would find it easier to escape the prison than it was to enter. Though, I will admit you smell horrible. Perhaps a bath can be drawn to get some of that dirt out."

Nic's heart caught in his throat. He turned to gape at the Flat-Nose, fear gripping every inch of his body. Would they punish a man for speaking with a prisoner? He knew the answer without asking. He opened his mouth to the councilor, then closed it.

He and Gaios... they both knew!

"Why so fearful? Curiosity never hurt anyone after all, as I'm sure that is the only reason you would venture to the cells. What curiosity may reveal, however... it would seem, we have much to discuss. Follow me, young man, and don't try running off. I fear that would only make things worse for you."

Chapter 15

Keoki

The noise woke Keoki – a sharp yelp of surprise by a grown man, followed by cursing from a woman. Keoki could hear Ivy calling out in muffled alarm.

He could see nothing. The taste of an oily rag caused his mouth to foam as he struggled to breathe properly. The girls must have been gagged, too. He smelled burnt meat and the woody smoke from a crackling fire. The cloth covering his eyes was rough and irritating. His skin burned beneath rope, and his back ached from being forcefully propped upright by some sort of wooden pole.

"Hey!" another deep voice called.

The sound of more rustling and movement in the area made Keoki anxious. He jerked sideways, trying to free his arms, which were bound above his head with thin twine that cut into his wrists. His shoulder flared in pain, and Keoki remembered the vicious spear wound. The yell he let out was barely audible through the gag, though with heaves of pain and spitting, Keoki finally expelled it from his mouth.

"Ivy! If you're out of your bonds, untie me!"

No response.

The clamor around him died down. Suddenly, someone ripped the blindfold from Keoki's eyes. He squinted as light filled the darkness. When the spots cleared, and Keoki's vision returned, he realized he was in a cave, dimly illuminated by a cookfire. Ivy and Maya stood before him, smiling and hugging a woman's legs affectionately. Five men were dead in the cave, burned, bloodied, and immobile. Clouds still hung in the sky outside, darker than before though the rain had subsided. It must have been nearing nightfall. His shoulder was still afire, though it bled no longer, blocked by woven bandages.

Keoki's gaze moved to the woman's face. She was pale, slender, and beautiful. Dark circles shadowed her blue eyes, which stared fiercely behind crimson hair. Her locks hung straight past her shoulders, speckled with dirt. Keoki realized there was blood there too, though it matched her hair color almost too closely to notice. A white scar stood out on her upper lip, curiously visible despite her fair skin. Her arms sheltered Ivy and Maya protectively, and there was no kindness in her eyes when she looked at him. Keoki wondered how she possibly killed so many of the thieves.

"How do you know my daughters?" the woman asked coldly.

"Uh, I found them in the woods. We met yesterday. I wanted to take them back home to you."

"This is Keoki!" Ivy said with excitement, overjoyed that her new friend was meeting her mother.

"I see," Ivy's mother said.

Ivy made to untie Keoki, but her mother grabbed her arm.

"Ivy, no. He cannot remember the things he's seen this evening. His memory..."

"Mother, he's Keoki! He's my friend, I want him to see the island," Ivy exclaimed.

Her mother's mouth twitched at the mention of her island. Maya took her mother's hand in her own and nodded up to her sweetly. What had he seen? Surely, she wouldn't expect him to blame her for protecting her children, even if it meant killing a few men. Keoki would have done the same.

The pale woman glanced at the fallen bandits. Her mind seemed to be working quickly.

"Listen, lady, I've had to kill one of these men myself. And I think your girls killed two of them in the woods. I'm not sure how, but it happened. Can you just let me down? My shoulder..."

The woman's face was a mask of unease, "Yes, they do know how to handle themselves. Knives, of course."

Keoki had no idea how Ivy and Maya had killed those two men, or how this woman had done the same with five. Knives seemed an explanation, though truthfully, he didn't care. He needed the pain to stop.

"Look, can you just cut me down. Use your knife."

The woman picked a blade up off the ground, and hacked the ropes to bits, allowing Keoki to struggle back to his feet. Maya patted his leg fondly when he stood.

"My children seem to like you, so up on your feet and let's get off this mountain. Take this."

She rummaged in a pack around her shoulder, pulling out a small vial. He drank cautiously, the pain in his shoulder immediately dulling.

"Uh, thanks," Keoki murmured, feeling that the woman disliked him strongly.

Ivy and Maya looked pleased, and Ivy picked up a blade from one of the dead men for good measure, stuffing it into the belt at her waist. Keoki picked up a fallen axe, too. He missed his stone knife and staff but figured a real weapon would do better than none.

Any daylight that could have peeked through the clouds had faded by the time they made it outside the cave. They were atop the low peak of a mountain, overlooking Helike in the distance. The place appeared to be populated by families. Men with garb similar to the bandits Keoki had fought earlier in the day wandered in and out of caves and tented abodes. Children sat around fires and played together quietly in the darkness. Their mothers held the smallest in their arms; Keoki could hear the gentle voice of one cooing to her baby as she tickled its nose lovingly.

The scene was so tranquil, Keoki almost forgot they were in

grave danger. He suddenly recalled that these men had beaten and captured him. He wondered why they hadn't killed him. Perhaps it was the girls. Had Ivy and Maya done something to make the bandits take him alive?

Shockingly, nobody had seen them exit the cave, and people seemed too busy to notice the four sneak behind an outcrop of rock, shielding themselves from view.

"How do you suggest we pass unnoticed?" Keoki asked the woman, "There must be hundreds of them."

"Once the fires are extinguished, it will be entirely dark. The women, children, and most of the men will be asleep. We need only pass a few guards."

"What if someone finds the dead men in the cave before then? Surely they'll send somebody to check about the noise."

She pursed her lips in frustration, as if weighing options that she did not relish.

"Then take my hand and try not to cry out."

Ivy and Maya already seemed to understand, each taking their mother's left hand in one of their own. Keoki took her right.

"What are you planning on – oh!"

Keoki had to stop himself from yelping. His body seemed to disintegrate before his eyes. A rush of air started at his hand, quickly washing over him. Keoki looked down in astonishment. All he saw was the stone below him. Where Ivy, Maya, and their mother had stood, there was nobody.

"Hello?" he whispered.

"I warned you not to be alarmed," the smooth voice of Ivy's mother responded.

Ivy and Maya giggled, "Kiki is scared!"

Scared didn't come close to describing Keoki's confusion. His body still felt the same. He could move his arms and legs normally.

But I'm nothing. How am I alive!?

Keoki wasn't just scared. He was horrified – stories of magic and that day in the square... all of it rattled through his head anew.

"Silence, children."

"I'm not one of your children, lady! What did you do? What are you?"

"I'll only warn you this once not to call me lady again."

"Okay, so what do I call you? And what did you do!"

The conversation was held in low voices, but Keoki tried to add an edge to his tone. He wanted the woman to respect him, maybe fear him a little. As it was, she seemed to find him an annoyance.

"Now isn't the time for any of this. I'll give you all you need to know as soon as we're not surrounded by men who would love to kill us."

Fair point.

"Fine. Tell me what we need to do."

"Walk. Down the mountain."

****

THE FIRST WAVE

Keoki did not notice the boat when they first approached the beach. His body had returned to its solid form as soon as he, Ivy, Maya, and their mother reentered the trees by the bandits' mountain. Ivy and Maya had led the way, though their mother directed them occasionally, ensuring that they were headed towards the sea. Keoki had not spoken much of the way, besides to ask the woman her name.

"Sapphir," she said, without looking at him directly.

"Your daughter is loud. Ivy is, and does Maya ever talk?"

"Maya is unique. My other children speak enough for her."

"There's five of them, right?"

"Yes."

It was there the conversation had ended. Sapphir asked nothing of Keoki's past, seeming to only care that he remained with them. Keoki just wanted to return to Agnes and Fil. He longed for his feather bed and a comfortable night's rest. It seemed an eternity since he had left with the girls to bring them back to their island, though only one day had passed. His shoulder felt entirely painless, and he even rotated his left arm once or twice to see if it could move properly again. What had Sapphir given him in that vial?

Keoki knew now what she must be. She was a witch – a sorceress, magician, mage, whatever the name may be. How else could she have made them invisible, allowing her children and their new friend to sneak past an entire camp of outlaws without trouble? He hated magic. The only magicians he knew of were the

Children of the Sea, and he despised the Children of the Sea; he despised them for their brutality, their promises of salvation from doom.

But they brought the doom upon Helike!

They were the ones who had killed men, women, and children for their refusal to trust the Children's fantasies. Even the most pious in Helike suffered.

But was that what Sapphir was? Were her girls raised as Children of the Sea? Keoki didn't know. Some people practiced magic on their own. Sapphir lived on her own with her family, so that was probably all it was. Did Maya and Ivy have the same powers? Keoki wondered how it worked. Growing up, magic seemed like just a story – only the gods were magic. Until his parents taught him about the Children of the Sea, Keoki assumed it was all made up. But that day in the square... and now he was sure it was real.

He was suspicious of Sapphir, but the girls were just normal children. Ivy was excited to introduce Keoki to her brother, Cy, and try to fish with him off the rocky shores of "their" island. Maya would smile back at her mother from time to time, tugging Ivy's tunic when Sapphir tried to tell them anything.

When they finally arrived at the beach, the black sky made the water shine eerily. There was no moonlight to reflect off its surface, so the world seemed to end at the coarse sand. So far as Keoki could tell, they were alone on the shore. The sound of waves breaking and wind whipping against water made Keoki feel uneasy. He usually appreciated the sea, with its sapphire-blue waters and gentle breezes. Tonight, however, the yawning black appeared menacing.

"Into the boat," Sapphir instructed, though her tone was less commanding as before on the mountain.

Boat?

Sure enough, a wooden rowboat floated in the shallow water.

"Come on in!" Ivy exclaimed, patting the open seat next to her.

Maya clambered in instead, curling up beside her sister. Ivy seemed momentarily disappointed, but then pointed to the seat across from her. Keoki sat down, feeling the boat sink a little deeper. Sapphir entered last, putting her hand on the side of the boat and speaking softly to herself.

"Sapphir, I can row. Hand me the oars."

The boat began to move in the darkness, gliding smoothly across the ocean's surface, unimpeded by any current. Waves lapped against the side, but only whispers of sea spray splashed Keoki's face.

"I see. No oars."

"Mother knows all the best tricks," Ivy said.

Maya turned away from discussion, eyes closed.

"She's sleeping?" Keoki asked.

"It *is* very late. Mother doesn't usually let us stay up this late. But I guess this was a weird day."

"Maybe we should be quieter, so we don't wake Maya."

"I'm tired, too, you know."

"Perhaps you can go to sleep then," Keoki offered, hoping she would follow Maya's lead and cease her chatter.

"Well, now it's easier to talk since we're sitting and not walking. Is your shoulder hurt?"

"No, I think your mother gave me a potion or something. I feel fine."

"You should say thank you."

"I did."

"Oh. That's good. I forget a lot. We got in a fight today!"

"Yes, I know. I have my shoulder to prove it."

"But your shoulder doesn't hurt."

Keoki sighed. He wondered if the girl was really more upset about the fight than she let on. Two men were dead, and Keoki had not been the one to slay them. Was this her first time killing?

"Ivy, I'm sorry. For the fighting. You didn't need to see that type of bloodshed."

"I know what happens when people die, Kiki. Or at least, I know how they can die. I thought they would kill you, but they didn't. I knew Mother would come."

She spoke so easily about the incident, yet Keoki knew firsthand how traumatizing it could be to see violence at such a young age. To experience a real fight.

"Ivy, did you... did you kill those two men?"

Perhaps it was not right to ask. Especially with Sapphir sitting nearby.

Ivy looked shyly at her mother. Sapphir finally spoke.

"Ivy, dear, it's okay. They would have hurt you and your sister."

Keoki felt embarrassed. He knew Sapphir might blame him for her daughters' capture.

"I promise, I tried to protect the girls. I'm sorry, Sapphir. Ivy, I'm sorry."

He couldn't make out her face without any light.

"Mother... I didn't... it wasn't Keoki's fault. They came from nowhere. And I never killed anyone."

"I saw both bodies, too, Ivy. Truly, it's okay," Sapphir said gently, though Keoki could hear the tightness in her voice.

She blames me.

"I never did anything, though. I tried to stop them, but they tied me up and I couldn't remember my words. They would have killed Keoki, too."

Realization began to settle over Keoki. He felt awestruck. He'd assumed Ivy had done the deed, the plucky little fighter that she was. He'd thought she must have performed some sort of magic, if she had the same powers as her mother.

"Maya?" Sapphir even sounded surprised.

"She didn't even say anything, mother. They were about to slash at Keoki's throat, about to tie her up. Then the two men next to us fell. And, and they would have killed Keoki, too after they tied us both up. But I think they were scared of us. They gagged us, too because I think they thought we couldn't do anything if we couldn't speak. Mother, I was scared. But it wasn't Keoki's fault."

T.J. VINCENT

Keoki didn't feel any better that a young girl had to stick up for him to her mother. He had failed two little girls, almost gotten them killed. And now, well, there was no way their mother would ever trust him.

Why did he even care? He would leave the next day, as soon as Ivy showed him her home. She seemed so excited to introduce her family to him, and he owed her that much. He didn't want to fail her again.

They drifted on in silence. Keoki may have even fallen asleep for a moment, as the lull of ocean waves and cool winds settled his nerves, despite its ominous appearance on the beach. Then, they were there. The island appeared just as the boat had, though this must have been shrouded merely by darkness.

How long were we sailing? Ten minutes? Two hours?

The beach was sandy where they made land – finer granules than the rocky shorelines of Helike. Cliffs and craggy rock faces jutted out around them, standing blacker than the night like city walls.

"We're here, Maya!" Ivy yelled, rushing out of sight, with her sister in tow.

Keoki stepped as if to follow, when a cold hand grabbed his arm. Her grip was strong, and her hands were bony. Keoki turned to face Sapphir. In the darkness, her face looked as intimidating as the ocean had.

"Keoki."

"Listen, Sapphir, I'm really sorry. For everything. I just found them a couple days ago and wanted to get them home. I never meant for them to come to any harm."

"You're right, of course. The girls would probably have run into much worse without you there. I... I wanted to thank you," she continued.

He hadn't expected that.

"I'm glad to have met them. They're great children. And you... thanks for getting me out of that cave. They would have killed me, I'm sure."

"Truthfully I wouldn't have paid you any mind if Ivy and Maya didn't seem to want you along. Perhaps that seems harsh, but you can understand how a mother feels the need to protect her children above all else."

"Of course, I do."

"Keoki!" Ivy called from the distance, "I want you to come meet the rest of my family!"

Keoki waited, expecting Sapphir to say more. Guilt still festered at the thought of Maya killing two men, saving his life when he should have been protecting hers.

Sapphir must know I didn't want this.

She said nothing however, simply waving a hand dismissively, permitting him to follow the trail of Ivy's voice.

Chapter 16

Melani

Xander parried the swipe from his opponent, responding with a downward slash of his blunted training sword. The other man, a member of Boura's infantry, barely lifted his shield to turn away the attack. Xander had him on his heels. He swept the man's legs out with a kick, pinning his sword hand to the ground as he rested his own blade on the man's chest.

The infantryman grunted. Then, laughed.

"Ya wield all the weapons ya make?" he asked, accepting Xander's hand to help him back to his feet.

"I've had my share of sword-swinging."

"Wishin' ya could share it with me, no?"

Xander smiled, "Again?"

They resumed sparring.

All around, Bouran men, some barely older than ten, were training. Many on the field were hefting a weapon for the first time, moving clumsily with spears or letting their shields hang uselessly while they attempted to swing a sword properly.

Melani stood near a few women, all practiced in medicine, waiting for their own newly minted tools – instruments of war that sang a different tune than swords. As Melani and Xander predicted, Ucalegon had called the Bourans to arms. All men save the crippled, priests, and those deemed too old for battle, were required to take to the field. Boura had an experienced militia, led by Parex the Hammer. Each man of that militia would take ten unseasoned fighters under their wing to train. Even with these numbers, they were surely outmatched by the Heliken forces.

The women were not all left out of the picture. Healers were a mix of both men and women, and despite Loren's fierce rebuking, Melani was allowed to join, being a former student. Her work on Aggio the fisherman had certainly helped her credibility. Now, she awaited the proper outfitting, requiring ointments, poultices, bandaging, and all the other tools of a Bouran healer.

She appreciated days like today, where she could watch Xander train, his prowess as a swordsman undeniable. He had learned to handle a blade with his brother, Rizon, years ago. Melani had met Rizon once or twice, and always thought he seemed the jolly type; yet Xander said he could never beat Rizon, no matter how many times they sparred. Truthfully, she didn't know what Rizon did. She had at first guessed he was a member of the League's Guard, helping to keep the peace of Helike from outsiders. It would explain his constant travel and rare appearances in Boura.

Xander claimed this was not the case, believing Rizon still lived in the countryside between Boura and Patras, tending the fields with their parents. Melani had met Xander's parents once before. They were a kindly couple barely past their fortieth year. Melani had never heard them speak of Rizon.

"Melani Atsali."

"Still just Melani, Loren."

Loren stepped beside Melani, dropping a sack at her feet that must have contained her supplies.

"Your tools."

Loren spoke with her usual coldness, pursing her lips haughtily and sticking her nose up to look down at Melani.

"Thank you. And I suppose I also have you to thank for my talents to help our troops in the battles to come."

She meant it sincerely, smiling to show her gratitude.

"Loren, I know you don't approve of my choices, but we both are able to do some good for Boura. Help our city win back its trade and its food."

Loren's shoulders relaxed slightly. She sighed, looking out at the training field.

"Indeed. For what it's worth, Thal has been asking after you. He still wants a painting, you know."

"He's a good child, I'll have to get to work on a gift as soon as the fighting is over."

"Yes, thank you."

ᏔᎯᎬ ᖴᏆᏒᏚᏔ ᎳᎯᏙᎬ

Loren's gaze wasn't fixed on Melani as she talked. She seemed distracted, and Melani soon realized her eyes were watering.

Finally, she spoke again.

"The war... you don't think it will last long, do you?"

"Truthfully, I have no idea. Xander thinks it should last only as long as it takes for Helike to allow trade again."

Loren wiped away a tear as it fled down her cheek, then nodded and straightened up again, "Good. That's good. We will talk again before the battles begin, I'm sure."

"Of course. Nice to see you as always, Loren."

Loren stuck out her chin, regaining her composure before walking away stiffly. It seemed to Melani that she had been so close to a breakthrough. The woman rarely showed her any kindness, or emotion besides smugness for that matter. Perhaps, she was scared for Thal. Who would watch the little warrior if his mother and father didn't return home? The latter seemed more likely to die, as Loren's husband possessed no talent in battle, meaning he would stand along the frontlines as a first line of defense.

One that could be easily breached.

The healers would probably survive, though the proximity to the fighting alone endangered them. Melani suddenly felt sadness grip her, considering what a miserable life would lie before Thal if his parents, or even one of them, were lost in the fighting.

She tried to imagine how different her life may have been without two parents. Unlike Thal, she had sisters and a brother who may have been a comfort to her. She had grown up in Patras, west of Helike and Boura. Her childhood had been simple. Her father was an apothecary, while her mother spent her days with the children. She could recall their home – three bedrooms above her father's store. They cooked and dined most days there as well.

Her pursuit of medicine began at her father's prompting, as he sold many of his formulas to the physicians around Patras. The city stood by the ocean, however, so Melani would find herself along the beach gazing into the vast expanse before her. It was here she met Hephes, a painter with a dark scraggly beard that matched his black skin.

She had been only eight when they first met. He caught her staring at him with curiosity – in truth, Melani had never seen a man with skin so black in Patras. Or at least, not that she could remember. Hephes smiled at her, beckoning for her to come look at his painting.

He called her princess and let her practice simple brushstrokes on his spare canvas. After that day, Hephes told Melani to return whenever she pleased.

"I'll always be right here, princess. Watching the gulls dive and the fish leap from the waves," he'd said, patting her head with a soft artist's hand.

Melani had returned to see Hephes many times after. He explained different painting techniques and shared his life story more freely than anyone she had ever met. He'd been everywhere – Persia, Egypt... he even claimed to have traveled farther north than any map. So, no matter how much her father pushed her into medicine, Melani's interest in the arts continued waxing.

Finally, she left Patras to receive schooling from the most capable healers in Achaea, the physicians of Boura. Though she learned invaluable skills from Loren, her heart was in the work Hephes had taught her.

Then she met Xander. She could recall the moment so clearly; it was as if it had been captured in one of her paintings. He was at the very same shop as today, face glistening in the glow of melting steel. She was on her way to the physician's school, a group of buildings adjacent to the Temple of Boura. A guard was testing the weight of a short sword Xander had handed him moments before.

"It's good steel, yes?" Xander asked, a little nervously.

"It'll get the job done. They say you're the best new blacksmith around here, so I was expecting some fancy tricks, eh?" he laughed, and Xander shuffled uncomfortably, "But it'll do."

Xander nodded, catching the bag of coins the guard tossed.

"A few more sales like this and you might be able to get yourself a girl like that, eh? Hey, you!"

Melani paused, looking back at the stout guard in his Bouran armor, a new sword clutched in his hand. She was used to japes and calls thrown her way, but they unsettled her, nonetheless.

"I've got a sword for you, eh? Just like this one!"

He laughed heartily at his own joke, grabbing himself below the armor and tugging. He spat on the stairs leading from Xander's porch to the street. Xander looked at her with a sad sort of compassion in his eyes. He clapped the soldier on the back firmly, sending him stumbling into the street.

"And it's just as undersized as the one I made him," he called jovially, waving his farewell to the embarrassed guard.

Melani had given him a shy smile then, blushing and turning away to continue on. After that, she greeted the new armorer every morning, eventually asking him for his name, though she had heard people call him Xander Atsali already. One day, she saw him at the city square, or rather, he approached her as she sat painting. He told her he liked the painting, and they began talking and laughing like they had known each other for years.

Though they weren't wedded under the eyes of the gods, Melani didn't care. She and Xander were perfectly comfortable being committed on their own terms. Her parents were skeptical when they first heard of Melani's new romance, but all their worries disappeared after the first meeting. His work brought in enough coin for hers to develop as well. She knew her father would be proud if he heard Melani was to be a physician in the Bouran military, but her mother would prefer she stayed well away from the fighting.

But she had to do it. She wouldn't let Xander's life slip entirely out of her hands.

The hours passed, and Melani walked along the riverside to buy fruits from the private vendors. Prices were higher than usual – Melani was sure the sellers wanted to protect their stock from running low with trade-waters blocked.

When she returned to the training grounds, she noticed

THE FIRST WAVE

Xander sitting on a low stone wall, cleaning his blunt sparring sword. Even with truly worthless items like this, Xander took gentle care to preserve them.

"Xander!"

"Mel!"

He slid off the stones, swinging the sword into a sheathe over his back, and jogged lightly to her.

"How are you? You get the stuff from Loren?"

She lifted the bag of herbs and poultices in answer.

"And I trust she was a bitch as usual?"

"Less so than you might think," Melani said, chuckling as they turned to walk to the baths which stood in a columned building only minutes away.

Xander shrugged, "That's nice, I guess. Maybe saving Aggio impressed her."

"Don't think that's it. She almost cried when we talked about Thal."

"Oh. Oh, you think she's scared then. I would be, too."

"You would?

"Well, I already am. I mean. Aren't you?"

"Nope, I guess I'm braver than you."

He snorted at that, though not rudely. They arrived at the baths in silence, Melani holding Xander's arm as she often did, though today she didn't want to let go. If she or Xander didn't come home from this war, at least they wouldn't be abandoning any children.

Only each other.

"Check that out," Xander said, tapping her lightly, and directing her to a man and a woman, who were pleasuring each other shamelessly in the middle of the baths.

"Xander! Gross! I didn't want to see that! Why do they feel the need to do that here?"

Melani glared back at Xander, whose face was tight with restrained laughter.

"Judging by the way he's standing, I think he's just helping her keep her hair dry."

Other people seemed to have noticed the two by now and were turning their noses away in disgust. Xander and Melani decided to move to a different bath.

"Here, we have this one all to ourselves," Xander commented, arranging their possessions fussily.

As they both undressed to refresh themselves, she noticed small scrapes and scars running across Xander's body, marks left from his day in the yard.

And these are only from training swords.

She looked down at her own body, unblemished and smooth, more delicate than she wanted. A smear of dirt clung to her thigh, so she licked her thumb and wiped it off.

Melani dipped her toe into the water, and Xander followed, jokingly grabbing her shoulder as if to push her all the way in. As he let go, wading in, the only thing Melani could see was the slightest trickle of blood, tracing its way down Xander's back.

Chapter 17

Sapphir

The children seemed to love Keoki. Cy and Ivy, being the wild fighters, probably admired his strength. He was muscular, Sapphir noted, much more so than her Yusef had been. Years of working on a farm, out in the field tilling soil and steering cattle, left him sturdy and powerful. Yusef had worked on a farm, too, Sapphir recalled, though his shepherding had been gentler – he was sweet rather than hardy. They both had the same curly dark hair, however. The same bronzed skin. Yusef always had soft brown eyes, while Keoki's seemed more suspicious and strangely weary for someone so young.

Egan showed as much fondness for Keoki as he did for anything. That is to say, very little, although he didn't show any signs of distaste. Celia seemed smitten from the start, as young girls almost always will be with handsome young men. She delighted in Keoki's willingness to feed Blackwing, which he did without hesitation. He did seem to have a way with the bird, perhaps from his constant proximity to other animals.

Maya, the sweet child, treated Keoki like a big pet bear. She liked to pat his legs and smile at him, a similar expression to the one she always gave her mother. Sapphir found this simultaneously adorable and sad, wondering if Maya would have loved Yusef the same way, and if she alone would always be enough for her children.

Cy and Ivy had left minutes before to show Keoki their favorite spot to fish, and they hoped to catch dinner for the seven of them. Keoki had at first been reluctant, wanting to get home to his farm family, Felip and Agnes. However, Sapphir relayed that Felip and Agnes would expect that he'd stay for a meal or two. It was only hospitable.

At least, that's what she had told Keoki. Truthfully, she was unsure what to do with him. The children *did* seem to love him well enough, and he seemed to be a harmless farm boy.

But a harmless farm boy could be our undoing.

It would not be the first time Sapphir ignored the potential dangers of an innocent witness, only to suffer greatly for it. She thought about Yusef, and how they'd tried to flee Helike after the Children of the Sea were sentenced to execution if they were seen anywhere in the city. If only she hadn't trusted that fur trader along the road.

But what could she do? The darkest inkling of a thought that crossed her mind was to kill him and be done with it. It would be so easy to tell her children he had simply returned home. She chastised herself for even considering it. She refused to murder innocents. Never. She had seen too much of that as a child.

For now, she felt waiting was the only possibility. Perhaps the solution would present itself. Whatever her ultimate decision, it would have to spare the feelings of her children, especially Ivy and Maya.

Sweet little Maya.

When she'd realized it had been Maya who slayed the two bandits — Maya who took not one, but two lives — Sapphir's heart had dropped into her stomach. Maya was far too young and innocent to understand the implications of such a thing – she may not have even known what happened. As Ivy described it, Maya hadn't spoken a single word and the two men died anyway.

It was typical for young magicians to have little control of their powers, which exploded out of them from time-to-time. Usually this was driven by pure emotion. If Maya had felt danger and terror, her magical energy may have reacted without her even knowing.

Or does she know?

Sapphir found Maya sitting on the cliffside, running a finger through dusty sand in concentric circles. Sapphir took a seat beside her.

"How are you feeling, dear?"

Maya looked up at her. It was the same look she always gave – gentle curiosity and unconditional infatuation.

"What have you made there?" Sapphir asked, nodding to the circles.

Maya stood, then spun in a quick circle before sitting back down.

She seems entirely unbothered.

"Why did you and Ivy run off, Maya?"

Sapphir had been so thankful to find the girls, she had yet to properly chastise Ivy for her recklessness. Ivy knew this would come; the clever girl must have considered that before taking Keoki to go fishing.

In response, Maya gazed shamefully at her circles.

"It's okay, love, I found you. But why did you leave? I just want you to be safe... if you want to leave, I'll take you anywhere you wish!"

"Ivy."

Sapphir sighed. She knew it had been Ivy's idea; she only hoped sometimes that Maya would speak more. She wondered if Maya struggled to read as well, perhaps it would explain her difficulty controlling her powers, even though she'd been studying for nearly a full year. Reading the words of a spell alone gave any magician greater mastery of it.

"But do *you* want to see more of the world, Maya?"

Maya cocked her head, unsure of what Sapphir was asking. The world is a nebulous thing for children so young to truly understand.

"I'll take you there some day. Take you back."

GHE FIRSG WAVE

Back where?

Sapphir had nowhere to go. There seemed to be no "back" to return to. But if that's what her children desired, it was what she would do. She would give them more soon enough, more than just the island and each other.

But will they ever be safe?

Sapphir stroked Maya's hair, and Maya leaned into her. She sniffled, and Sapphir wondered if she was crying. Then she sneezed. No tears.

A sea osprey glided noiselessly over foamy swells in the water, on a never-ending quest for prey.

✷✷✷✷

Keoki, Cy, and Ivy returned around sunset. Keoki held two large trout with ease, allowing a faint smile to creep into his hard features when Ivy and Cy kicked at each other and raced towards their mother.

"Welcome back, hunters!" Sapphir called, ruffling her rambunctious children's hair as they skidded to a stop by her side.

Keoki sauntered in. "Where should I put these fish?"

"It's quite a catch you have there, who was the lucky fisherman today?"

Keoki raised an eyebrow.

"Put them on the stone table in that cave," she said, gesturing to the biggest cavern with the kitchen.

188

He walked off, the kaleidoscopic scales of the trout shimmering in the sunlight.

The farm boy puzzled her, she had to admit. Besides her five children, Sapphir interacted very rarely with anyone. She must have forgotten how to converse properly with someone nearing her own age. Or at least, someone older than eleven. She wanted to treat him nicely, even though she would need to rid herself of him in some capacity eventually.

"Keoki's such a good fish catcher, Mother!" Cy said reverently.

"Yeah," Ivy agreed, "And he's so strong he carried the fish all by himself and I couldn't even carry one."

"How impressive."

"Can I show him my new trick, Mother?" Cy asked, "Egan taught it to me! I can jump really high, like higher than a person!"

"Perhaps later, Cy. Keoki is going to help me with dinner."

She thought it best that Keoki knew as little about their powers as possible. He probably suspected all the children could perform magic, but she was the only one he'd seen in action. Yes, the less he knew the better.

"Did you tell him much about your magic, Cy?"

"Only the fun parts! Like I told him I could try to hold my breath a super long time and catch the fish and that I could make a sword with a rock."

"Cy, what have I told you about sharing your abilities with people?"

He held his head down and let his blonde hair hang over his

blue eyes, "I shouldn't. But Mother!"

"Keoki too! Keoki shouldn't know these things."

"I'm sorry, Mother."

Ivy chimed in, "I didn't tell him a single thing."

"Yeah! You told him you could swim underwater for longer than me!"

The two began to bicker as always. Truthfully, Cy hadn't told Keoki much more than any normal child would tell someone they wanted to impress. But Keoki would have connected the dots, unless he were thicker than the cattle he tended.

"Enough quarreling! Ivy! Cy! Enough! Go get Celia and Maya, I'll tell Egan to give you a lesson to practice today."

They continued to snap at each other, Cy balling his fists.

"Children!"

"Sorry, Mother!" they said, before dashing off to retrieve their sisters.

Sapphir watched them disappear into their cave, then entered the kitchen.

"Egan!" she called, knowing he would be in the room nearby with the natural light spilling in from a hole in the ceiling above.

He strolled in, a few scrolls tucked under his arm, "Yes, Mother? And hello Keoki."

"Hey," Keoki said, waving with two fingers.

"Would you mind giving your brother and sisters a lesson while Keoki and I get dinner ready?"

"You want me to help with dinner?" Keoki asked.

"Yes, please. Farmhand like yourself, you should be useful around the kitchen."

Keoki shrugged noncommittally and Egan agreed, leaving the kitchen to find his siblings.

"So, what do you want me to do?"

"Um, how about we start by cleaning these fish? I don't like the bones in them. Children might choke, you know."

"Sure," Keoki said, "You got any knives?"

"Pot behind you."

They went on like this for a while, peeling away the reflective scales of the fish and cutting off the heads and tails. Deboning was tricky but Sapphir enjoyed these kinds of tasks to ground her. Sometimes it was better than using magic.

"So, where should I sleep tonight?" Keoki said.

Sapphir had not thought about this.

"How about we make a bed up for you over there?" Sapphir pointed at Egan's favorite room with her elbow.

"Sure. And I'll leave tomorrow morning? Will you take me on the boat?"

Sapphir had not thought about this either. She had no plans to let Keoki go back tomorrow.

"I won't be taking you on the boat tomorrow."

Keoki moved away from the fish, wiping some of the juices onto his frock, "So, how am I going to get back?"

"You won't be going back tomorrow."

"Uh, yes I will. Fil and Agnes will start to worry."

GHE FIRSG WAVE

Keoki was still holding the carving knife in one hand. Sapphir collected herself before responding, squaring off to face him.

"Keoki, I can't let you go back yet."

"Why?" he said, suspicious anger creeping into his voice.

"I... I can't risk you telling about us. The island... this is the only place we're safe."

"Then blindfold me. I don't know where we are and I wouldn't be able to find this island again, even if I tried. Even if I wanted to give away your secret, which I don't. And what's going... why aren't you safe?"

His voice was rising, so Sapphir tried to keep hers steady.

"It's a long story... Listen Keoki, I just don't know if I can trust you."

"Trust me? What, you think I'm going to rat you out? You're worried I'll tell someone there's magicians on an island *somewhere* in the middle of the sea?"

That's exactly what I'm worried about.

"I'm an exile, Keoki. Magicians can't be found in Helike!"

"You're not *in* Helike! You're on an island!"

Sapphir was growing frustrated. How could he not understand?

"Just stay for now! Stay until I figure out what to do with you."

"Figure out what to do with me?" Keoki took a step back, "You planning on getting rid of me? Like you did with the bandits?"

Is that what I want?

"No, no! I'm not going to hurt you, Keoki. I just need to work out a solution. Or you can stay long enough until I know I can trust you."

"You can! I promise."

"It's not that simple!" she yelled this time, and Keoki retreated another step.

Sapphir leveled her voice, "I'm sorry. It's not that simple. I've... I've been betrayed before. And I have even more to care about now."

Keoki grimaced, and she could see in his eyes that he knew what it was like. Loss or betrayal. Both maybe. When he spoke, it was with a careful sincerity.

"Okay... okay. I won't go back tomorrow. But I have to know why, Sapphir. I need to know why you're so scared of being found out here. You have to tell me why."

Sapphir had hoped it wouldn't come to this. But she knew she had to do it. She would have asked the same of Keoki. She felt afraid again – a different type of fear than that of losing her children. She hadn't shared herself with anyone, not since Yusef. She'd have to explain everything about him, too, she supposed. The thought of that made a tear jump to her eyes.

"It's a long story, Keoki."

"It seems that I might have a little time. How long do you think it will take for you to trust me anyway?"

"Maybe you can start by telling me your story, too."

It was Keoki's turn to pause.

"After dinner then. Once the children fall asleep."

THE FIRST WAVE

Sapphir nodded, "Thank you, Keoki. Thank you for trying. It's... it's for the children. You understand."

He gave a sad smile, then returned to deboning the trout.

Chapter 18

Nicolaus

Nic's body tensed as he followed the Flat-Nose. They were in a part of the castle he'd never seen before, several corridors tucked behind the wing where Orrin's living quarters stood. Finally, they arrived at a great tapestry, supposedly weaved by Arachne herself, though Nic knew this to be false. There was no such thing as a giant spider-lady hybrid. If that was the type of monster that came with the Olympian gods, Nic was thankful they didn't exist either.

Simon undid the bottom right corner and folded it up to reveal a door.

"Here we are, Nicolaus. Enter at your leisure, and please mind the furnishing, I like to keep my spaces tidy."

The Flat-Nose hadn't lied. A perfectly ordered stack of tomes and scrolls were tucked away on a desk, and candles were already lit, each marking equidistant spots around the room. There was a table in the middle with a chair on either side.

"Sit, please."

Nic sat, and the Flat-Nose took his place opposite. In the candlelight, Simon's face seemed skeletal – hairless with skin pulled tight over every bone. His thin eyes bore directly into Nic's, though it was somehow not intimidating.

Nic decided it would be best to let the Flat-Nose make the first move.

"Orrin has you running errands now?"

"I'm always attending Lord Orrin," Nic responded, choosing his words with care.

"Well-met, Nicolaus. But let us not quibble over wordplay. Councilor Orrin has you fishing for information."

It wasn't a question, Nic realized.

He already knows.

"Yes."

"Our dear Orrin does not trust that the Council made the right decision blocking trade. An act of war, he says."

Once again, not a question.

"Yes."

"Ah, finally dear Orrin has decided to become a politician. Do you know how long I've had to pull the weight of the Council? Gaios is far too mischievous for one man to bear, you know. Poor dead Euripides certainly couldn't handle it, hero that he may have seemed."

"Wait you and Gaios aren't? You... handle what?" Nic asked.

"Politics, Nicolaus! Kyros is worthless. Orrin has been, up

until this point right now. He's as predictable a councilor as he is skilled a battle general. Yes, until now it has been only me keeping Achaea from Gaios."

"I'm sorry, sir, I'm not quite sure I understand."

Simon ran a finger over some melted wax next to one of his candles.

"But you do, Nicolaus," Simon began, "Otherwise you wouldn't have agreed to follow Orrin's orders and learn about the prisoner, Rizon Atsali. I observe the meetings of the Council, Nicolaus, and I can see when a man is listening. You know more than you realize."

"So, you're on Orrin's side? Is that why you aren't going to arrest me for talking with the prisoner?"

"I have no *side*, Nicolaus. Orrin is an honorable man, always on the side of what is good, what he believes is right. In fact, every man is on the side of what he believes is right. And every woman. Gaios believes Achaea would be safer under a single ruler, or a single council. He is correct; naturally, twelve cities cannot coexist as they are now for much longer. But war is not the answer either, and I fear he believes Achaea needs conquering."

"So, why don't you stop the war? You voted to block trade. Why?"

Nic felt lost. Even though Simon insisted he was more capable than he believed, all this information was swimming aimlessly in his head. He couldn't make much sense of it.

"Gaios will have this war, Nicolaus. He won as soon as

ᏃHE FIRSᏆ WAVE

Euripides agreed to execute the Children of the Sea and exile magic. I warned Euripides not to do it. Pleaded with Gaios not to convince him," Simon flicked at the candle flame, "But it was written then."

"So, magicians killed Euripides? Through Rizon?"

"It matters not who killed Euripides, do you not understand? King Ucalegon has always been weak in Boura, and he would never follow through with the systematic execution of criminals – even those such as the Children of the Sea. As a result, Boura already slighted Helike for accepting some of those savages into their midst."

Simon let that sink in before continuing.

"And we can't forget they already leach away at our food supplies and foreign trade. War was already brewing by the time Euripides was killed. Anyone could have killed him then, and Gaios would have spun it as reason enough to start a war. It was all he needed to break the tension."

Simon explained all of this methodically, but quick enough that Nic knew he must be telling the truth, or at least his interpretation of it. Nic's leg shook nervously, and he tried to steady it before Simon noticed. The Flat-Nose still seemed too distracted by the candle to care, however.

"You know all this... why didn't you try to stop it earlier? And why haven't you told Kyros or Orrin?"

"Gaios was a step ahead of me the whole time. He's smarter than me... and he knows how to, uh, distract me," Simon stumbled for the first time here.

Distract him?

What could Gaios be up to that was enough to draw the Flat-Nose's attention?

"Kyros and Orrin?"

"What could Kyros have done? Tried to kill Gaios by out-drinking him? And Orrin would have tried to do the honorable thing. The *good* thing. Perhaps he would have charged Gaios with crimes, though I'm not sure what he could cite specifically. Manipulation? This is no grounds for a sentence."

"Then, why don't you just kill him yourself?"

"Alas, if it were only that simple. I mentioned he knows how to distract me, yes?"

Simon finally took his eyes off the candle flame.

"Yes," Nic said, wondering again what this meant.

Simon laughed, "Then you can guess why I would never act against him on my own accord."

Nic truthfully could not, but he decided to move on, "So, what? War is inevitable? What will happen to Rizon Atsali? He said he had to choose between murder and his family, or something."

Simon seemed to be calculating how to respond, closing his eyes and drumming his fingers lightly against the table.

"I suppose I've told you just about everything else. There's something funny about a servant, yes? You just know how to listen. It would appear poor Rizon Atsali found himself in a spot of trouble with the Fishermen. You remember them?"

"I do," Nic said, the wheels in his mind beginning to turn.

"And what do you suppose they do to people who wrong them?"

"Something bad?"

Simon laughed again, a hoarse chuckle that seemed unnatural.

"Yes, quite bad. Quite horrible. It would seem someone wanted Euripides dead. The Fishermen often handle requests such as these, so they offered Rizon Atsali the life of his family in exchange for that small favor. You know what happened next."

"But... the Fishermen brought him in to Gaios? Even though they hired him. Why did they bring Gaios the real killer?"

"I am still trying my best to work this one out myself. Who knows how that mysterious bunch operates? Perhaps they thought we would be hard-pressed to punish the people who brought us the true assassin."

"And he'll be executed for this? For protecting his family?"

"For murdering a councilor of Helike."

"A councilor who sentenced hundreds to death and doomed the city to war? Why don't you punish the Fishermen?"

Simon returned to the candle, this time picking at the hardened wax until his fingernails were caked in it.

"If we could find them all, perhaps. But do you punish a wolf for eating a deer? It's what they do."

But Gaios can find some of them at least.

"You're starting to understand though, Nicolaus. What do you think I'll have you do now?"

Nic bit his lip. He wished he had an answer. Why was the Flat-Nose telling him this? What could he possibly do to help?

"You want me to tell Orrin about Gaios?" he guessed, though he knew it was too pedestrian an answer to be correct.

Simon coughed out another hoarse laugh, "No... No. I'm afraid he wouldn't understand nor approve of my next move. No, Nicolaus. I want you to watch. Watch Orrin, watch Kyros, and most importantly, watch Gaios. And live through the war, Nicolaus. I need more people to understand how this city works, how Achaea runs, and how it will survive."

"And what's your next move?"

The Flat-Nose leaned back in his chair, breathing noisily through his flat nose.

"I'm going to free Rizon Atsali. It will give me an excuse to leave Helike. The councilors will let me pursue him because they know I've spoken with him. They think I oversee his torture, but I just talk. Others have dealt him enough physical damage already. The man yields less than I would like, unfortunately. That will give me two days, maybe three, before Gaios realizes what I've done and gets the heart to act. I have... matters to attend to in other cities."

He said all this with the exact calmness that he exercised throughout the rest of the conversation. Nicolaus was coming to respect the Flat-Nose. He wasn't sure he liked him all that much, but Rizon deserved to live, and Simon was going to help him. Nic understood why Simon didn't want to tell Orrin. Orrin wouldn't approve of releasing Rizon, even if the murderer had unselfish reasons.

"Okay. Okay, sir, I can try. But I have to ask, why are you telling me this?"

"Well, I did catch you consorting with a murderer, Nicolaus. I thought I'd test you and see if you were clever enough to keep up with me. If not... well, I could just have you arrested, yes?"

"Oh," Nic said, surprised. He'd forgotten he was talking to one of the most powerful men in Helike.

Simon the Flat-Nose gave him a thin smile, "Seems that won't be necessary though, Nicolaus. I'll bid you good luck in the war with Boura. Helike will win. I do hope you survive."

Simon waved his hand, bidding Nic to leave. He pushed the door open, slipping past the tapestry into the hallway. He still wasn't sure where in the castle he was but began to walk. It took nearly twenty minutes to find a hallway he recognized, though Nic was having trouble paying close attention. There was too much on his mind!

He tried to organize his thoughts as he passed the angry statue of Poseidon, staring disappointedly at Nic, as always.

The Children of the Sea?

Bad. They were sentenced by Euripides at Gaios' encouragement.

But this decision?

Also, bad. It left a population of exiles fleeing Helike, some caught and executed, while others made it to nearby cities in Achaea. This caused tension between Helike and the other cities. Especially Boura, as it was the closest to Helike.

And Helike already hates Boura, though the feeling is probably mutual.

Nic arrived at his room. He didn't even remember climbing the stairs to get there, but he was in bed before he could register it.

Gaios. War. Inevitable war. The Flat-Nose is releasing Rizon Atsali and fleeing to other cities. To find... to do... what?

The last thought to cross Nic's mind before he fell asleep was the only task Nic could fully wrap his head around right now before the war he now knew to be inevitable.

Survive.

Chapter 19

Keoki

"Good night, Mother. Keoki."

Egan shuffled out the cave. The boy amused Keoki. He was somewhat of a behemoth for his age, towering over all of Sapphir's children; he was even taller than Sapphir herself. However, his ungainly size matched quite a shy personality. He seemed dreary most of the time, though Keoki noticed he was affectionate with Maya.

Keoki had been a tall child as well, but he was always more rambunctious and boastful. Time had changed Keoki, and he wondered if Egan would experience the same. Maybe he'd become an unbearably enthusiastic adult.

Keoki remained in his seat at the round table, facing Sapphir. She twiddled her fingers nervously, though her face betrayed nothing. She looked at him with a similar hardness as she had yesterday, when they'd first met.

Yesterday? Damn.

"So, this magic thing. How does it work?" Keoki asked, deciding he would start the conversation as bluntly as possible.

Sapphir eyed him curiously, "You know of the Golden Age, I assume?"

"My parents taught me all that stuff. They were the perfect humans, the gods' first attempt at life."

Keoki's parents had made sure he was well-versed in the history of the gods and all of mankind. He could clearly picture his mother's face as she read to him about the Golden Age and the war between the Olympians and the Titans.

"Those are the essentials. It was said they didn't need to eat or suffer – they spoke with animals and were always happy. If the stories are to be believed, they all died in their sleep. Peacefully. Then, the Titans came."

She paused, crossing one leg over the other.

"Do you think they all died, Keoki?"

"I'm guessing you want me to say no."

"Do you believe in the Titans? The gods?"

"Less now than I used to."

"It matters not. The magic I have – the magic my children have. It all comes from there. We have the blood of the Golden Age in us."

"How?"

Sapphir smirked, "Truthfully, I don't know. It's what my father told me."

"So, you were born with magic?"

"Yes, I suppose I was. That's all it is, random chance. Though my father and mother would say it was because the gods had chosen us. Father gained a lot of followers by telling people they were chosen by the gods."

Followers.

The thought had crossed Keoki's mind several times throughout the day, but he hadn't wanted it to be true. She couldn't be one of them.

"Followers... you're from Helike? Right?"

"I'll make this easier for you. I'm a Child of the Sea. My father, he was the first of the Children," Sapphir said this wearily, but an undertone of spitefulness accompanied the word "father."

Keoki clenched his jaw, and the look he gave Sapphir must have been too harsh.

She chuckled, "This upsets you. It should. Everyone in Helike despises the Children."

"You're an enemy if it's true."

"An enemy, am I? How did you come to this conclusion?"

Sapphir looked at him with a mixture of amusement and concern, and her eyes told him this was the reaction she'd expected.

"I was raised in the Sons of Poseidon. My father was a high priest. He and my mother raised me as the Sons do, and I believed it all. I believed the gods would reward us for being pious and that we could save Helike with good deeds and faith."

"Believed? Do you not anymore?"

"Why should I?" Keoki snapped, angry tears welling, "He was perfect. He and my mother, they were perfect. Kind, honest, faithful. And... and they..."

He hit the table. Why couldn't he talk about it? How many years had it been? Ten? Eleven?

Sapphir said nothing, bidding him to continue.

"You're one of *them*, Sapphir. And *they* killed my parents."

She wasn't looking at him now.

"You knew already?" he asked.

"How could I have known?" she tossed her hair to one side, "But... I do believe you. We did horrible things, all of us. How did it happen?"

Keoki took a deep breath, "We were in the city square. I was eight. My father was speaking to the city... there were so many people there. I can remember being so excited. I think I bragged to my friends all week beforehand."

He gave a humorless laugh at the irony of this, and Sapphir stayed silent.

"Anyway, that one councilor – you know, the one they murdered. Or I don't know who murdered him. He'd just come to the temple to talk with my father about the Children of the Sea. The Council was exiling all of them on pain of death. My father had resisted at first... he didn't want people executed, but he hated the Children's violence as much as anyone. So, he agreed to speak about it."

ᏀᕼᎬ ᖴᏆᎡᏚᏀ ᏔᎪᏙᎬ

Sapphir kept her features hard as stone.

"He had just started talking when it happened. I guess I still don't know *what* exactly happened, but the next thing I remember, there was stone and dust everywhere."

He felt the first tear streak down to the corner of his mouth.

"And then they died. I broke my foot, I think," Keoki said simply, flexing his toes to remind himself of the pain, "And my father made me close my eyes so nobody bad would check if I was alive. I don't know if that would actually have worked, but they never came. I think they already knew their job was done."

He paused for a minute. He was angry at himself for crying, even though he couldn't help it. He'd told so few people the actual truth, it still felt fresh every time he shared. He wiped his face, waiting for Sapphir to speak.

"I'm sorry, Keoki."

That was all. He shook his head. The Children had murdered the two most wonderful people in the world, and Sapphir was *sorry*.

"Sorry? Is that it?"

He stared at her. The woman who'd killed so easily for her children – she must have done it many, many times before.

"Were you one of the people... one of the magicians in the square? One of the people who killed them."

"No. I didn't kill before the exile. I may as well have, but I never did," she looked at the table again, letting her red hair block her eyes.

"You may as well have? What does that even mean?"

"I didn't stop them. Only a minority of the Children truly had magic, but my father worked so many of them into a frenzy, almost any would murder for the cause. But I never did."

Keoki believed her for some reason, "What did you do then?"

"Father raised me to become like him. He trained me. He beat me," she pointed to the white scar on and above her lip, "There's more like this. Did your parents ever?"

Keoki was startled, "Of course not!"

The only physical torture his mother had ever inflicted on him was tickling. He'd hated it as a child, but he would laugh anyway. And his father? He was far too kind and gentle.

Sapphir smiled, "Lucky you. My mother would do nothing to stop them, though she was horrified. He used magic almost every time, of course. Why would he get his hands dirty?"

Keoki began to feel sorry for her, then remembered what she was. Still, he felt conflicted.

What would Father and Mother say of her?

"Father only trained me. He taught me how to use my powers, how to harness the energy without hurting myself. But I only knew bits and pieces of what they did. I was a child, after all. As I grew older, I became rebellious, as all children do when they reach a certain age. As Ivy is now, I guess. That's when I met Yusef, a farmer from the Heliken hills. He was so gentle and kind. My father hated him."

It was Sapphir's turn to let her eyes turn glassy with tears, a sad smile playing across her face.

"How long have you farmed?" she asked.

She's trying to change the subject.

He didn't resist, "I've been with Fil and Agnes for three years now. I was an apprentice for Mako, the smith, since my parents died. But I hated the people – all those soldiers think they're better than everyone. And all those rich snobs who want beautiful swords just to have beautiful swords. I like the cattle and the grapes much more."

Keoki pictured Io, the clever heifer whom he'd lost somewhere in the Heliken forest. He wished he'd been born in the Golden Age, so he could have spoken with her.

"Yusef liked farming, too. He loved to be out on the land."

"He sounds like a man I would get along with."

Sapphir's blue eyes looked at him with a sort of wistful longing. Her red hair was still swept to one side. She was quite pretty for her age.

How old is she?

He hadn't considered that too much, as she had a child of thirteen. He supposed she could be both a mother and a young woman.

"So, Yusef," he said, trying to break the tension.

"Yes. Yusef changed me. I spent more time with him than with my studies, and my father grew sour. Eventually, he forbade me from seeing Yusef, threatening to act with force if I resisted. But the Children all struck me as different now. They cared for nothing besides the gods. Every one of them wanted to cleanse the world, to show the true might of Poseidon. But Yusef had shown me more, and that's what I wanted."

"Did you run away?" Keoki asked, curious now.

He realized that she was sharing much more than him, even though it was he who needed to gain her trust. Perhaps, this was one of her first times sharing her story, the same way Keoki had rarely spoken of his parents. She needed it as much as he did.

"No, I didn't. I knew my father would find me, and I was terrified of what he'd do to Yusef. I just stayed and trained. Then we were warned of the exile."

"They gave you warning. Who?"

"Your father, Keoki. It must have been him. A man with hair like yours, tall and strong. He came and told us all we were being cast out of the city or we would be killed. I heard my father talking with my mother that very night. She wanted to leave, but he said his business in Helike wasn't done. The city hadn't been properly cleansed. I fled that night with nothing. I found Yusef, and I took him with me."

"And then your father killed mine?"

Sapphir nodded, "If it wasn't him, he ordered it."

"You could have stopped him."

"I could have."

Keoki wanted to be furious, he wanted to lash out at Sapphir and tell her exactly what she had let happen to him. But he couldn't, and he suspected she already knew. He tried to consider what he would have done in her shoes, and he couldn't see himself acting any differently. She had fled to find a better life for herself with the man she loved.

"What happened to Yusef? You came here and had your children with him? He was happy to leave Helike? Just like that?"

"Yusef wanted to stay, but I knew if my father escaped the city, Yusef would be the first person he would look for to find me. We were on our way out of the city when we passed the fur trader. Everyone was on the lookout for people fleeing, hoping to get a reward for capturing one of the exiles who hadn't left the city fast enough. All of the Children of the Sea were criminals now. Yusef didn't want to harm the man, so we let him pass. They found us the next day, scores of Heliken guard."

She closed her eyes, drawing shallow breaths, her neck muscles tightening.

"You don't have to tell," Keoki said, knowing exactly where the story was headed.

"They took everything from me, Keoki. They did it in the same square as your parents. I had to watch as they walked him to the foot of the stairs, right under Poseidon's statue. My energy was too tapped from the night before, I could barely muster enough strength to break free of my bonds before the axe fell."

Her voice had changed to a shaky monotone, the emotion entirely gone.

"I'm sorry, Sapphir."

He watched her steady her hands. She seemed so hurt, so

broken. He wondered how she possibly raised the children on her own so well. But if Yusef had died, they couldn't all be his.

If not his, then whose?

Keoki's heart sank in sorrow for the woman before him, but bits and pieces of what he'd learned of her family began to fall into place. An old story that plagued Helike since the Children of the Sea were exiled, and one that Fil and Agnes found particularly disturbing, needled into his head.

I shouldn't say anything.

"Ivy says she never knew her father... have any of your children met both of their parents?"

Sapphir met his eyes, shaking her head slowly. Her skin was somehow paler than before, the scar now barely visible.

"Keoki..."

"Helike took everything from you."

Not just everything from her past, everything that could be in her future.

She was straightening now, blue eyes still locked with his. They were still filled with sadness, but shame was beginning to creep in.

"Sapphir... these children... Egan, Maya, Ivy... all of them."

Stop. I need to stop.

He began to inch his chair backwards, muscles in his legs tensing. It was finally making sense to him – why Sapphir really hadn't wanted Keoki to leave the island, why she stayed so close to the city that had exiled her and executed her husband, when her children could be raised anywhere else in Achaea, and why they looked nothing like her.

"You wanted to take something back from them, didn't you?"

She stood now, and Keoki knew he wouldn't be able to stop whatever magic she could conjure at him. But he had to confirm, had to be sure.

"They're not yours, are they? You took them and raised them as your own."

Would she kill him for knowing? Why hadn't she just wiped his memory clean from the beginning and sent him on his way. Her hand shook as she extended it towards him, and her whole body mimicked the pattern. He needed to do something, but he couldn't wrap his head around his new discovery, and he hadn't formulated a full response to it.

"Sapphir, wait," he started to say as she stepped forward.

He raised his arm defensively, and she grabbed it. He could feel his body begin to go limp, and his voice no longer worked. But he could still see as she dragged him, floating, out of the cave, towards the side of the cliff.

Chapter 20

Melani

Melani should have told him days ago. She paced the length of the cozy room with a cookfire frying eggs for the both of them. She could hear Xander shifting in the other room, packing a couple changes of clothes in his bag and checking that all the pieces of his leather armor were in order.

All the commotion as Xander prepared to leave with his unit, and Melani retrained her skills in medicine, had left her too distracted to tell him that she hadn't bled this month. She touched her stomach as the eggs crackled in the pan. She didn't need to check her healing tomes to know what it meant.

I'm in the same position as Loren now.

"Mel," Xander said from the bedroom, "is breakfast ready?"

"In a minute, dear."

He emerged in full armor, smooth leather perfectly molded to his figure, with hardened glass stamped in a mosaic to strengthen it. The armor was light enough for Xander to move normally, yet hard enough to deflect arrows and spear-points. A sword placed just right would certainly pierce it, Xander said, but he seemed unbothered by this. He carried a simple leather helmet to match.

"How do I look?"

"Like a proper soldier."

She stepped closer to him, running her hand over the leather and glass on his shoulder.

"You'll need a proper breakfast, too."

He kissed her, then picked up the pan, plating eggs and bread for both of them. They ate slowly, as if it would delay what was about to happen.

"When do the healers set out to make camp?"

"Tomorrow. I guess we'll be between you all and the city."

She tried to maintain composure, and she could tell Xander was doing the same, despite his ferocious appearance in armor.

"Xander, there's something I have to tell you."

He nodded, speaking between mouthfuls of egg, "What is it, love?"

"I should have told you sooner, I just... I don't know."

"Well, don't wait any longer," he laughed, "It might be a while before I see you again, you know."

Her face reddened, and she tried to laugh alongside him. But she felt strangely scared.

"I didn't bleed this month."

Xander dropped his fork.

"And?"

"And what?"

"So, you're..."

"I think so. I mean, yes. I think."

"Are you sure?"

"Yes."

She was sure. She tensed, wondering what he would say.

When he jumped out of his chair, Melani thought he was angry, then she looked at his face. His mouth was gaping, and his eyes were equally wide with surprise. Joyful surprise.

"We're going to have a child?"

He walked away, then spun in a tight circle and came back to her, grabbing her head excitedly, yet with his usual gentleness. He kissed her forehead.

"Why'd you wait so long to tell me? We're having a child!"

"Yes," she said, before a smile broke across her face. "We are, Xan, we're having a baby!"

For a moment, the war didn't matter. She was happy. And he was happy. And she stood to embrace him, and he spun her around with elation. He pulled her close, and they kissed once more, though she held onto him longer this time.

When they broke apart, he stared at her for a moment as a tear rolled down her cheek.

Then he grimaced, "And I'm leaving."

"It's okay, Xan, I'm leaving, too."

"You should stay behind, we have too much at risk now. Don't be a healer, just stay here."

Her face fell, "Xander, no. I'm coming. I won't be in any danger, you know that. I can't let you go out there alone, not when I can do something, too. If you get hurt... and if they can't help you... I have to know I tried."

"I *have* to go though, Mel. You don't!"

"You don't *have* to do anything!" she exclaimed, "Why don't we both just stay?"

Xander shook his head, "It's too late for that, I can't abandon my post."

"Then, I can't either."

When they looked at each other again, any frustration they had melted away. They both knew they wanted to stay in this room, to go back to their bed and fall asleep in each other's arms. But it was too late for that. Xander would be arrested, more than likely, if he stayed, and she refused to let him go alone. They stayed silent for a while.

"I love you," he said.

That was all that needed to be said.

"I love you, too, Xander Atsali. And if you don't come back, I swear to all the gods..."

He has to come back. He's a father now.

"I'll come back to you," he declared.

He kissed her one last time, then picked up his bag, slung his sword over his back, and walked through the door.

T.J. VINCENT

✳✳✳✳

Melani sat on her favorite bench by the Bouran city center. She couldn't handle the empty house for one more minute, so she'd walked down the cobbled stone streets and bought a plate of cheese and olives. She nibbled at the green morsel, working her way around the pit cautiously. She loved olives, especially when she could take a bite paired with her favorite cheese. Boura was bustling, as men and women went about their business. A street performer dazzled two younger women with a levitation trick, though Melani could see how his staff had a seat on which he could perch.

She hadn't painted in weeks but thought about doing some food pieces when she returned. She rarely saw those; perhaps the rich would like them.

A colorful arrangement of vegetables, with a nice wheel of cheese, maybe.

She was just about to pop the perfect bite in her mouth, when a familiar voice cut through the humdrum of city noise.

"Ah, do my eyes deceive me? Is that Melani, lover of Xander Atsali?"

She turned just as Tarlen the fur trader stepped into view. His muscles were visible once again, as he stood bare-chested with another ornate, jeweled skirt around his slender waist.

What's he doing here?

Melani hadn't thought about Tarlen much since their

219

conversation, and she wasn't entirely pleased to see him. In her recounting with Xander, she may have been overly harsh of the man, but he still struck her as suspicious.

A trader, traveling between Helike when trade has ceased...

"Tarlen, isn't it?" she asked, pretending she wasn't sure.

"Yes, yes, Melani. And I'm sure you meet a lot of dark-skinned fur traders in your days around Boura. It must be difficult to keep us sorted."

A glint of mischievous humor flashed across his eyes. He had called her bluff. She decided to move on.

"What brings you to Boura, again? I thought you were merely passing through last time."

"It seems the town is quite taken to my pelts, here. Though, I'll admit, I may have been motivated to see an old friend."

"Who would that be?"

"Why you, of course, Melani. You, and Xander Atsali."

Melani gave him a weary look, "How lucky that I'm right here, then. I'm afraid Xander has already left Boura."

"A brave warrior, yes? He's off to fight the battles of lords and kings?"

"I suppose that's true."

Tarlen looked her up and down, reading her emotions. His hand rested against his skirt, fingers tapping a red ruby.

"I sense you don't want him gone."

"Of course, I don't want him going to war, Tarlen. War is dangerous."

"Tarry. My friends call me Tarry."

Subconsciously, Melani had stood, and was already beginning to walk in the general direction of her home. She realized her mistake too late.

"Where are you off to? Surely, you can't leave a friend who's come all this way."

"Home, I'm a little tired. Perhaps, after I get some sleep, we can talk."

Melani hoped Tarlen would get the message. Instead, he began walking with her. She pined to quicken her pace but knew it would do no good. She felt an urge to stay in the city square, but if he wanted to follow her, he'd do so when she left later as well. Better to head home in the light of day, while men and women still meandered the streets.

If only Xander were home!

"Business has been good, I take it?" Melani asked, trying to revive conversation.

"Indeed. Quite good, indeed. I may have enough coin to make some deals with Xander Atsali. If only he were home."

She immediately regretted informing him of Xander's absence – however, for some reason, she suspected that he already knew. She recounted her last meeting with the man.

He shows up, just as tensions rise between Helike and Boura. Then Aggio and his friends are filled with arrows.

They passed shops and houses, but the number of people thinned as they continued radiating from the main square. Melani needed to speak now.

"Tarlen, why are you following me?"

"Following!" he exclaimed, almost offended, "I merely wish to accompany a friend home!"

His hand dropped to his waist again, and it was only then that Melani saw the dagger hilt. She cried out, throwing her fist at his groin before breaking into a run.

The move caught Tarlen by surprise, and he folded as she made contact with his member. She was only a few paces ahead of Tarlen when he recovered. And he was much faster.

She had been running for barely ten seconds when he caught her, grabbing her shoulder. She twisted and dropped to the ground hard.

The baby. I'm hurting the baby!

She scrambled back on all fours as he loomed over. His torso eclipsed the already waning sunlight, creating a fiery glow around his muscular body. Melani felt small and powerless – she was just a child again.

I'm just a little girl. And that's Hephes, getting ready to show me how to paint the sky.

Melani nearly laughed, thinking of Xander on his way to war while she lay on the road so close to death.

Our child will grow up without a mother.

Of course, Melani knew that the baby would not survive a dagger to her mother's heart. The fragility of her existence, and the codependence of her baby, struck before the knife ever could.

Melani realized her daughter would never have the full life she herself wanted to live.

Daughter... no... I think I'd rather have a son.

Melani had always wanted both.

Xander and I should have left Boura together.

Tarlen clicked his tongue disapprovingly, as if Melani had upset him in some way. He lifted his arm to make a quick, deadly cut, when a blade exploded from the back of his neck. It withdrew in the blink of an eye.

The fur trader – or whatever he was – fell to his knees, grasping at his throat as blood fountained out of both sides.

Behind him stood a slender man, muscles taut as a wild animal. His beard was trimmed roughly over a chiseled face that somehow drew her attention to sharp eyes. She recognized this face, though he looked more disheveled than she recalled.

"Melani. You remember me?" he asked, his voice graveled and unused.

"Rizon?"

He reached his hand out, helping her to her feet. Melani felt invigorated. She couldn't tell if it was relief, or some kind of sadistic happiness. All the fear she may have had drained at the sight of Tarlen's bloodied body.

Is this... wrong?

"You look the same," he said.

"You look... worn."

He laughed, then coughed, "Well, pull yourself together. This one isn't the only person they sent after you and my brother."

"Who? After us?" she said, bewildered.

After me... and Xander? Why would they... me?

"The Fishermen. Look, I'll explain as soon as I can. Let's get out of the city and try to find Xander."

"He's on the move with the Bouran army, Rizon. What do you expect us to do?"

He shrugged, "Find him before they do, I guess. Grab anything you might need, and let's get going!"

Melani was frozen. Cold fingers brushed her neck as the truth of her situation, and the danger it put her baby in, finally grasped her.

Yes... we need to find Xander before they do. Find Xander.

"I'm ready."

Melani touched her stomach lightly. Besides the father of her child, she had everything she needed.

Chapter 21

Nicolaus

Orrin huddled over his map of the beachfront, murmuring under his breath as he traced his finger along the ridged shoreline. He had finalized battle plans earlier in the day with the other officers but seemed in grim spirits despite the numerous advantages held by Helike's army.

They were camped on a hillside just outside the outer walls of the city, meaning any approaching Bouran would have to press across the beach below before arriving at the gentle uphill incline. Scouts had informed Orrin that the Bourans had fractured into two cohorts, one led by Parex the Hammer – a name Nicolaus recognized as King Ucalegon's own champion.

Parex's forces planned to trap Helike in a pincer movement, approaching the city from the northwest, while other Bourans attacked from the southeast. Given the limited size of Boura's army, Orrin regarded the move as a good one; it forced Helike to split its own forces to defend the walls and meet them in the open field.

However, Parex would need to funnel his forces across coarse sand and pebbles along the seaside in order to reach Helike. Here, the Golden Spear waited, with an army almost double the size of Parex's own.

Orrin had a larger, better-positioned command. Yet, he still seemed on edge. Nic couldn't blame him. He was terrified himself.

"Nicolaus, can you fetch my water?"

"Yes, sir," Nic responded, grabbing the cup that stood on a table across the tent.

Orrin took a sip, letting the water sit in his mouth a moment before swallowing.

"Nicolaus, I realized I never properly thanked you for trying to find out more about Rizon Atsali. You acted bravely for your city."

"Thank you, sir. I'm not sure I deserve it, though. It did nothing to stop the war," Nic said, feeling his cheeks redden.

"You are being too hard on yourself. This war... I fear I was too late in trying to bring an end to it. I received word that the prisoner escaped, too."

Nic feigned surprise but said nothing. He was afraid he might give away his secret meeting with the Flat-Nose.

"Alas. Another guilty man escaping justice, while we fight a battle he caused. The Flat-Nose is in pursuit of the murderer. It's curious, he seemed so sure he could find him."

T.J. VINCENT

Guilt washed over Nic. He wanted to tell Orrin that Rizon Atsali didn't want to start a war; he wanted to tell him that Gaios had foreseen this from the beginning. It was Euripides who doomed the neighbor cities to violence. Though, he had been hard-pressed by the Children of the Sea. Nic's face suddenly flushed, beads of sweat budding on his neck and forehead. Orrin had been nothing but kind to him, and he was withholding information from him.

He was breaking Orrin's trust by saying nothing. But, what good would it do? Orrin had enough on his mind without learning of Gaios' conniving.

Yes, they had to win tomorrow's battle first.

"Perhaps, the gods still have other plans for Rizon Atsali," Nic offered.

Orrin smiled, "Very wise of you, my boy. We know not what they have planned for us."

Nic didn't know if the gods cared what happened to Rizon Atsali. Or if the gods cared what happened to anyone, for that matter. Why would they allow wars, if they wanted only good for the people of Achaea?

"Sir, do you have everything you need for the evening?" Nic asked, wanting to be dismissed so he wouldn't need to lie any longer.

"I believe so, thank you. I'll have you here in the morning, then? Just before the sun rises. I will need assistance with my armor, I'm afraid. Far too many straps for an old man."

"Of course, sir."

"And during the battle... are you certain you are prepared to act as my steward?"

It was customary for high-ranking officers to have with them squires or stewards, someone to stay by their side during battle and refill their arrow quivers, or something. Nic thought this was a ridiculous practice, though he had completed the required training. He had almost no experience with weapons aside from a few lessons from a Heliken guardsman years ago. It appeared Nic's servitude was beginning to take on a whole new level of danger.

"Uh, yes. I mean, sir, I'm afraid I might be... unhelpful?"

He couldn't find the right word for, "completely and utterly useless."

"You have already proven to be a brave man, Nicolaus. And what's more, you are loyal to me. You always have been. Why do you think Gaios, Kyros, and Euripides have had so many attendants in their days? They can't find someone they can trust, who is humble enough to help them perform menial tasks. *You*, Nicolaus, are a good man. You are clever enough to offer advice, but you do not presume to know more than your elders. You have received the necessary instruction in the duties of a steward. I want you by my side tomorrow because I need men I can count on, as well as skilled soldiers."

Orrin stood as he spoke, his head well above Nicolaus. He walked around the table with his map of Helike and put a hand on Nic's shoulder.

"I believe in you. But I do not want to ask too much of you. I do not want to endanger you without cause."

Nic heart swelled. He couldn't remember the last time he felt so flustered. However, it was a strange sort of embarrassment.

Is this pride?

"Sir, I... I'm honored."

Honored.

That was an understatement. The Golden Spear, one of the greatest heroes in all of Achaea, trusted him... truly valued him.

"Will you attend me tomorrow, as you have so admirably for these past years?"

Nic straightened, throwing his shoulders back, "Yes. I'll do my best."

"I believe you, son. Get a good night of rest, now. I'll need you sharp tomorrow."

Nic exited Orrin's tent, looking for his sleeping pad nearby. Six other attendants sat around a fire, making light conversation and laughing. One had a cup sloshing with ale, looking as if it were not his first.

He had no interest engaging with their merriment. He wasn't sure he could formulate a proper sentence. He felt simultaneously empowered and terrified; how could he live up to Orrin's high praise?

Nic slipped under a blanket on his pad. The air was crisp this evening, though the skies were clear and starry. Once, when Nic was younger, he and his sisters had tried to see what shapes they could find in the stars.

Gabrielle always saw animals – a bear, a scorpion, even a lion. Ibbie couldn't figure out what she saw, usually just squealing when a sparkling dot would shoot across the sky, propelled by some unknown force.

He missed his sisters. Maybe, if he served well enough in the battles, he would be allowed back home. He wondered what his mother would say if he showed up, so many years later. Would she pinch his cheek and tell him how tall he'd gotten?

More likely, she'd poke his stomach, "You're too damn skinny! Didn't they feed you in that fancy palace?"

He supposed she didn't know he'd been living in a fancy palace.

Would he even be able to find his way home if given the opportunity?

I could certainly find Egypt...

And the village outside of Memphis would be easy to locate from there.

Will Ibbie recognize me? With my hair so shorn and clothes so clean?

He needed to live through tomorrow first. He realized his family would never know how he died if it happened in a foreign war like this. Would they weep for him as Helike would weep for the Golden Spear, if he perished?

Nic thought of Elfie now, the homely wife of Orrin, who had been so kind and generous as he recovered from the beating that night. Maybe Nic would suffer a wound like hers and live the rest of his life with only one arm.

Ibbie would like having a one-armed brother.

He remembered Orrin's daughter, Rosie. He wouldn't soon forget her pretty face, nor the shame that came with his attraction to her.

It could never be, she has a husband. And children.

Well, she'd had children. Grandchildren of Orrin, whom they'd lost somehow.

Had they died?

Nic recalled the sadness on Orrin's face as he spoke of his lost family, the tears in his green eyes.

Did my family cry for me, too?

Rosie had given him stew that night, and he longed to share another meal with her. Really *with* her this time, though. For some reason, his mind jumped to Opi now, and he imagined her caramel skin and short hair, like Nic's.

She had always been so kind to Nic, but he never opened up to her.

Why didn't I want friends? I only ever talked to Krassen. She might have been my friend.

Or more, perhaps. Nic realized then, that he'd never kissed a girl. He was sixteen now, and somehow never managed to. Would Opi have wanted to kiss him?

What if I die tomorrow, without ever kissing a girl?

When he returned to Helike, Nic vowed the first thing he

would do is ask Opi to have a drink at Krassen's pub with him.

Would she like that? No... Maybe a meal in the palace courtyard.

He lay there, staring at the bear in the sky, letting dreams of Opi, his family, and home, wash over him.

****

Nic was up before the dawn, aroused by birds chirping. The sky was still dark, though the horizon was tinted blood orange. A gentle breeze tickled Nic's face, and he took a deep breath to take in the scent of the sea. Sand and salt greeted him.

He slipped carefully out of his blanket. He felt surprisingly well-rested. His thin mail armor was in Orrin's tent. He could hear the giant man snoring from inside and lifted the tent flap carefully. He nudged the mound beneath a pile of furs; Orrin woke almost immediately.

He wore loose linen, a flexible finery that would fit comfortably under his armor.

"Good morning, sir."

"We shall see if it is good soon enough. I hope you were able to sleep well."

He stretched, pulling himself out of the temporary bed Nic had set up in his tent. Nic stood awkwardly to one side, fidgeting with the pile of Orrin's armor on the floor, though he didn't know how the pieces fit together.

"Here, have a bite of this," Orrin said, tossing a meat-filled pocket of bread to Nic.

Startled, Nic fumbled it. He managed to catch the pastry before it hit the floor. The food was not hot, but Nic realized how famished he was as soon as he bit in. He ate quickly.

Orrin began pulling on thick leather boots. Nic still wore sandals. Most of the men still did. Nic thought this may have been an oversight. Certainly, boots would be superior for battle. It was too late now.

"Would you mind assisting with my breastplate? The straps in the back," Orrin asked, pointing over his shoulder and turning.

Nic helped fasten the massive steel sheet to Orrin's hulking form. His gauntlets and mail kilt were extremely heavy, and Nic was barely able to push all his weight into propping them up for Orrin to handle.

A thin sheen of sweat collected on Nic's skin already; he wasted too much energy on this task. The entirety of his own mail armor was considerably lighter than Orrin's kilt alone, but it still weighed him down when he slipped into it. He took a deep breath to reduce his heart rate. Orrin seemed to notice his discomfort.

"Catch your breath, son. There's no need to let your nerves get the best of you before the battle even begins."

Nic acknowledged nervously.

A case standing two feet taller than Orrin stood propped against the table with the map of Helike. Orrin snapped it open, gazing reverently at the contents. He reached a hand the size of a water pitcher inside and brought out a sturdy golden staff, tipped with a fierce, razor-sharp tip.

The Golden Spear and his golden spear.

Orrin spun the weapon around effortlessly, pointing it at an invisible foe.

"I suppose I've missed this part," Orrin said quietly, as if he weren't addressing Nic, "The thrill of it all."

Nic was the furthest thing from thrilled. He was disturbingly aware of his own intestines twisting inside his body.

Orrin took another item out of the case, a spear approximately a head higher than his steward. He handed it to Nic. The hardened wood was pliable, yet strong. It was tipped with a wicked iron point and banded with a taut leather grip.

"Er, thank you, sir," he said, moving the weapon from one hand to the other.

"It is no trouble of mine to arm my steward. Are you ready?"

No.

"Yes."

Orrin gestured to the tent flap, and Nic walked through, holding it open so Helike's great general, the Golden Spear, could be revealed to his army. Orrin's armor was dyed sea-green, a similar color to his formal himation. However, he seemed much more confident in steel than fine cloth. Poseidon's trident decorated both the front and back of his breastplate, and his helm was a crowned masterpiece beset with a sapphire. He was truly a magnificent sight to behold.

Unfortunately, a disorganized mob of tired soldiers were the ones to behold it. They meandered aimlessly throughout the camp, half-dressed in their battle attire and sporadically armed. Orrin's mouth tightened with concern. Nic knew the councilor worried about his force's discipline.

"Hira, Julan, Furel! Where are my officers?" Orrin bellowed, capturing the attention of hundreds.

The soldiers began moving with more intention, readying themselves further. However, they were slow on the uptake.

"Men! Form rank! Hira! Damn my officers!"

He swept through the camp, stomping past hundreds of Helike's finest men. His three senior officers, Julan, Furel, and Hira were gathered around a cookfire, warming water for tea.

He will not be happy about this.

Nic watched with disappointment, as Orrin berated his most trusted military minds for settling in for breakfast tea, while the enemy could approach at any moment. Julan, a barrel-chested man in his forties with a hairy moustache, reacted first, throwing down his cup and standing to attention, his spear bouncing against his leg as it fell from his waist.

After a few minutes, the four men returned to the edge of camp, and faced their troops, the majority of whom finally appeared prepared enough. Hira and Furel looked similar to Nic, both thin men with wispy beards, though Furel's was blonde, while Hira's was black. Each commanded a different specialty.

Furel would have control of the archers, staying on higher

ground and raining arrows to the foes below. Hira, a famed swordsman, but not renowned for his leadership, would command troops on the left flank, closest to the cliffs to press the foes into the sea as they approached. Julan led the front lines, mostly spearmen and javelin throwers, who could get extra range with their long weapons.

Orrin would control forces from the middle. Infantry fighters with swords and spears alike. There was no cavalry in today's battle; the horses would struggle on the slanted hillside and sandy beach.

Nic stood next to the handful of stewards behind the commanders. Before them stood ten thousand men, roughly a fifth of Helike's strength. It would be more than enough to fend off the Bouran attack, or so Orrin and the others thought. Five thousand more soldiers waited at Helike's northern walls, while the remaining forces protected against the other Bouran assault.

"Form rank!" Julan shouted in a wheezy voice that certainly didn't inspire Nic.

Those who had not already found their place amongst their platoon scrambled to do so, until a semi-organized mob of soldiers stood in loose rows before the four leaders.

Orrin paced in front of them all, his helmet's visor lifted to show his worn face. Compared to Julan, his voice boomed, filling the camp atop the hillside.

"Brothers! Soldiers of Helike! Today, men threaten your home. They mean to endanger your wives, your children, your mothers, and fathers!"

He beat his chest with a steel hand.

"But the day is not theirs to win! We have the position; we have the numbers! We have the skill to smash Boura for trying to take what is ours – for trying to overthrow the great city of Helike!"

Nic felt a chill inch down his spine. The air still smelled of salt and sand, the freshness of the ocean wafting across what would soon be the site of endless death.

"Men! I ask you. Will you defend your honor? Will you defend the honor of your families? The honor of your great city? Will you defend Helike, as the gods will you to?"

Nobody answered his rhetorical question, but a tense excitement glowed in the eyes of many of the men. Some swelled with bloodlust, while others yearned for the chance to prove their heroics to whomever would witness.

Nic wanted a drink. He wanted to play Senet in Krassen's pub, and he wanted to entertain Ibbie with her dolls.

I wonder if I could still make her laugh until she cried.

"Soldiers! Prepare to deliver Boura to Hades or make the trip yourselves trying!"

A roar of approval greeted Orrin, and the Golden Spear pounded the hard ground with his weapon. The crowd mimicked, banging swords against shields, mailed hands against metal armor, and pounding spears against the Earth.

Nic tapped his lightly against the ground, noticing for the first time that his helmet didn't quite fit, and that his mail armor made his skin feel soggy, like boiled crab.

Chapter 22

Sapphir

The sun peeked above the cliffside, bathing Sapphir in a red-orange glow that melded into her hair. She had woken before dawn, choosing to walk to the seaside and wade into the salty water. She liked how the delicate spray leapt playfully against her skin. The coast of Achaea stuck out sorely from the vast blue, signifying the edge of her world.

Still, she enjoyed starting her morning this way. Now, she could hear Ivy stirring. She always woke before her siblings.

My children are competitive indeed.

"Good morning, Ivy," she said.

"Good morning, Mother. What are we having for breakfast?"

"Figs? Bread? I found some fruit at the village yesterday, how does that sound?"

"I like figs and bread!"

She kicked a pebble as hard as she could, elated at the way it skidded across the dust cliff. It stopped in a shrub not far away, and she pumped her arm, satisfied.

"Would you like to learn today?" Sapphir asked, hoping her daughter would say yes.

"Mmm, I don't know. Maybe Cy and I can go diving for shells?"

"It has been too long since I gave you any lessons, dear. You and Cy dove for shells yesterday!"

Ivy shrugged, "Okay, maybe if Cy and Celia want to after lunch."

Sapphir tried to cover her disappointment. At her age, she had not always wanted to train either, though she was rarely given much choice. It had been over a week since she last taught her children anything or spent proper time with them for that matter. Now that she thought about it, her last lesson with Ivy was the day she and Maya had taken a boat and fled the island.

Then, of course, he had arrived.

Sapphir would never be able to forgive herself for revealing her secret to that boy. She had wanted to learn about *him*, but the moment she began unveiling pieces of her past, it had all tumbled out of her. She had never told anyone about Yusef and couldn't stop herself from sharing the details of his death.

In truth, Keoki reminded her too much of her Yusef – that was why he now lay in a cave on a hidden part of the island, rather than the bottom of the ocean.

If only she had been more careful! She could have covered her tracks at any point; she could have lied about her parents, about Yusef, about the children. She could have said the children were sons and daughters of fishermen she never saw again, or men she paid for a night of pleasure.

But he had read her too easily. As soon as he knew Yusef could not be father to all five of them, he knew they could not have truly come from her. Perhaps her eyes gave away that Yusef would always be the only one she could love in that way.

Still, Keoki did not know the whole story. Helike owed her a debt that it could never repay, but the children were not part of this trade. They were *hers*, the same way she was theirs. They had the blood of the Golden Age running through their veins, just as she did – she could sense it whenever they were close.

And so could her father. Teremos surely would have found them all and taken them for his own. By the time Sapphir found Egan, three children had already been recorded missing; Sapphir knew her father was collecting, trying to use children whose blood boiled with mystic energy to revive the Children of the Sea.

Her children had needed her protection from the day they were born.

Keoki had not listened when she tried explaining this to him a week ago.

"You took children from their mothers! Their fathers! Their brothers and sisters. Just because they could do magic?"

"He would have found them, Keoki. They needed me."

He had just shaken his head. He thought the situation was

simple! She was a thief of the worst ilk. She had separated mothers from their babes out of pure revenge.

But I'm no thief! They would be dead without me. Or worse, with him.

This is what she told herself every night before she fell asleep.

They love me, and I love them. I would do anything for them.

One day, she would convince herself fully that she had done the right thing.

"What will you tell the girls?" Keoki had asked.

"That you went home."

They had believed her, as they always did, when she had told them Keoki left without saying goodbye. He wanted to get home before morning, and they had already gone to sleep. Maya frowned when she told her this, and Ivy pouted the next day, wondering when she could go see "Kiki" at his farm.

As she watched Ivy kick pebbles aimlessly, waiting for the brother she loved so much – a brother that was not truly hers – Sapphir tried to stop herself from bursting into tears.

"Are you happy, Ivy?" she asked, feeling awkward that she sought solace from her eleven-year-old.

"Today? No, I'm bored."

"But it's just the morning."

"Yeah, it's just the morning. Can we eat now?"

She wanted Ivy to say yes... yes, she was so happy. Happy to live on a beautiful island with her family. Happy to learn her powers and play without worry.

T.J. VINCENT

If she were happy, would she have run away?

Ivy poked Sapphir in the thigh, then shut her eyes, letting the sea breeze tousle her hair gently. She breathed in the crisp air, anxiously awaiting her mother's answer.

"Yes, dear. Let's go have some figs. I'm hungry, too."

****

Once all her kids were awake and fed, Sapphir told them to play until she got back for a lesson. She packed away leftover figs and barley bread and marched down to her rowboat.

"I'll be back soon, children. Just going to pick up food for tomorrow."

She got in her boat, out of sight from the children, but instead of rowing towards the villages across the sea, she hugged the cliffside, paddling to the opposite side of the island. She could let the boat row itself, of course, but sometimes it felt better to do the work herself.

Caves peppered the rocks, but she searched for one in particular. A pointed rock jutted twenty feet high at the very tip of the island, blocking the inlet behind it from view. A small cavern was situated just above high tide, so it remained almost completely dry, save for the occasional splashing wave.

She moored the boat against the rock and climbed her way up the natural staircase. He sat inside, leaning against the cushion she had given him, chained to a padlock that fused to the cave walls with a spell of Sapphir's own invention.

Some days, he didn't eat and pushed the cushion away, sitting defiantly on the hard ground. Today, however, he seemed not to care how she perceived him. There was a strange bravery in this unpredictability, as if he wanted her to know it was still his choice to accept whatever she sent his way.

"I have food," she said, holding up the sack.

"Thanks," he responded, catching it and picking carefully at the figs with his dirty hands.

"You still have enough water?"

"What's it to you?"

"I'd like you to live."

"Is that why you've set me up in such a comfortable home?"

He scowled. His hair remained a wild mess of curls, but he had not shaved his face in over a week, and rough patches of black were now visible. Sapphir checked the canteens scattered around him. He still had plenty of fresh water.

"You know I had no choice," Sapphir tried.

For some reason, she still needed to justify everything to him. Why was that?

"What? To imprison me? Or to kidnap the children?"

"I'm doing it *for* them."

"You did it for you. You thought you couldn't have kids anymore, so you took them for yourself. Did you ever look to see the families? Who they belonged to? Before you took them.... Whose children are they really?"

244

T.J. VINCENT

Sapphir stamped her foot against the stone lightly. She did know whose children they were; but he already knew she didn't care. Part of her had wanted them because Yusef was gone, she couldn't deny it.

"Why didn't you just wipe my memory? You could've erased my knowledge of you, and that would've been it."

"It doesn't work like that. I would've had to take them all."

It was true. Memory charms were among the most advanced Sapphir knew, requiring intense focus and compliance from the subject. Because they could only cloud the truth, the spells waned with time. It did take many, many years, but strong-willed people could eventually piece back the knowledge they once had. If any memories remained after the spell was cast, the rest would soon come back.

"Is that what you did to Egan? To Maya and Ivy? To Cy and little Celia?"

The heat that sweltered within her whenever her temper escalated began to bubble. It was magical energy awakening, unconsciously preparing to defend her.

I don't need it right now.

"Yes."

There was no use lying.

"And you *still* think you did the right thing?"

"I love them, Keoki."

His face told her he understood this. It did not, however, change the fact that he saw her as some sort of monster.

ᲗᏂᎬ ᖴᏒᎥᏒᏚᏖ ᎳᎪᏙᎬ

He knows nothing of monsters.

"So, I'll just live my days out in here. Staring at stalactites and the ocean. If that's the case, why don't you just kill me?"

"I can't."

"You did just fine killing those other men who threatened your family. How am I different?"

"You're innocent."

"Right. And *you* are not."

Keoki smirked as he let the last word sink in. He picked up a fig, biting into it and chewing slowly. A seed stuck in his beard when he set the fruit back down.

Am I guilty?

"If I were to let you go, my family could be torn apart."

"You're an expert at that."

"If you told anyone... if word got out about the island at all... He'd come for them. You'd be dooming them."

Keoki leaned back, considering this. He took out the hunk of bread, gnawing at the crust before wolfing down the middle. Then, he closed his eyes.

Sapphir sighed. She left him there to sleep, climbing back down to her boat. She sat there silently, letting waves rock it back and forth. Water lapped in sometimes, and she raised her hand to let it dance in front of her eyes. It was one of the first tricks she learned as a child, playing with water in her cup at dinner. Whatever she thought about, the water seemed to do. Maybe this was because it was so simple, just tiny drops obeying her commands harmlessly.

Maybe her father had been right. Poseidon could have chosen them. She was a Child of the Sea, able to perform miracles as the gods could.

If the gods chose us, why are we so evil?

She did not know how many Children remained. Certainly, her father was alive, and a few more fled to Boura or Olenus. Or Dyme or Patras. But there had been hundreds before the exile, and only those who stayed behind or were already imprisoned were executed.

The Children's numbers swelled further as more newborns were blessed with the blood of the Golden Age, and the Children discovered them.

Stole them.

Father had always told her the Golden Age was a peaceful time. Everyone was well fed and lived in perfect harmony with their surroundings. *If only we could revert to that paradise, instead of suffering in the age of iron and war, poverty and famine.*

This was how Teremos built the Children of the Sea. They were to be the new Golden Age of men, chosen by the gods, by Poseidon himself, to save their people. Was he wrong?

Of course, he is wrong.

Every now and then, Sapphir could hear his voice, smooth and sweet as honey, in her head, calling to her.

"Daughter, you know what you are. Let me find you and save you; bring your children and let them become true Children

of the Sea."

She never responded, fearing that he would be able to break the veil she had created around the island for her family's safety. After all this time, he still wanted her to be his champion, to rule with him over the new Golden Age.

"Let me find you and save you."

She wondered often if she had made the right choice abandoning her father and the family she grew up with. But her new family meant more, and she could not bear to become what her father had. She ran a finger over the jagged scar above her lip and felt the heat of magical energy return.

Chapter 23

Melani

The night sky glittered with stars. Melani tried to keep her eyes open from the back of her horse. She was an adequate rider, having learned from her father at a young age. Rizon seemed at home on the back of his spotted steed. He said a man called the Flat-Nose had given it to him after releasing him from Helike's prison cells. They would ride to meet him at a cove a few miles west of Helike's shore.

Melani hadn't asked why Rizon had been imprisoned; she didn't want to learn he was a killer like Tarlen. She knew the Flat-Nose was one of Helike's four councilors and was further puzzled at why the man would go through so much trouble to set Rizon free. However, if it meant safe passage away from the so-called Fishermen, Melani felt no need to question it further.

They just needed to find Xander.

The ride from Boura to the camp where Xander and the others

were stationed was not far but procuring horses had taken more time than they'd planned. It was perhaps two hours until morning.

Their horses cantered to a stop, and Melani could make out hundreds of tents and men lining the ground, sleeping or drinking. A few fires still flickered in the darkness, enough to illuminate the entirety of the camp and for Melani to realize that finding Xander would prove more difficult than she had expected.

Rizon stayed out of sight from the soldiers, keeping the horses together in the trees that bordered the camp. Melani strolled in, attempting to look as confident as possible. Multiple sentries stood watch, though they seemed distracted by their drinks or each other. One even noticed her but brushed aside any confrontation – she was only one woman after all.

Wonderful to know how careless Xander's comrades are.

She picked her way through the grounds, looking for any recognizable faces or pieces of armor. Nothing.

Dim light was beginning to fill the sky. She had miscalculated the time – it appeared morning was fast approaching. The low light helped Melani navigate the sleeping forms and odd weapons that littered the ground, and she noticed the men begin to stir. Where was Xander?

She was reluctant to peek into tents, assuming that Xander would be on the ground and not wanting to see anything she would regret. However, it seemed the only proper course.

After a thorough combing of the tents and bodies around the winking fires, Melani became worried. It was difficult to tell how many soldiers were spread around the camp, but she realized it was not all of Boura's forces. Perhaps Xander had broken off with a fraction of the men to another encampment.

Shit.

It was dawn by now, the sun rising to glare between the trees. More soldiers yawned and stretched. Some gave her the odd look, and a couple snickered. They probably thought she was a pornai, a woman hired for the night, who hadn't quite left in time to pass unseen. Melani averted her gaze shyly.

The scout who had noticed her from before finally approached. Melani recognized him vaguely but couldn't quite place it.

"Ma'am, you seem to be in the wrong place. Is there any way I could help?"

His tone and words were polite enough.

"I'm a healer, I arrived before the rest. I'm actually looking for someone. A soldier."

"Who would that be?"

"Xander Atsali. You wouldn't happen to know if he's here, would you?"

"Oh! Xander, I do know!"

He seemed overjoyed to be able to help, and Melani finally realized where she'd seen him before. He was the same soldier who had sparred with Xander in the training field, the day she'd last spoken to Loren.

"Is he here?"

"No, ma'am, I'm afraid not."

"Would you be able to tell me where, then?"

He shifted uncomfortably, not making direct eye contact.

"Sir?" she prompted.

"I... well, how can I be sure you're really a healer with the Bourans and not some spy?"

"Why would a spy be looking for one soldier in the Bouran army?"

She could think of a few reasons, but hoped the man was as dim-witted as he appeared. He lifted his left foot, pointing his toe to the ground as if it would direct more thoughts to his head.

"Um, I don't think I can. I suppose... well, I guess I could tell you."

Melani smiled sweetly, touching him on the shoulder, "Thank you, sir."

"There's a force headed to the beach just north and west from Helike's walls. I saw him leave with them. It's only the best fighters of course, and if you know him, well, he's one of the best we've got."

Melani thanked him again, wondering why the man never even asked why she sought Xander.

This army is full of novices.

She found Rizon in the same spot. He looked impatient but calm enough.

"Well?"

"He's with another group, northwest of here, up by the beaches. Should be hard to miss, I'd assume. Let's g–"

A distant bang ripped through the quiet woods, startling Melani. The noise sounded far off, but she knew it must have been deafening.

Her eyes met Rizon's. The noise had come from the northwest. A battle had already begun. Without speaking, the two pulled themselves onto their horses, and urged them forward, racing in the direction of Xander and the carnage of war.

****

A cliff overlooked the beach nestled between two slopes. Helike's northern walls were behind Melani, though surrounding villages spotted the coastline. The ocean was calm today, and and seagulls glided above the water. However, the sand and rocks below were soaked red. Melani tried to adjust to the horror, barely believing what she saw.

Over a thousand bodies littered the beach, Helikens and Bourans alike. Spears and arrows protruded from their chests, necks, and stomachs. A large, blackened spot dominated the center.

The explosion.

Soldiers were still afire from it, smoke rising from their lifeless forms. The air smelled of burned flesh and death. Melani gagged.

Rizon was wordless, too, his face a stony mask. She could see the gloom in his eyes. They were too late.

"What's happened?" she asked, hoping Rizon would give her

some creative explanation to counter her fears.

"War. A bloody battle."

Obviously.

"Xander?"

"I don't know."

He couldn't be gone. Melani refused to believe it. There were more Bouran soldiers than dead on the beach. She was unable to make out any faces from so far away, but she feared that the closer they got, the more grotesque the scene would appear. And so many of the figures were mangled, certainly unidentifiable.

"Look there," Rizon said, pointing to the hill on the far side, which sloped up towards one of Helike's gates.

Soldiers were slogging in that direction, lugging away the wounded on stretchers, while others led a few hundred chained prisoners. She realized they must be Bouran soldiers. Helike had won the first battle.

As her eyes turned back to the desecration of the seashore, she noticed shapes moving slowly. Perhaps, they were healers or more soldiers from Helike, checking to make sure everyone below was truly dead.

"We lost," she said simply, emotionless.

It occurred to her then that she didn't care at all who won the war. Not really. She just wanted Xander.

Xander.

Her hands began to shake. The shock of the scene below was wearing off, allowing the truth of the matter to settle in.

"Xan... Xand..." she choked, trying to get his full name out.

"Dead. Or a prisoner."

Rizon's voice was leaden, totally even. But she could tell he was forcing it to be this way. His face tightened unnaturally, as if he were straining to keep his mouth from twitching, his eyes from watering.

Dead or a prisoner.

"No. That can't – what if he escaped?"

As she spoke it, she knew it couldn't be true. Xander would never abandon his companions. He would have been right in the middle of it all.

But he's abandoned me.

She couldn't start thinking like that. He hadn't abandoned her, not really. He left for his duty. She thought about the clumsy soldiers on the training field and the incompetent guards at the other Bouran camp. Certainly, they weren't worth dying for. Not when he could have lived for her!

And the baby.

She leapt off her horse, racing to the beach.

"Melani!" Rizon called, spurring his horse in pursuit.

What did Rizon care? She was going to find his body, she needed to know. If he wasn't on the beach, she would know he was alive. Just a prisoner.

Just a prisoner.

Would they torture them? Melani had no idea how Helike treated their enemies after capture. He *must* have been taken prisoner.

She was just reaching the rocky hill when Rizon caught up to her, pulling his horse to a halt beside her.

"Melani, you can't go down there. Those are Helike's men, probably putting the wounded out of their misery."

"I have to know, Rizon! Don't you care? Don't you want to know what happened to your own brother?"

"Melani, don't..."

"Don't what!" she exclaimed, rounding on him, "You leave your family without word, for years! I don't know you! And you show up; the first thing I see you do is murder a man right in front of me!"

"He would have done the same to you!"

"I know that! But... why? Why was he after your family!"

"I can explain more once we're away and safe."

"Your brother could be alive down there, and you're just going to ride away? With the mother of his child? No. I'm not coming with you until I know he's alive."

"And... and what if...."

His face twisted, and he slid off his horse, patting it to stay put. He glared at her. Then, he looked to his feet.

Melani realized in that moment that he was miserable. It wasn't that he didn't care, Rizon couldn't bear the thought of seeing his brother's dead body. He refused to even consider facing the notion.

"We have to know, Rizon."

"The Helikens. What of them?"

Melani pointed to a knife strapped to his leg, "You know how to use that."

She'd seen him use it and hoped it wouldn't come to that. Maybe they would let them search the site without even bothering to ask questions. Surely, they had all suffered enough losses as it were. Why would they need to confront two common folks?

They descended to the bottom. It took all of Melani's willpower to hold down the last food she'd eaten. The sickly aroma of burnt men and shit filled the air. In her days healing, Melani had witnessed plenty of death, so she was familiar with the basics of it. Men always smelled horrible when they died, but in this magnitude, it was entirely overwhelming.

Horrifying wounds surrounded them, and most of the soldiers were contorted in terrible positions, their arms akimbo or smashed behind their heads, while their legs skewed out, bloody and immobile. Flies buzzed around, too, rejoicing at the fresh food.

Even Rizon looked queasy, though she was sure he was more familiar with this type of violence than her. One soldier had his head smashed in so badly, it looked almost flat. His brain spilled all around him. He could have been of Helike or Boura – she never would have known.

Either way, he's someone's child.

As they passed, no recognizable faces stood out to Melani, and the ones far too destroyed to even try weren't attached to Xander's body. She would recognize his body, if not his face, she was certain.

ᴳHᴇ ꜰIRꜱᴳ WᴀᴠE

Only five men had the unfortunate duty of combing the bodies. The closest was only thirty feet away, stepping gingerly over a burned corpse. One of his companions drove a sword into a dying man close behind. Melani winced when she heard the squelch as he pulled the blade out from his chest.

"What's your business here, you two?" the closer one called, a tired sense of resignation in his voice.

Rizon stopped moving, setting his hand lightly on Melani's arm.

"We're from the village nearby, heard that raucous explosion. Quite a scene here, sir!"

"Yeah," the man responded, "Haven't we sent word to all you folk nearby about the battle? You were told to stay far, far away."

Melani let Rizon continue, not wanting to add any further story to the conversation. It would be easier that way, she thought. The soldier continued approaching. He was a diminutive man, looking unbalanced in his armor.

"I know, but you see, my wife here is a healer. Thought she might come take a look and see what she could do. Lots to learn from the dead and alive alike, I fear."

Melani nodded to confirm the statement.

"Ah, I see. I'd think you should still stay well away, but we could use good women like you in the city right about now. Perhaps, I'd tell you to gather up your things from that village and come to the city center."

Melani responded, "A good suggestion, perhaps I will do that.

Though, if you don't mind, I'd like to add to my notes a little more about burn wounds... I'd suspect you have a lot of that to deal with."

"You'd be correct in that. Be quick about it."

"Won't take more than a few minutes."

Melani and Rizon walked past the man, thanking him as they did. She tried her best to examine as many forms as she could. Her hopes continued to rise as she scoured more and more of the dead, without spotting any signs of Xander. Unfortunately, almost a hundred bodies were charred so badly from the explosion, she couldn't even make out the shape of them.

She urged herself not to cry. He couldn't be one of those blackened bodies, crisped far past the point of being remotely human. No, they must have marched him into the city with the rest.

After a couple minutes, she whispered to Rizon, "We should clear out. No signs of him."

Rizon agreed, and they left the way they came, waving in acknowledgement to the soldier who'd let them pass so easily. They mounted their horses. Melani's shoulders tensed as she shut her eyes, taking long, deep breaths in an attempt to remain calm.

He's alive. He's alive and I'll come back for him.

"Melani, let's go. The Flat-Nose will be waiting some miles to the West."

Her horse galloped at full speed, the wind stinging her face with flecks of sand and sea spray. The sky was perfectly clear, aside from a single white cloud. She hated that. She hated how beautiful the day was, while so many lay dead. She hated that Helike won the battle at the beach – not because Boura lost, but because Xander was either dead or captive.

He's not dead. He's alive. And I'll come back for him.

Her horse was lathered from sweat, and the way he bounded away from the city made her dizzy. Or was she dizzy from misery? Anger?

She passed Rizon, gritting her teeth and digging her heels into the horse.

He's alive.

A speck of wood and canvas bobbed in the distance; it was the ship they sought, moored by a protrusion of rocks offshore.

"That's him?" she called to Rizon.

I'll come back for him.

Nobody was around – there were no witnesses to see them board the dinghy and catch the rope ladders to board the sloop. They had escaped the Fishermen, at least for now. Rizon shook hands with a thin man. He had the look of a man from the East, with a bald head, tan skin, thin eyes, and indeed, a very flat nose.

Melani couldn't hear what they said to each other. She fixed her eyes on the shore in the distance, where smoke still plumed into the sky. Had he escaped somehow? No, she was certain he hadn't. She rubbed a hand over her navel, assuring her child what she didn't believe – that everything would be okay.

He's alive. He's alive, and I'll come back for him.

Chapter 24

Nicolaus

The blade barely missed Nic's chest, swinging wildly past. He stumbled backwards, eyes wide, opening his mouth to yell. But no words came out. As the steel-clad soldier approached, lifting his sword to deliver the final blow, he was barreled to the side by two men in Heliken garb. They disappeared into the crowd, and Nic pushed himself to his feet.

Nic had blood smeared on his cheek, but he was unsure if it was his or another's. The Bourans had swarmed the hillside only minutes before, and the two armies finally clashed. Arrows rained down from behind Nic as Furel called for barrage upon barrage. There was no discernible front line anymore, as the forces of Boura and Helike intermingled into a chaotic mess of spears and swords.

Nic had watched an enemy arrow thud into Julan almost immediately, replacing the officer's right eye with his dark lifeblood. Hira still had reasonable control over his swordsmen, though it was nearly impossible for Nic to tell what was happening outside his direct field of vision.

Orrin still stood tall, skewering any Bouran who dared to come within spear-length of him. He was an easy target for archers, but they seemed unable to find chinks in his solid armor.

For the millionth time, Nic wondered why he even needed to be there. Orrin only used his spear, so there was no reason to replenish arrows, and it was laughable to suggest that Orrin needed his help in the actual fighting. Nic's own spear had been sliced in two by a zealous Bouran infantryman, who had shortly after been felled by an arrow.

Why are the arrows still being fired? They could hit any one of us!

Just as he thought it, an arrow landed two feet to his left, shaft tilted in the direction from which he came. Nic's body seemed unable to properly respond to his thoughts. Each footfall took him in the direction of a foe, forcing him to backtrack until they were inevitably met by some other soldiers.

I'm going to die today.

He was certain of it. He had made no use of his half spear, and the point remained its stony-gray color. Every other weapon he could see was spattered red with blood.

Dazed, he fell again, tripping over a pair of dead bodies. He wondered if he had seen either of the men the day before wandering about camp. He realized he couldn't tell whether they were Bouran men or his own.

What does it matter now? Dead either way.

"AHHH!!" a soldier screamed, thrusting his spear at Nic.

His instinct forced him to step sideways, barely dodging the strike. He threw his broken spear shaft at the man, who batted it away in alarm. The soldier charged again, and Nic hopped backwards over the dead bodies. In his heat, the man didn't see the obstruction, and lost his footing as Nic had.

He's just as dumb as me.

Nic prepared to finish him off, poised with his spear pointed directly at the man's neck. It would only take one movement.

Do it!

He paused a second too long. The soldier rolled away, kicking out at Nic. He missed, but Nic was too startled to fight back. Just as the Bouran struggled to stand, an arrow buried itself in his throat. Nic yelped, watching the blood spill from his neck and mouth. He moved his lips as if he were praying or asking Nic for help. Nic shook his head, terrified. A horrible stench filled the air, and the man collapsed, face first into the rocky sand.

Stunned, Nic kept his feet planted in the ground. He didn't want to be there, didn't care if Helike won or lost. No, he *did* care. Right? The Bourans deserved this fate, right? He knew it wasn't true. He couldn't convince himself. He tried to remember why the battle was even happening in the first place.

All around him, men were dying. Or dead. The wounds were too horrible to look at. Clothes were stained brown and red, some bodies floated aimlessly in the shallow sea, while others stacked on top of each other.

"Nicolaus!"

It was Orrin. Nic looked for his massive friend but was suddenly pulled to one side.

"Oh, sir! Sir it's..."

"I know, son," he spoke quickly, bleeding from a cut in his forearm. His visor was pulled up, so Nic could see his green eyes.

"Are we winning?"

"They're running out of men, if that's what you're asking. I haven't seen Parex the Hammer, though. There were fewer of them here than we thought."

Orrin seemed bothered by this. Why would Boura have sent even fewer men, if they already knew they were outnumbered? Where was the famous Parex? Nic wasn't sure he cared about the answers.

"Sir, we have to end this. Do something to end this!"

Orrin looked at him sadly, as if just now realizing his squire wasn't ready for war. Nic knew he was letting him down. He simply couldn't bear to see any more destruction and death. Orrin put his hand on Nic's shoulder, then flipped his visor back down.

The two of them were positioned by the cliff, facing the sea. In front of them, a few thousand soldiers still clashed, though there were many more Heliken men. His eyes were curiously drawn to one Bouran soldier. He had short brown hair, matted to his face with sweat. He wore leather armor, but it seemed to shimmer in the light.

Glass crystals!

His sword and helmet were simple designs, but the blade flashed marvelously. All around the Bouran, men were falling.

He's ruthless.

Nic wondered if this were Parex but cast that notion aside.

Parex has a hammer. This man has a sword.

The man suddenly caught sight of Orrin, the hero of Helike, towering above his small attendant. Orrin met his gaze, stepping forward with his spear poised for battle.

He's going to lose.

The Bouran charged, lean and fast. Orrin still greatly outsized his foe, but the Bouran was muscular and quick. When Orrin slashed with his spear, he slid under it, slicing at Orrin's leg. The blade caught his shin, and Orrin cried out.

Nic was compelled to join, leaping stupidly at the warrior from behind. He seemed to notice at the last second and swung an elbow around to catch Nic square in the face. Nic scrambled back to his feet, slashing with his broken spear as Orrin stabbed with his golden one.

The soldier blocked Nic's blow and ducked away from Orrin's, bringing his sword up to parry the Golden Spear. Orrin's armor was stronger, but Nic soon saw the advantage of the thin leather. Orrin's movements were clunkier, his natural slowness magnified in comparison to the speed of the Bouran.

The warrior leapt at Orrin, stabbing him in the gap between his breastplate and steel gauntlets. Orrin yelped in pain, smacking him with the shaft of his Golden Spear. The man fell towards Nic.

Orrin was bleeding now, and the warrior seemed unfazed. He danced lightly between Nic and Orrin, catching strike after strike with his sword and pricking Orrin at every chink in his armor. The Golden Spear yelled, hoisting his weapon in preparation to throw.

Don't throw it! He'll kill you!

A rush of Bouran soldiers swept Orrin away, as four men took their chance to take down the vulnerable hero. Nic raced to help without thinking. The warrior with his shimmering armor blocked Nic's path. One kick to the chest, and Nic was on the ground, staring up into the hard eyes of his foe. There was something familiar about those eyes and the muscular build of the man. But what did it matter?

I never even got to kiss a girl.

The man hesitated. His face confused Nic.

Sorrow? Is he sad to kill someone as young as me?

He kicked aside Nic's spear, then extended a hand to hoist him to his feet.

What?

Before Nic could process the mercy being shown, a blinding light filled the beach, followed by an ear-splitting bang. Nic's head rang, and he was lifted from the ground along with the men surrounding him. He felt as if he had just been thrown into a swath of flames – his blood boiled within and the smell of burnt *something* was overpowering.

Nic could hear screams of pain, but everything was dulled by the unrelenting ringing. It took him a few moments to realize his clothes had caught fire. Nic rolled over the rocks and sand, hoping to suffocate the flames. He touched his face with a shaky hand. He was alive, and he was amazingly unharmed – or as unharmed as he could be.

What had happened?

Clearly some explosion. But who would set off such a weapon? Certainly, men on both sides were suffering. To Nic's left, the warrior from Boura was groaning, his left leg badly burnt, singed nearly black. He had cuts and scrapes from the battle, but his *leg*. It smelled like overcooked fish.

Nic pushed himself to his feet groggily, taking in the scene. Whatever had been left of the Bouran host was lost. Men stood close to the eastern hillside, surrounded by Heliken soldiers, who didn't look much better. It seemed the explosion had affected every soldier on the beach, sparing those along the hill.

Strange, it looks as though most Helikens are okay. We must have set off the blast.

It was then that Nic wondered when they had all retreated, leaving Orrin and his command vulnerable along with the Bourans.

Orrin!

Nic limped weaponless and aimless until he saw the mound of steel that could only be the Golden Spear.

"Sir!"

He rushed over to his friend. Nic knew right away that

something was amiss. Orrin wheezed quietly, his breath ragged and uneven.

"Sir, are you hurt?"

It was a dumb question. Orrin chuckled then coughed, before finally responding.

"A bit. Just a bit."

Nic crouched to examine the damage. Orrin's linens were darkening by the second, right in the space between the breastplate and back. His armor was warped from heat and torn to bits by repeated sword strokes. Another pool of blood began to ooze from a wound between Orrin's neck and shoulder.

"Sir, you need help."

Nic tried to maintain composure, standing and waving his arms to call attention to other Heliken soldiers. Few noticed, and all were too preoccupied to care.

"It's going to be okay, sir," Nic said, his voice cracking, "I-I promise."

"You going to carry me by yourself, Nicolaus?" Orrin grunted as he tried to shift to a seated position, "That little Bouran soldier was a piece of work, eh?"

Nic hardly would have called the leather warrior *little*, but he supposed that was all relative, "We got him in the end, though, didn't we, sir?"

"No, I'm afraid I was whisked away before then. You must have handled it all yourself."

Orrin gave a weak smile, that quickly turned into a grimace.

Nic thought of the fight once more. Truthfully, he hadn't handled anything. The soldier had let him live. He wanted to tell Orrin – about the merciful soldier, about the victory Helike had just won. He also wanted to ask why they hadn't known to retreat. Who set off the explosion?

But he couldn't trouble Orrin with all of that. Not now. He struggled to find the right words.

I let you down; I was supposed to protect you, and now....

How could he say that?

"Nicolaus..."

He coughed violently, then winced, clutching the wound on his side. His hand turned red seconds later. Nic eased him gently into a seated position, propped up against two dead Bourans.

"Sir, it'll be okay... just lie back... HELP! ANYONE!"

He yelled as loud as he could, watching soldiers on both sides holding their fallen brothers, as the unscathed on the hillside rounded up Bouran survivors. It was almost comical how nobody seemed to notice their leader, dying in the middle of the blackened beach.

Or do they notice? Do they not care? Or...

"Nicolaus."

"Sir?"

"I..."

He was trying to tell Nic something, but no words came out. Nic could feel panic roiling within him, his body clenching at the ignorance and carelessness of Helike's army. All around, men were calling out for healers, pleading for someone to help them carry the burned bodies of their friends as life drained from them.

Nic tore a piece of fabric from his clothes. Maybe he could bandage the wounds. Orrin watched him work, his face tight with pain. He swatted woozily at Nic's arm.

"Leave it."

"We can still stop the blood loss. You could live."

You have to live.

Nic ignored him, prepared to stuff the cloth over the gushing wound.

"Don't... Help them." Orrin said, catching his wrist.

"Sir, I... who? Help who?"

"All... all of them."

Orrin was gritting his teeth now, so his words were barely intelligible. Could he mean it? Did he really think a scrawny sixteen-year-old from Egypt would be able to fill his massive shoes?

Hot tears streaked Nic's face, and he could feel veins sticking out as he restrained himself from breaking down.

"Orrin. Sir. Don't you want to see Elfie? Sir? Sir!"

Orrin's eyes glistened with a mix of pride and sorrow. And fear?

Nic clutched Orrin's thick arms, burying his head in the one huge bicep. He felt The Golden Spear's body go limp.

✳✳✳✳

G.J. VINCENT

The rest of the morning was hazy and surreal. Hira and Furel had the remaining Helikens round up the Bourans, roping them together in a line of prisoners hundreds deep. Nic and other stewards were tasked with carrying the most grievously wounded on stretchers.

The two ranking officers lamented at their fallen leader, instructing the soldiers to bear Orrin on a litter back to the city. Their tragic demeanor seemed false to Nic. He would have to find out more about these two. Why had nobody cared to help Orrin moments ago? They must have noticed their leader, lying in a bloody heap in the center of the beach.

Nic's movements did not seem like his own; perhaps the gods were forcing him to walk and lift and carry for their own entertainment. He took one step in front of the other without thinking about anything.

He's really gone.

As he and one of Hira's attendants headed to the city walls, passing the winding line of Bouran prisoners, Nic heard a soft voice croak from the stretcher. He looked down, finally realizing who the wounded man was. He had a wounded leg, burned and scarred, with bruises on his handsome face and muck in his short, brown hair. There was a peculiar sunspot on his right hand. He was whispering something, though it didn't seem aimed at anyone. Hira's attendant didn't turn around.

Nic strained to hear. It sounded like one word, repeated over and over again. A name perhaps? Nic couldn't be sure. He felt validated by his task now, as he brought the man who'd shown him unnecessary mercy to salvation. Nic was suddenly transported back to that moment, as he lay on the ground looking up into the face of a skilled warrior. And the warrior had offered him his hand.

Why?

Hira's attendant came to a halt, and Nic stopped.

"Wounded Bourans to the right," a man said, pointing to the heap of injured men, groaning and wheezing.

Hira's attendant nodded, and made to move in that direction, but Nic's feet remained planted. Helikens were being taken to a building on the left, in which Nic could see numerous healers tending to wounded soldiers.

"Why separate them?"

"We need to tend to our soldiers first, servant."

Nic felt strangely wronged by this order.

"These men will die."

"Well, then it'll be fewer enemies, no?"

Hira's attendant glared at Nic, giving a sharp tug to the stretcher. Nic gave in, setting the warrior down in the dirt. When he met the earth with a slight bump, the man's eyes opened, meeting Nic's with resignation. Nic wondered once more why his face seemed so familiar.

He knows. He knows he's going to die here.

Nic wondered if the soldier recognized him. Did he know he was looking at the man he'd spared? Guilt washed over Nic. Why did he deserve to die now? What was the difference between Nic and this man, besides the city in which he lived? Nic didn't even come from Helike, for gods' sake!

Frustration and misery clashed within Nic, and he felt an intense hatred for the city of Helike. Hira's attendant had walked away now, and Nic was alone with all the wounded. What would Orrin have wanted him to do in this situation?

Help them. All of them.

"You don't deserve this," he muttered, though the soldier certainly couldn't hear him.

Once again, the gods Nic didn't believe in took over. Nic picked up the soldier, allowing the Bouran to use him as a crutch.

"Wha?" the warrior murmured, nearly falling back to the ground before steadying himself with his good leg.

"Keep silent and walk with me," Nic said sharply, half-dragging the Bouran to a side street behind the pile of injured men.

The man said nothing, mustering enough strength to walk with Nic's assistance in a direction he didn't know.

"Come on," Nic said under his breath, mostly to himself, "We're getting you somewhere they'll take care of you."

And where they'll truly care about Orrin.

He just hoped Orrin's family would forgive him. He was taking the man who had fought so valiantly against Orrin straight to them. But Orrin respected this man, right? And he hadn't truly killed him; something else had. It had been that explosion, and the Heliken soldiers who ignored him. Nic needed to find out if it had been one of their own who'd set off that explosion, without warning Orrin and his men. He had the most uncomfortable suspicion that it was by design that Orrin had died. Who would benefit from the Golden Spear's death?

He was compelled to run, as fast as he could, far, far away from Helike. But simultaneously, desire for revenge and justice for his fallen friend weighed on him. If he were completely honest with himself, intrigue in the forces that moved Achaea also urged him to remain.

Help them. All of them.

Nic's eyes were still dry though he felt like bursting into tears. He didn't want to do it in front of the Bouran warrior. The two trudged on, acknowledging nobody as they made their way to Orrin and Elfie's cozy home.

Chapter 25

Keoki

Keoki stood on the pedestal beside the statue of Poseidon in Helike's city center. The cold, salty water reached his ankles, climbing slowly up his legs. The entire square was submerged. A tapestry depicting the weaving contest between Arachne and Athena floated past, borne alongside wooden chairs and scraps of food.

Then, they came. The bodies. They rose from the depths as they did every night, leaking water from their mouths and noses. Pale faces with tangled hair stared sightlessly at Keoki. He watched, horrified, as countless dead men and women were swept towards the sea. The water rose faster now, pouring in from side streets and alleys, bringing more lifeless forms.

Keoki's breath quickened. Most of the people were unrecognizable – strangers of the city he once called home. Then, most horrible of all, two of the dead began walking atop the water, bloated and waterlogged like the rest, but somehow still moving.

"Fil... Agnes..."

His voice was scarcely above a whisper as his farm family came closer, extending dead arms to him, mouths moving wordlessly...

Keoki woke in a cold sweat, thin sea spray misting in from the opening of the cave. A dream. It was just another dream. He'd been having the same vision every night – Helike in ruins, flooded from some unseen disaster.

It's this damn cave. I'm going mad!

How many nights had he been chained here? Ten, maybe eleven? He'd lost count, even though he was confident he could count past ten; the days just ran together.

He felt weaker than usual, his face gaunt and eyes sunken. Some days, he chose not to eat, just to bother Sapphir. He couldn't tell if it worked, but having a little control gave him as much satisfaction as the scraps of food she brought.

Well, it wasn't scraps. Truthfully, Sapphir had cooked some delicious meals for him. That was strange. Why did she try to keep such good care of a captive?

Flies buzzed around his beard, which was scratchy and unkempt. Keoki hated that. Maybe Sapphir would give him a shave if he asked nicely. Gods, what got him into this mess?

Keoki hated the cave, hated the hard ground that was way too uncomfortable to sleep on, hated the chains that weighed down both his arms and felt too cold on his wrists. But somehow, he found it hard to hate Sapphir.

Yet he certainly did. She was a Child of the Sea, after all, one of those fanatics who'd helped kill his parents. She hadn't explicitly done the deed, but Keoki knew it was enough to simply be a part of it. And her children. Maya, Ivy, Cy, Egan, and Celia – none were truly hers!

Perhaps she had protected them *somehow*, but that excused nothing. Or did it? It was too much! And the whole time, Sapphir was acting out of love *and* spite. Keoki knew what that was like. Thinking about it hurt his head, but what else was he to do? He was chained in a cave, alone with his thoughts and the occasional spider crab, who did not make as good of companions as cows.

So why was it so hard to hate her? The lonely part of him looked forward to every visit she made to the cave, though he tried his best to appear aloof. And she *was* beautiful, though that shouldn't have mattered.

That's gross, she's Ivy's mother.

But she wasn't. Not really. Her "children" did love her though, and she took good care of them. They seemed happy enough and safe. But they hadn't seen any of the world besides this island, so what could they really know?

Keoki flicked a pebble at the wall, watching it collide with a puff of dust. He missed Fil and Agnes. They were surely worried sick about him. Agnes had probably tried to make Fil go out and look for him, and she had probably asked every man, woman, and child around Helike if they'd seen him. He hoped the cattle were okay without him to take care of them. But he was sure Fil could handle it. Keoki suspected that the two old farmers needed him less than he needed them.

He wished Agnes could meet Sapphir. She'd really let the witch have it for chaining up her Kiki and letting his beard get so disgusting. He thought of what he'd say to Agnes when she somehow found a way to scold him about it.

"You did want me to find a girl, didn't you?"

The sun inched over the horizon, leaking golden rays into the cave and illuminating the sea. His view was magnificent in its own way, and Keoki did love solitude. Were he unchained, the cave might have been a lovely place to relax. Most days, Sapphir came around first light. It would be any minute.

When she finally arrived, Keoki couldn't help but admire the way her fiery hair looked in the orange sunrise. He felt strangely embarrassed by his own disheveled appearance.

That's stupid.

"I have eggs today. Will you eat?"

His stomach growled at the thought of eggs, but he acted as if it couldn't matter less, merely nodding and reaching out his hand. She placed the plate at his feet instead, and he had to reorient himself into a seated position to pick it up. As he ate, Keoki kept his eyes fixed on the food. The eggs tasted amazing, salted perfectly with just a hint of spice from some sort of pepper.

"Good?" Sapphir asked.

"Yeah."

"You slept well?"

"Fine."

Keoki wanted to tell her about the repeated dreams he'd been having. Something about them felt too real, almost prophetic. After considering for a minute, he spoke.

"Do you dream?"

Of course, she does. What kind of a question is that?

Sapphir inclined her head, slightly caught off guard, "Um, yes. Every now and then, yes. Why?"

"Do you ever *really* dream. Like magic dreams where you see what's going to happen?"

She ran her tongue along her front teeth, causing the scar to stick out from her upper lip.

"Are you asking me if I see the future? In my dreams."

"I guess it sounds foolish when you say it like that."

"No," she said, truly baffled by his interest in the topic, "it's a good question. My father would sometimes claim he saw visions of the future. I think he just wanted people to be intrigued by his power."

"He sounds like a real sack of wine."

"Usually."

She sat herself down opposite Keoki, crossing her legs and folding her arms into her lap. Keoki suspected she wanted to take the opportunity to converse further with her prisoner, since he tried so hard to remain silent. However, Keoki was getting bored of talking to himself and the spider crabs.

"Do you dream, Keoki?"

"I... yeah. Doesn't everyone?"

"You just asked if I do."

"Oh. No, I just meant dreams where you see the future."

"Ah, I see."

"I've had dreams here every night. Way more than usual. Maybe because you've got these damn chains on me."

He held up his wrists to show Sapphir the shackles.

"That's nice."

"No, no, the *same* dream."

"You're a talker today."

"I'm bored, and the crabs never respond to me," he paused, considering the peculiarity of that sentence, "So, I keep having this really terrible dream, right?"

"Okay."

"Helike is completely underwater and everyone's dead, floating around and staring. Every night, all dead. What do you think that means?"

Sapphir's eyes flashed with alarm, but she covered it quickly, "I guess it flooded."

Why did that scare her?

"No, I know it flooded in the dream. But why do I keep having it?"

"I... I don't know..."

Her eyes were unfocused, as if she were looking past Keoki at something he couldn't see. It took almost two full minutes before she broke the silence.

"My father spoke of that same thing, you know. Helike underwater. Bodies everywhere."

"He told this to you when you were a child?"

"Actually, yes. All the time. I... I've had the same dream."

An odd sensation washed over Keoki. He could hear his heart beating. What did this mean? Sapphir ran a hand through her red hair, twisting one of the strands in a tight loop around her finger.

"Do you think I'm evil, Keoki?"

It was Keoki's turn to be caught off guard. What did he think? Sapphir had thrown him in a cave for discovering the secret of her stolen children. Those seemed like evil things to him. Yet...

"No. I... no."

Sapphir had no reaction.

She spoke slowly, "My father... This dream you're having; I know it's all connected."

"You're not going to try to tell me he's not evil, too."

"I'm not."

"If I ever get out of these chains," he shook them at her again, "I'd kill him."

"I'd like that," she said dryly.

"Then let me out. Let me go find him."

"You wouldn't find him. And if you did, he'd kill you."

Damn.

He thought that might have worked. Sapphir hated her father, he knew. But he could tell that part of her still loved him, too.

Parents were tricky that way, he supposed.

She stood, pacing the cave and muttering to herself. Something about the dream had disturbed her, and Keoki found himself extremely grateful that his boredom had driven him to talk today.

"What are you thinking?" he asked, letting hope edge into his voice.

"The dream. Why'd you have that dream?"

She didn't seem to expect an answer, and when he did it was barely audible.

"Sapphir, we both hate your father."

She waved away his point, "Helike underwater..."

"Why don't we–"

"Keoki, who do my children belong to?"

He paused, wanting to snap that he didn't know, and they didn't either. No, she wouldn't like that. She was testing him, trying to learn if they could work together.

"They're yours."

"And you are at peace with that?"

No.

"Yes. But you have to let them see more than just this island. They have to know what else is out there."

Ivy would like that.

"You know it's too dangerous."

"What about my farm? Fil and Agnes could show them some of Helike's countryside. Can't you put some protections over it?"

T.J. VINCENT

She tapped her foot anxiously but made no retort.

"We can take them to the farm," she said under her breath, "Yes. And go find him."

Keoki watched, hoping she was reaching the decision he should have asked for ten days ago. He had been too angry at first, too stubborn, and too betrayed. The waves lapped against the side of the cliff, bringing with them a soft wind that cooled the inside of the cave.

"I won't say anything about it, I promise. You're their mother."

He could figure that out later.

She took a step towards him, then another. He couldn't wait to shave and wash the cave smell off of him. She extended her pale right hand to Keoki, and he took it.

The chains fell from his wrists.

Epilogue

The cityscape disappeared from view as Gerros descended to the inky shore. Moonlight reflected across the ocean, illuminating the vast nothingness before him. He was on the outskirts of the Olenus territory, a few miles north and west from the walls. The trek to this remote seaside had once frightened Gerros, but he was too old for fear now.

The boat was moored in a hidden cove, completely out of view, even in the light of day. He entered, running a skeleton-thin hand over the smooth wooden skiff. No matter how many times it was used, the boat remained in immaculate condition.

He began to row methodically, propelling himself along the beach until it became a sheer rockface, over forty feet tall. This sea was rarely traveled, but the placid waters of low tide made the journey easy enough. The skiff bobbed up and down, calming Gerros' usually sporadic heartbeat.

The sea revives me every time.

Gerros had been rowing for nearly thirty minutes before he

saw it. The cave entrance was only visible at these low sea levels, an eerie grotto that always had a curious purple hue on the inside. He directed the boat with caution, passing under the craggy archway. He came to a slow stop on the glassy waters inside and had to row a few more strokes until the keel bumped into the staircase.

The steps were carved from the stone itself, and a rope hung down so Gerros could tie the boat before exiting. He climbed the slick rock, his hip making a familiar popping noise with each stride.

If only I could row myself everywhere.

Gerros had only recently begun to limp like this. His quivering bones were becoming wearier with each passing day. He often used a cane, but it pained him to appear so feeble. The gods would give him the strength he needed if he prayed with enough diligence.

Rhea never sincerely believed that.

Maybe if his wife had been more pious, she would be walking the caverns with him, instead of sitting in an urn in the catacombs of Olenus. It had been her idea to join the Children of the Sea, years ago. She'd heard Teremos preaching outside the Temple of Poseidon, back when they were mere numbers within the Sons of Poseidon. Rather, Gerros had been a Son, while Rhea was one of the many women who prayed and studied alongside their husbands.

That was one of the reasons she had wanted to join Teremos.

"I could be a Child of the Sea, same as you. We would be alike under the eyes of Poseidon."

Gerros had resisted. Their life with the Sons was happy. Then, he heard Teremos speak. Teremos was handsome and tall, with a rich voice, blonde hair, and intense blue eyes, flecked with purple and yellow. The man had such a way with words, he should have become a storyteller or playwright.

No. No, those roles are beneath him.

Gerros and Rhea were entranced by the promises of a better Helike, a better Achaea. They would become just like the men and women of the Golden Age. But Rhea had not been ready.

She was too gentle to act as we needed to secure a future of peace and prosperity.

Then, the doom came for the Children of the Sea.

Gerros had to make a conscious effort to stop himself from grinding his teeth. He became so distracted, he almost slipped on the damp stone floor. He was hunched over, treading through the second tunnel with care. Every ten feet, a torch hung on the wall, keeping the space warm and well-lit.

Although the maze of tunnels spread beneath the mountainsides and farmland that surrounded Olenus, the torches led to one cavern. Many of the passageways had existed for thousands of years, but they lay uninhabited and jumbled – their purpose unclear. Gerros marveled at the incredible refuge Teremos had created after the Children had fled Helike to disperse across Achaea.

The most loyal followers of Teremos, such as Gerros, were

called by him soon after. Somehow, the brilliant leader spoke to them in their dreams, informing them of the new sanctum beneath Olenus. Rhea had not received this message, but Gerros pleaded with her to join him. She refused, wishing to start anew in Olenus.

I should have forced her to come with me!

The last words she had spoken to Gerros haunted him from time to time. One simple phrase – "I loved you." He had still loved her.

She was a distraction. She would have driven me away from the gods.

Gerros plodded on, his knees aching from the journey. He wished the Children could meet in a less arduous location, but that was wishful thinking. Most had to travel long distances to reach the sanctum; at least Gerros resided in Olenus. He wondered where Teremos spent his days when he wasn't with the Children.

Finally, a ring of torches revealed the wide entryway that led to the final cavern. It was huge, with stalactites and cracks in the ceiling through which natural light could pour.

Today, silvery moonlight allowed Gerros' old eyes to admire shelves of books and scrolls. The readings ranged from the histories of gods and men, to the tales of great heroes, to stranger mysticisms, which Gerros would never fully understand.

Teremos had powers he could not hope to fathom, and he knew some of the other Children possessed similar abilities. When the Children of the Sea were exiled, many of these magicians were executed; they had thought themselves powerful enough to remain in Helike. Gerros knew his life was a gift from the gods, if so many men and women had perished, despite their strength.

Perhaps they did not truly live for the gods.

Gerros did not see anyone in the cavern and assumed most had gone to sleep in smaller caves fitted with beds and blankets.

I will be able to speak with my brothers and sisters in the morning.

He prayed that Teremos would come the next day, to share his wisdom and relay the words of Poseidon.

Just then, he heard shuffling in a room to his left. He hobbled towards the noise, noticing torches and candles winking beyond. A cramped archway led to a much more comfortable cave with chairs and tables.

At the front of the room, a boy Gerros did not recognize was in a seated position facing the main cavern. He was thin and blonde, and his eyes were closed, but it was too dark to make out other features on his face.

This one is new. Teremos must have found him today.

Gerros wondered if Teremos had saved the boy yet, erasing the poisons he may have learned in his early years.

If only Teremos would do the same for his older, faithful Children. Then I could forget Rhea.

More boys and girls sat in the room with scrolls unrolled on the tables, reading them carefully. None of them turned to face Gerros.

What dutiful Children. They will bring about an age of glory.

T.J. VINCENT

He was about to leave to find an empty bed, when a voice as smooth as honey filled the room.

"Children, which of you would like to awaken your newest brother? He came to us today, all the way from Helike."

Appendix

Helike

◊ Orrin, the Golden Spear: Councilor of Helike

◊ Simon, the Flat-Nose: Councilor of Helike

◊ Kyros: Councilor of Helike

◊ Gaios: Councilor of Helike

◊ Furel: Commander of Heliken Army

◊ Julan: Commander of Heliken Army

◊ Hira: Commander of Heliken Army

◊ Nicolaus: Attendant to Orrin

◊ Opi: Attendant to Simon

◊ Perl: Attendant to Gaios

◊ Krassen: Pub Owner

◊ Keoki: Farmer

◊ Felip: Farmer

◊ Agnes: Farmer

◊ Rosie: Daughter of Orrin

◊ Gerrian: Husband of Rosie

◊ Elfie: Wife of Orrin

◊ Philomena: Trader of Helike

◊ Mako: Smith of Helike

APPENDIX

Boura

◊ King Ucalegon: King of Boura

◊ Wyrus Warren: Nobleman of Boura

◊ Parex the Hammer: Commander of Bouran Army

◊ Sir Farlen: Officer of Bouran Army

◊ Melani: Artist and Healer

◊ Xander Atsali: Smith of Boura

◊ Loren: Healer of Bouran School

◊ Loren's husband: Soldier of Bouran Army

◊ Marlo: Baker of Boura

◊ Aggio: Fisherman of Boura

◊ Mari: Fisherman of Boura

◊ Tarlen: Fur-Trader, Fisherman

The Children

◊ Teremos: First Child of the Sea

◊ Gerros: Senior Child of the Sea

◊ Sapphir: Daughter of Teremos

◊ Ivy: Daughter of Sapphir

◊ Cy: Son of Sapphir

◊ Egan: Son of Sapphir

◊ Maya: Daughter of Sapphir

◊ Celia: Daughter of Sapphir

A Preview of:

The

Children of

the Sea

Book Two of The Secrets of Achaea

Coming soon...

Prologue

A gentle drizzle began to fall, causing Gaios' normally well-groomed hair to cling to his forehead. The loose tunic he wore had a black hood, but he left it draped over his shoulders. Gaios always chose to leave his head uncovered. For some reason, people kept a keen eye on men who tried to hide their faces. It was much easier for him to steal away on nights like these under the guise of total normality.

Gaios had left the Heliken castle shortly after dark, using a cramped tunnel to exit unnoticed. The passageway led to a steep slope, which ended at the river.

Gaios and his Bouran visitor had met in secrecy thrice before, always on the damp riverbank. Gaios had little love for the man, but he never let antipathy get in the way of judging a person's value. Affection was the bane of progress; and progress was to be the subject of tonight's meeting.

Progress... tragic progress...

He still admired the late councilor. The Golden Spear had

1

rarely agreed with Gaios, challenging him vocally on most every proposition. But he had respected this strength of will, knowing that Orrin's concerns were born from a love of their city.

However, Councilor Orrin had been fearfully clumsy with his grasp of the city's politics. Helike would never advance under such a ruler.

He saw too much good in the world.

Gaios noticed the danger of Orrin's bungling positivity when ruthless magicians had plagued Helike. Orrin had viewed them as naught but outliers among more peaceable men and women.

The fool... knowing the power those magicians held?

Gaios had understood that dealing meekly with the Children of the Sea would allow their grievances the chance to fester. Yes, despite Orrin's disagreement, the Children had needed to be expunged. Thankfully, Gaios avoided becoming the face of such a bold endeavor.

Euripides was more than willing to take the hero's role.

While Orrin and Euripides had bickered over how to deal with the Children, Gaios focused on Helike's bright future – a future that would soon become reality. The war with Boura edged ever closer once the Children of the Sea were removed, but Orrin had suspected nothing until the soldiers were already sharpening their blades.

It is truly a shame. The Golden Spear became cleverer just as his days became numbered.

The thought of the great General Orrin swallowing his pride

to spy behind the Council's back amused Gaios.

He must have felt so devious... so dishonorable.

And his efforts had been futile.

But the Egyptian... the boy is another story.

Simon had warned Gaios to keep a close eye on Orrin's little servant months before.

"That one listens, Gaios. More than he knows," he had said, fixing his thin eyes on Gaios as they stood in the palace courtyard, the fountain bubbling melodiously.

"Simon, what does it matter? He is naught but a boy. A foreign one, at that."

Simon's mouth had twitched at this. "Foreign boys become Achaean men after living in this city long enough."

The Flat-Nose, of course, had once been a foreign boy himself.

I should have listened, should have addressed the boy earlier.

Now, he was certain that Orrin's servant had released Helike's most prized prisoner. He must have struck a deal with the assassin in their brief conversation. The Golden Spear would not have known. Certainly, he could never condone anything so drastic.

Gaios was uncertain if the boy had survived the explosion. Perhaps he perished alongside his councilor. Informants had given mixed reports on the matter. If all were to be believed, the boy had been stabbed earlier in the battle, killed himself after seeing Orrin's lifeless form, and run away as other soldiers tried to save their leader.

It cannot be all three.

ᏦᎯᎬ ᏟᎻᏆᏞᎠᎡᎬᏁ ᎾᎨ ᏦᎻᎬ ᏚᎬᎯ

But Gaios had a strong suspicion that the servant was alive, somewhere in Helike. Gaios closed his eyes, listening to the river. The Bouran would arrive any minute. Gaios brushed a drop of water from his brow.

Perhaps the Golden Spear had ordered the boy to release the prisoner. He could have thought it would end the war, somehow.

Gaios knew that Orrin was perplexed by the fact that Rizon Atsali was not a known Bouran soldier, nor a Child of the Sea. To Orrin, those had been the only options.

Perhaps he still believed Rizon Atsali to be one of Ucalegon's men. Releasing him could have been a... peace offering of sorts.

Gaios picked up a pebble, wiping away the grime with a long finger. He rotated it slowly, sliding his thumb along its rough edge before flicking it towards the river.

Only a fool would think a Bouran soldier would kill a councilor of Helike.

The rock splashed, indistinguishable from the falling rain.

A fool who refused to learn the most unsavory of Achaea's secrets... and Orrin never bothered to learn the true nature of the Fishermen.

This, of course, was what Rizon Atsali had been – a Fisherman who had lost sight of the catch, and nearly paid with his life. The Fishermen knew how to negotiate with desperate traitors.

When a man knows he has been caught, he becomes very easy to use.

Perhaps, something about Rizon Atsali captivated Orrin's

sympathy and attention – enough to send his little steward to finish the dirty work. More likely, in Gaios' mind, the boy acted of his own accord.

Gaios picked up another pebble. The rain fell harder. The mystery of Rizon Atsali's escape bothered him.

If the Egyptian boy was alive, surely, he would turn up.

Gaios skipped the pebble gracefully and picked up another. He would determine the truth when he had the boy.

Unless...

The Flat-Nose had left during the Battle at the Beach, assuring the Council he would only return with Rizon Atsali. Simon's eagerness to find the escaped prisoner would make even more sense if he were trying to cover his own treachery.

No... no, Simon knows Rizon Atsali's importance. He would have been a vital prisoner for me. Helike continues to love Euripides. The people long for justice for his assassin.

Rizon's execution would have been a great triumph for Gaios and the Council.

No, it could not have been Simon.

Gaios' long, spindly fingers tapped lightly against his ever-dampening robe, as if laughing at him. Gaios took a deep breath, annoyed at himself for doubting that the servant boy was the culprit. He whipped the rock into the river; the splash was audible.

Or am I annoyed for ignoring what could be true?

Another light splash caused Gaios to refocus. He straightened as he noticed the skiff gliding down the river. Inside, a broad-shouldered man paddled as another sat huddled beneath a dark cloak. The paddler wore black chainmail, which reflected curiously under the moonlit rainclouds. Gaios could not see it in the darkness, but he knew a hammer was branded on his left bicep.

Parex the Hammer.

The Champion of Boura, general of their military, and one of the most impressive warriors in Achaea – Parex looked unnatural without his great Warhammer. As he approached, Gaios spoke first.

"I hear you're wielding a battle-axe these days, friend."

"W-What does it matter, C-Councilor?"

Parex spoke with a shaky voice, that Gaios always found humorous. It was discordant with his confidence and splendor.

"I worry that our friends might not recognize Parex the Hammer on the battlefield. That is, if he isn't wielding a hammer."

"M-My hammer isn't th-the thing that p-people recognize when th-the fighting begins."

He leapt off the boat, landing beside Gaios before tying it to a nearby tree.

"Careful there, Parex. The ground's slippery. We wouldn't want Boura's champion meeting an untimely death at the hand of a light rain."

Parex sneered, touching the dagger at his belt. The message was plain enough.

"I mean no threat. Wouldn't dare it, in fact. I fear my talents with a knife leave something to be desired."

Gaios could feel the cold steel of his own dagger beneath his cloak and hoped there would be no need to draw it. He was more able than he let on, but diplomacy would be easier than killing Parex the Hammer.

Parex reached an arm out to help the second man off of the boat.

"Ah yes, and a good evening to you, my Lord," Gaios said, letting the politeness in his voice cover the small insult.

The man huffed, replying shortly, "Greetings to you, as well, Gaios. I continue to wonder why you don't send messengers and letters. It would be easier than meeting on a rainy night."

"Yet... here you are. Messengers and letters leave too much out of my own, capable hands," Gaios said wiggling his spindly fingers.

The man snorted, removing his cloak to reveal a regal robe. He was short and thin, which must have factored into his ever-suspicious attitude.

Easy to be suspicious when a gentle breeze could be the death of you.

His head was balding, which Simon joked was the reason the man had crowned himself. Gaios knew he couldn't let these preconceived notions of the man affect his manner. He extended his hand to shake the short man's.

"I do apologize for the weather; I'm sure you understand the need for us to be covert."

King Ucalegon of Boura accepted the gesture, then wiped his hands on his robes.

THE CHILDREN OF THE SEA

"Yes, of course, Lord Gaios. I believe we have much to discuss, and precious little time."

Acknowledgements

Before I go, there are a few people I would like to thank for this thing.

My editor, Francie Futterman, for helping to make sure the word "thing" doesn't come up much in my novel.

My illustrator, Aven Jones, for illustrating – which is something I cannot do. She also took the photo of me on the next page.

My readers: Allie Schneider, Elise, Kari, and Patrick Vincent, for having my back both in and outside writing; you've given me support even when I don't deserve it.

About the Author

Theodore Jacob "Teddy" Vincent is a mathematician from the University of Georgia. *The First Wave* is the premiere installment in *The Secrets of Achaea* book series, documenting a fictional (probably) history of the First Achaean League, a largely forgotten part of Ancient Greek History. Theodore is from St. Louis, Missouri, and currently lives in Athens, Georgia – though he is finishing this while in quarantine during the coronavirus pandemic.

Printed in Great Britain
by Amazon

23430756R00178